文学通诠

On the Exercise of Judgment in Literature

〔英〕巴西尔·沃斯福尔德　著

罗选民　全译/导读

商务印书馆
创于1897
The Commercial Press

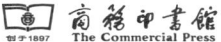

图书在版编目(CIP)数据

文学通诠/(英)巴西尔·沃斯福尔德著；罗选民全译、导读.—北京：商务印书馆，2021(2022.5重印)
ISBN 978-7-100-20460-6

Ⅰ.①文… Ⅱ.①巴…②罗… Ⅲ.①外国文学—文学理论 Ⅳ.①I106

中国版本图书馆 CIP 数据核字(2021)第 222339 号

权利保留，侵权必究。

文 学 通 诠

〔英〕巴西尔·沃斯福尔德 著
罗选民 全译、导读

商 务 印 书 馆 出 版
(北京王府井大街36号 邮政编码100710)
商 务 印 书 馆 发 行
北京中科印刷有限公司印刷
ISBN 978-7-100-20460-6

2021年12月第1版　　开本 880×1230　1/32
2022年5月北京第2次印刷　印张 9
定价：58.00元

严复(1854—1921)

譯著

美術通詮

篇一

藝術

英國倭斯弗著
候官嚴復譯

行平都邑之間所見者莫不有鑄像畫圖文史典籍而文明之國其所有者尤侈富即在通衢巷陌其園柱方坫或以銅或以石高者聳霄漢卑者掩映林木間其接於遊人之目者皆其國男女之肖像也入其居懸於牆者則有畫庋於几閣者則有壺瓶册牘及他古器而書史卷帙縱橫琳瑯乃至富家舊族往往關堂室齋宇專以待所搜奇圖像簡册鼎彝異珍必臻文明既進之民藝術又其生服其人生最急者非歟顧既足之餘何爲有此以兒治化已廣羅殘缺收拾細碎者鳥所取耶之所待使神明之地不貴是諸物者以爲養疲精力費貨財以

是故藝術文章之事起則有鑒別之學窮耳目心思之用以識別藝事文辭之正爲高下是謂孤力狄實沁 criticism 而具學識神智有以別乎事文辭之正爲高下而不譯者謂之衡鑒家曰孤力狄克 critic 考孤力狄克字源於希臘其義爲判斷爲許騭此當亞烈山大世學者自紀元前三百四十六年

而已然當此時有以五事讀書之說所謂五事者一曰底哇噯悉斯（一）第其次序次日安

寰球中國學生報　第三期

《文学通诠》的解密与发现

（代序）

一

我必须说明，《文学通诠》不是一个最忠实的译名，但在我看来，它是最合适的译名。"通诠"一词，很可能乃严复所造，我在《辞海》《汉语大词典》《现代汉语词典》《新华词典》中都未查到此词。"通诠"的大意应该是"原理""导读"，义与英文的 introduction 相近，属于入门类的理论书籍。我之所以取《文学通诠》之名，是希望从一个宏大的语境即中外文化交流史的角度去看待严复的译本、英文原著和最新的全译本。

本书由三个部分构成，根据顺序为本人的全译本《文学通诠》、严复的节译本《美术通诠》和沃斯福尔德（W. Basil Worsfold）的英文原著 *On the Exercise of Judgment in Literature*。沃斯福尔德的英文著作发表于 1900 年，严复的三章节译本出版在 1906 至 1907 年之间，从年代来看，全译本与原著、严复的节译本相差多达一个世纪，所以我今天的序可以看作是两位译者和作者的跨世纪对话。我希望《文学通诠》这个译名不仅能卓尔不群，还能与严复的译名产生某种互文关系，让读者明白商务印书馆的全译本不是一个独立的学术或商业行为，而是一种历史的递进行为。我们可以视其为中国现当代思想史和文学史研究上的一次寻根活动,是有关严复研究的考证之旅,是对中国现代文学的一次重新认识。

二

20世纪初的翻译语境与今日相去甚远。那时候翻译可能是摘译,可能是译述,可能是改写,还可能是"豪杰译",甚至出现移花接木,译著与专著浑然一体。这在今日,万万不可。一是当下精通外语的人多,对于翻译质量的要求自然非常高了。二是译文出版常常会遇到读者的苛刻批评,读者甚至可以把手指分别点在原文和译文之上,于行距之间检查译文的忠实度,严复的翻译就屡遭此待遇。所以,当今的翻译批评大都是语言和文化的差异性问题,不像20世纪初期的翻译,由于其多样性和不稳定性,会涉及思想史、一个时代的社会语境等问题。

早在《美术通诠》之前,就有严复的《政治讲义》一书为学界质疑,最终得到考证。该书被公认为中国近代第一部政治学著作。1905年,严复应上海青年会之请,共做讲演八次,合集最终于1906年由商务印书馆出版,取名为《政治讲义》。严复的写作是否参考了前人的成果?参考的是哪些人的成果?学者们过去对这部书的思想来源和演说意义都缺乏深入研究。

尽管严复(2014:7)在《政治讲义》"第一会"中开宗明义地说:"不揣寡昧,许自今日为始,分为八会,将平日所闻于师者,略为诸公演说。非敢谓能,但此所言,语语必皆有本,经西国名家所讨论,不敢逞臆为词,偏于一人政见。"《政治讲义》基本依据西方学者的言说是板上钉钉的事情了。但依据的是什么书?严复却语焉不详。萧公权(1998:754)在其专著《中国政治思想史》中指出,严复的《政治讲义》"其中虽多袭取西说，鲜有创解，然不失为中国人自著政治学概论之首先一部"。萧公权依旧没能解答该书的出处问题。戚学民（2004：95）认为，"目前严复研究中比较流行的方法趋向是严译文本的中西文比较研究。……在研究实践中也产生了一些偏向，比如研究重心大都落在探讨严复翻译的准确程度和寻找严复译文与其西方原典之间的差距上。"

严复1905年撰写的《政治讲义》被认为是中国人自己撰写的第一部近代政治学著作，然清华学者戚学民却从中发现一些端倪，他指出从其文本渊源来看，该书基本上参照19世纪英国剑桥大学近代史教授约翰·西莱（Sir John Seeley）的著作《政治科学导论》（An Introduction to Political Science）写成。他的研究和考证结论是："鉴于《政治讲义》全书体例、篇章结构、材料和语句都与《政治科学导论》基本相同和相似，我们应该肯定前者基本根据后者写成。"（戚学民，2004：91）他甚至将严复的《政治讲义》与西莱的《政治科学导论》切分章节，逐一进行对比分析。这些分析结果印证了他的观点。他呼吁，"严复政治思想之来源比较复杂，研究严复思想，不仅应从中西文比较的角度探讨严译文本，同样也要关注晚清时期的政治语境。"（戚学民，2004：85）戚的研究无疑解决了严复研究中的一个重大难题。

三

以上个案告诉我们，严复一部专著被解读，让人们看到了其专著乃是译著，至少是译述参半。此例说明，在严复研究之中仍然存在诸多不确定性，而其中最突出的，则是对严复的未竟译著《美术通诠》的种种质疑和猜测。

严复用《美术通诠》的命名来统称他于1906—1907年刊载在《寰球中国学生报》(The World's Chinese Students Journal)的三篇译文——《美术》《文辞》《古代鉴别》，这三个文章名对应的英文分别是"Art" "Literature" "The Criticism of the Ancient World"。署名是"英国倭斯弗著，侯官严复译"。英国作者倭斯弗是何许人也？《美术通诠》的原著名叫什么？这些严复都没有提供。学者们努力去揭开此谜，但都以失败告终。于是有人怀疑，莫非此书乃严复自撰，英国作者之名实为借用。

这种疑虑的产生完全可以被理解。因为至2010年以前，能找到的相关信息寥寥无几，最多的是在皮后锋的《严复大传》之中。书中记载了严复在上海期间的教育活动，他曾任《寰球中国学生报》主编，与全球华人学生会创始人李登辉关系密切。皮后锋（2003：308）还在书中提供了严复手稿的图片以及在报纸上发表的译文图片，甚至还引用第三篇文章《古代鉴别》中的一段，来解释严复之所以选择翻译这本书，是因为他意识到中国人忽视了教育中艺术对词曲和小说的重要意义。皮后锋对《美术通诠》的引用和论述虽不过寥寥几行，但这已经是有关《美术通诠》的资料中最为详细的分析。陈平原（2007：62）也略有提及："《寰球中国学生报》，1906年6月创刊于上海，双月刊，兼收中英文著述，由寰球中国学生报馆编辑发行，李登辉、严几道等主编。……除创刊号外，其余各期上均有严复的译撰。而1907年6月刊行的《寰球中国学生报》第5、6期合刊上，载有严复译述英人倭斯弗著《美术通诠》第三篇《古代鉴别》，以及自撰的《英文百科全书评论》。"有人提出，仅凭严复译著的书名和作者姓名很难找到英文原著（吴小坤、黄煜，2010：39）。皮后锋（2003：308）也有类似结语："这（指《美术通诠》）是严复一种重要的未竟译著，大多数从事严复研究的学者至今尚未发现这一译著,更谈不上利用。"

大约是2007年的5月,在一次会议上,清华历史系蔡乐苏教授跟我谈到严复的《美术通诠》,说此书一直是学术界的一个谜、一桩悬案。《美术通诠》到底是严复写的,还是翻译的?如果是翻译的,严复根本就没有提到译本的英文书名。而且"倭斯弗"仅为一个英国人的姓而已,所以,找到其英文原作者的名字已非常之难,更不要说凭《美术通诠》一名去找到原著的英文全名。莫非严复是借"倭斯弗"之名来阐述自己的学术思想?不管如何猜测,不管如何努力,当时的实际情况是《美术通诠》就是谜一样的存在。

蔡教授建议我来完成这个解题。探索真理的火炬从历史学者手中传到了外文学者的手中,真可谓机缘巧合。我考虑再三,把这个课题交给了我指导的研究生于蕾,作为她的硕士论文选题。于蕾2007年本科毕业于清华大学外文系,同年被保送本系攻读硕士学位,跟随我做翻译研究,是一位我信得过的学生。

研究的第一步就是寻找严复《美术通诠》的底本。此时我们才发现,偌大的北京,这么多的图书馆,居然在国家图书馆、北京大学图书馆、清华大学图书馆、北京师范大学图书馆都找不到1906和1907年的《寰球中国学生报》,那时还没有电子版,信息远远不如现在通畅。我们阅读了大量的过刊、传记、论文,希望发现有用的线索,从一鳞半爪的叙述中由此及彼地迂回寻找严复的译文底本。但一切努力都没有结果。鉴于《寰球中国学生报》是在上海发行,我们后来把目光转向了上海,大学图书馆依然没有。于蕾最终在上海图书馆搜索到了这个报刊。由于报刊老旧易碎,图书馆不同意提供复印件,经请示后提供了扫描电子版。这一天定格在 2009 年 7 月 17 日，上海图书馆账单流水号是 20090717010002。

接下来就是寻找《美术通诠》的原著。尽管已从阅读的文章传记中得到些许提示，在寻找严复译文时，我们仍然花了好几个月的时间。原著之所以困惑我们许久，因为《美术通诠》译本封面上只留下几个字"英倭斯弗著"，再无其他任何英文信息，这给还原作者英文姓名带来极大困难。首先，"倭斯弗"只是作者的姓而已，如果作者像莎翁那样出名，事情也就简单了；或者，如果严复给出作者全名，部分用了英文缩写字母也是好的，都可以极大地减少寻找的难度。再者，严复给出的译名，是根据韦氏音标来注音的吗？译名是否有受到福建闽南方言的影响？就如我们凭一个 Wang 姓找某人的出版物，可以从王姓中去寻找，也可以从汪姓中去寻找，如果遇到广西方言，还可以从黄姓中去寻找。总之，这种检索难度是不可估量的。

《美术通诠》的译名误导了几乎所有学者，大家认为原作是有关美术的著作，而没有想到实际上是文学批评的著作。译著名的学科属性就迷惑了大量的研究者，当然也包括我们。

于蕾做研究生开题报告时，这个研究课题的可行性曾遭到外文系论文评审小组个别人的质疑，认为译著底本都没有找到，就没有必要开题，并建议改做"正经"的翻译课题。我鼓励于蕾不畏困难，坚持做下去。她通过各种手段寻找原著，包括严复当年就读的英国格林威治大学图书馆、华威大学图书馆等，并随时向我汇报进展情况。因为 2009 至 2010 年这两年间，我在伦敦政治经济学院的伦敦商务孔子学院任中方院长，每年有一半时间待在伦敦，于是我也帮着在大学图书馆现场寻找英文原著，在 V 和 W 字母开头的作者中寻找相关书籍，付出了种种努力，但还是没有找到。几乎就在要放弃的时刻，于蕾居然从一个免费网站上偶遇了 W. B. Worsfold 的 *On the Exercise of Judgment in Literature*。多么神奇，真可谓苍天不负有心人！

严复《美术通诠》的底本和原著的发现，在大数据风行的今天算不上什么稀奇。但在十多年前，这是一件不可思议的事情。于蕾的硕士论文填补了国内关于严复研究的一个空白，是一项具有标志性的学术成果。

首先，严复的《美术通诠》有了最清楚的考证，这就避免了学术界的种种猜疑，算是了结了一桩学术史上的公案。其次，原著的发现有力地否定了过去那些顽固的断言，即严复不翻译文学作品，他的兴趣点仅在法学、经济学、社会学、政治学等领域，它的出现为严复研究开拓了新的领域。再次，原著的发现意义非凡，因为《美术通诠》应该是二十世纪第一部根据英文翻译过来的文学理论著作，它的出现让中国文学批评家需要重新审视 20 世纪初的中国文学发展运动，过去的教材于是也需要被修订或者改写。最后，严复的《美术通诠》也是中外文化交流史方面一个重大成果，可以由此窥见 20 世纪初，在严复一批启蒙先驱的带领下，中国知识分子开始全面向西方学习，其中就包括文学在内的文艺美学批评。

当然，发现不是我们的终点，我们还要通过《美术通诠》去思考一些问题：严复为什么选择 W. B. Worsfold，是出于一种雅兴，还是有意而为之？严复为什么把这本译著取名《美学通诠》而不是《文学通诠》？严复的《美学通诠》对中国近代之文学起到了什么样的作用？严复为什么只译了三章，没有完成全书的翻译？严复的《美术通诠》在清末民初起到了什么样的作用？《美术通诠》与严复提倡的"三民说"有什么关系？这些都不曾有现成的答案。

四

严复（1854—1921），是中国近代史上最具影响力的启蒙思想家、翻译家和教育家，为中国近代启蒙运动作出了不可磨灭的功绩。尤其是他翻译的西方学术著作，传播了新的社会价值体系，成为近代西学东渐的转折点，推动了中国现代性的发展，他因而被誉为向中国"介绍近世思想第一人"。遗憾的是，严复的八大译著中并没有文学译著，因此一个世纪以来，人们普遍诟病严复只注重社会科学，轻视人文科学。

然而《美术通诠》一出，让人文学者为之一振，研究者必然陡增。人们能够预感到，《美术通诠》英文底本的发现将给学术界带来的新视角和研究空间。

《美术通诠》（*On the Exercise of Judgment in Literature*）的原著作者叫巴西尔·沃斯福尔德，1858年生于英格兰约克郡，1883年获牛津大学文学学士学位，三年后获牛津大学文学硕士学位。他热心于政治，也涉足经济学、法学与教育学，曾广泛游历四大洲。他在1883—1890年间受聘于开普殖民地（Cape Colony，今南非、纳米比亚）、新西兰、新南威尔士，足迹遍及纳塔尔、维多利亚、昆士兰、爪哇等地。1891—1900年间在牛津继续教育代表会（Oxford Extension Delegates）和伦敦联合委员会讲授经济学和文学。1898—1899年间出访埃及，1903年出访希腊。1939年逝世。他一生著述颇丰，但绝大多数与他在南非、新西兰、爪哇等地的受聘和访问有关。除《美术通诠》外，沃斯福尔德还有《批评的原则》(The Principles of Criticism)、《南非联邦》(The Union of South Africa)等著作。与严复翻译的绝大多数作品相比,《美术通诠》的作者可能是名气最小的。但我认为,严复选择这部书,至少有四点值得参考:1. 沃斯福尔德是非常符合严复喜好的那类作家:视野开阔,谙熟经典,旁征博引,言辞优美。2.《美术通诠》这部书少有学究气,作者的大局观好,而且以"通识"来展开,便于理解,便于接受。3. 本书前面三章,包括艺术、文学、古典批评,相对完整。译文既有内容,又符合严复的民智、民德、民力之说。4. 节译此书几个章节,总共不过数千字而已,并不需要耗费严复太多的时间。从 1903 到 1909 年的六年间,严复的主要精力在翻译《法意》一书,能够抽空翻译《美术通诠》三章,依时间耗费而言,实属奢侈。若不是这些章节与《法意》原本产生某些共鸣,他断然不敢有如此的精力投入。"此前的研究往往重视考察某些重要思想家比如斯宾塞和约翰·穆勒对严复思想的影响,那些不太知名的思想家则相对被忽视。"(戚学民,2004:94)[1] 沃斯福尔德应该就属于戚学民提及的"那些不太知名的思想家",值得我们进一步去研究。

---

1 与《美术通诠》的原作者 W. B. Worsfold(沃斯福尔德)相比,《政治科学导论》的作者 Sir John Seeley(约翰·西莱爵士)就比较有名了。英国剑桥大学近代史钦定讲座教授外加爵士,那绝对是一张响当当的名片。在英国,举凡拥有爵士头衔的,一定是该领域最出类拔萃之人,如伦敦政治经济学院院长 Sir Howard Davis(霍华德·戴维斯爵士),是英国金融界响当当的人物;英国著名足球俱乐部曼联队主教练 Sir Alex Ferguson(弗格森爵士),是英超俱乐部的一个神话。

五

严复的《美术通诠》中的"通诠"一词如何理解？如我在前面提到，"通诠"一词，很可能是严复所造。"通诠"的大意应该是"原理""导读"，义与英文的 introduction 相近，属于"总相类"、入门类的理论。"通诠"一词多用在文章标题、书名之中。1898 年严复在《天演论》中曾用到"通诠"一词，1904 年严复译爱德华·甄克斯的著作 *A History of Politics*，取译名为《社会通诠》。此后有张岱年《文化通诠》、《吕氏春秋通诠》等论著名，不过用者屈指可数。

依《汉语大词典》，"通诠"二字之用，前者倾向"没有阻碍、懂得、传达、普遍"之释义；而后者"诠"更倾向于"真理、系统知识"此类阐明事物意义、诠释人世真理的言论。两字合用，我们可以理解为"普遍、系统的知识"。《美术通诠》则意为"关于文学艺术的普遍、系统的知识"。

"通诠"两字不胫而走，但也招来批评之声。如章太炎（2015：48）在《菿汉微言》中有言："严复又译《社会通诠》，虽名通诠，实乃远西一往之论，于此土历史贯习固有隔阂，而多引以裁断事情。是故知别相而不知总相者，沈曾植也。知总相而不知别相者，严复也。"在章太炎看来，严复虽有许多总体性的概括，但重在西论，难以照应到本土之实际；他的"总相"指向社会的共同点，而"别相"则指向本土的特性或地域与文化的差异。他指责严复将中学与西学进行盲目比附。

客观地说，章氏的批评有些偏颇。首先，以严复之译为，在整个清末民初，无人能与其比肩；其二，翻译本身就是"一往之论"，不敢背离原文；其三，严复（2004：106）根据中西语言之差异对于翻译西文做了说明:"新理踵出,名目纷繁,索之中文,渺不可得,即有牵合,终嫌参差。译者遇此,独有自具衡量,即义定名。"真所谓,评论易,翻译难。好在章太炎批评的另一人为沈曾植(1850—1922),同为清末民初的高人,治学严谨,综览百家,博古通今,学贯中西,以"硕学通儒"蜚声中外。如此看来,章氏这样的批评,倒可视为一种善意的抬举。当然,三人之中,当以章太炎站位最高,一语甫出,就把"总相"和"别相"两者尽揽怀中。

六

严复为什么舍"文学"而取"美术"?是理解错误,还是有意为之?严复不可能将literature错译为"美术",这是普通译者也不会犯的错误。严复将书名的"literature"译为"美术",但他将原著第二章标题literature译为"文辞"。在书中也是一样,他把literature译为"书"和"章"。根据这些现象,唯一的解释就是,严复有意而为之。

清末民初的"美术"一语,系翻译名词,相当于现代人所说的"艺术"(张宜雷,2004:73)。严复(2014:553)在《美术通诠》的按语中指出了美术在国外教育中的重要地位:"故美术者,教化之极高点也。而吾国之浅人,且以为无用而置之矣。"惜国人常从俗入流,抱残守缺,不求思变,需要引入新的风气,新的理念。因此严复节译此书,希望唤起国人的审美意识。

严复的这一行为恰好符合他极力提倡的"三民说"。"所可悲者,民智之已下,民德之已衰,与民气之已困耳,虽有圣人用事,非数十百年薄海知亡,上下同德,痛刮除而鼓舞之,终不足以有立。"(严复,

1994：12）严复为旧中国的积弱和匮乏感到痛心，提出"鼓民力、开民智、新民德"，希望从这三个方面来强国盛世，这些对后来的知识分子都产生了极大的影响。

汪晖对严复的描述有一定的参考价值。他（2004：193）认为，严复在构思和理解宇宙和道德行为的过程中，试图在归纳与演绎的逻辑和概念体系（所谓"名学"）之上建立一种"学"的谱系，在这个意义上，作为分类学的"理"概念与近代的科学概念之间存在着某种内在的关系，这种关系不仅表现为近代中国科学家或科学教育家用"穷理学"、"理学"，以及与此密切相关的"格致"概念指称科学的语言实践，而且还表现为科学的知识谱系也被运用于政治、经济和道德的实践。

如果我们把这与严复论艺术与美的另一段话放在一起来看，这个意思就更明显了。这段话见于严复译著《法意》第五章之按语：

> 吾国有最乏而宜讲求，然犹未暇讲求者，则美术是也。夫美术者何？凡可以娱官神耳目，而所接在感情，不必关于理者是已。其在文也，为词赋；其在听也，为乐，为歌诗；其在目也，为图画，为刻塑，为宫室，为城郭园亭之结构，为用器杂饰之百工，为五彩彰施、玄黄浅深之相配，为道涂之平广，为坊表之崇闳，凡此皆中国盛时之所重，而西国今日所尤争胜而不让人者也。而其事于吾国则何如？盖几几乎无一可称者矣。（严复，2014：322）

严复从1903年起，全力翻译《法意》，前后耗时六年。不难想象，他之所以选择沃斯福尔德的《美术通诠》(*On the Exercise of Judgment in Literature*)来做翻译，是因为该书恰恰与他读到孟德斯鸠《法意》中有关章节的精神相符。在他看来，中华盛世曾经有的审美精神和礼乐风俗，在经过 19 世纪西方列强对中国的霸凌和压迫之后，已经不复存在，反观曾经在历史上落后于中国的西方，如今对美术的追求已经蔚然成风。严复为之而痛心，希望通过翻译来加强国民对美的追求。下面一段《法意》中的文字比较好地说明了他当时的心境：

> 美术者，统乎乐之属者也。使吾国而欲其民有高尚之精神，誅荡之心意，而于饮食、衣服、居处、刷饰、词气、容仪，知静洁治好，为人道之所宜，否则，沦其生于犬豕，不独为异族之所鄙贱而唤讯也，则后此之教育，尚于美术一科，大加之意焉可耳。东西古哲之言曰，人道之所贵者，一曰诚，二曰善，三曰美。（严复，2014：322）

其实，诚善美即我们平时所说的"真善美"。美是行为美、服饰美、言谈美、饮食美、环境美。追求美，是一个国民提升自身素质的必经之路。这就恰好印证了严复的"三民说"。我们再看看《美术通诠》中的第一段：

> 行乎都邑之间，所见者莫不有铸像画图、文史典籍，而文明之国，其所有者尤侈富。即在通衢巷陌，其圆柱方坫，或以铜，或以石，高者耸霄汉，卑者掩映林木间。其接于游人之目者，皆其国男女之肖像也。入其居，悬于墙者，则有画。度于几阁者，

则有壶甑尊彝,及他古器。而书史卷帙,纵横床榻。乃至富家旧族,往往辟堂室斋宇,专以待所搜牢者。图像简册,触目珍异,其美若不胜收者焉。(严复,2014:541)

前面三段引文,它们的主旨、精神、语调都十分一致,上下贯通。英文原著虽系文学批评书籍,但其开头并没有做文学叙述,倒是有了一段有关艺术的描述。这是因为艺术统领其他文学音乐等,作者首先领读者入林,然后再观木。人类艺术在这里得到了总体的描述。在严复看来,船坚炮利固然是强国之器,文学之诚、美术之真、风俗之善才是真正国富民强的表现。开民智、新民德、鼓民力,如果国民之审美得到提升,国民素质则必然得到升华。这恐怕是严复的良苦用心所在。

七

在严复看来,美术实乃文学艺术的最高表现,它包括文学但不能等同于文学,关于这一点,严复(2014:542)在《美术通诠》中有这样的描述:"……艺术可别为二类也,其一谓之美术,其一谓之实艺。美术如营建(Architecture),如刻塑(Sculpture),如绘画(Painting),如音乐(Music),如诗赋(Poetry)。实艺如匠冶梓庐之所操,乃至圬者陶人红女车工之业。"他对美术内涵和地位的认识,无疑是受西方长期以来观念的影响。其实,在清末民初,文学之代言者唯诗赋不可,那时的小说等尚未进入文学和士大夫的大雅之堂。抓住了美术,就抓住了严复的改良要害之处。严复(2014:542)在《法意》中继而言之,"然美术之关于民德、民智尤深,移风易俗,存于神明之地;而实艺小术,则形质养生所不可废,而于人理为粗。"严复希望借助美术,来移风易俗,滋润民心,良苦用心由此一览无余。

严复说《美术通诠》是未竟译著,但他最后没有花时间来翻译余下的章节,也许他觉得本书前面三节,分别探讨了艺术、文学、古典批评,而且三者各有侧重,古典批评乃经典之论,处于"原"或"元"之初,意义可以演绎,其最容易激起共鸣。他就此停笔,也不失为一种明智之举。

商务印书馆建馆百余年,出版翻译经典的传统深厚。我应胡晓凯编辑之邀翻译旧典《文学通诠》,并将译稿与严复的节译、英文原著合集出版,倍感荣幸。我希望这本书既是一本阅读的经典,也是一部研究的范本。适逢严复逝世100周年,商务印书馆出版这部合集,功莫大焉!

罗选民

2021年10月7日于西大镜湖斋

参考文献

陈平原.晚清辞书视野中的"文学"——以黄人的编纂活动为中心［J］.北京大学学报，2007（3）：59-74.

狄霞晨，朱恬骅.严复与中国文学观念的现代转型——以新见《美术通诠》底本为中心［J］.复旦学报，2021（1）：26-36.

关爱和.晚清：以报刊为中心的文学时代的开启［J］.复旦学报（社会科学版），2020（3）：132-143.

姜荣刚.现代"意境"说的形成：从格义到会通［J］.文学评论，2019（2）：31-39.

罗选民.严复《美术通诠》的底本和原著的发现［J］.亚太跨学科翻译研究，2021（1）：1-10.

皮后锋.严复大传［M］.福州：福建人民出版社，2003.

戚学民.严复《政治讲义》文本溯源［J］.历史研究，2004（2）：85-97.

汪 晖.中国现代思想的兴起（上）［M］.北京：生活·读书·新知三联书店，2004.

吴小坤，黄煜.严复与《群己权界论》：密尔自由观对严复新闻思想的影响［J］.中共浙江省委党校学报，2010（01）：38-43.

严 复.原强［A］,《论世变之亟——严复集》［M］,胡希伟选注.沈阳：辽宁人民出版社，1994.

严 复.法意［M］,严复全集［C］（4）.福州：福建教育出版社，2014.

严 复.美术通诠［M］,严复全集［C］（5）.福州：福建教育出版社，2014.

严 复.政治讲义［M］,严复全集［C］（6）.福州：福建教育出版社，2014.

严 复.天演论译例言［A］,严复选集［A］,周振甫选注.北京：人民文学出版社，2004.

萧公权.中国政治思想史［M］.大连：辽宁教育出版社，1998.

于蕾.译者可见性——严复《美术通诠》的个案研究［D］.北京：清华大学（未发表）.

曾小凤.何谓"美术"？怎么"现代"？［A］,2021年先锋的寓言："美术革命"与中国现代美术批评的发生［M］.桂林：广西师范大学出版社，2021.

章太炎.菿汉微言［A］,章太炎全集［C］.上海：上海人民出版社，2015.

张宜雷.严复与中国文学的现代化变革［J］.理论与现代化，2004（05）：71-74.

周兴陆."文学"概念的古今榫合［J］.文学评论，2019（5）：64-70.

Worsfold, W. B. *On the Exercise of Judgment in Literature* ［M］. London: The Temple Primers, 1900.

总目录

文学通诠 1

美术通诠 115

ON THE EXERCISE OF JUDGMENT
IN LITERATURE 145

文学通诠

On the Exercise of Judgement in Literature

〔英〕巴西尔·沃斯福尔德 著

罗选民 译

目录

第一章	艺术本质之哲思	5
第二章	文学智慧之洞察	17
第三章	古典文学之批评	25
第四章	现代文学之批评	39
第五章	如何唤起想象力	51
第六章	当代文学之批评	61
第七章	文学判断之运用	79
第八章	形式方法与风格	101

科隆大教堂，最著名的哥特式教堂之一

第一章 艺术本质之哲思

批评和批评家的定义——批评原则与道德原则相似——区分"美的艺术"与"次要艺术"——美的艺术可分为(1)"眼"的艺术和"耳"的艺术,(2)与物质基础相关——艺术的定义——建筑——雕塑——绘画——音乐——诗歌近乎所有大城小镇，尤其是文明国都，都藏有许多雕像、绘画和书籍。即使六街三陌，也随处可见由大理石或青铜铸成的男女雕塑，高耸于基座之上，迎接往来人群的凝视与瞻望。而且，近乎每家每户，皆有绘画妆墙，花瓶饰架，书籍置案。遇大户宽宅，则辟有专室存放绘画、雕像之类的珍品，斗室充栋，可谓琳琅满目。凡此种种，皆已明示，艺术乃文明人生活之重要组成部分，因世人希冀时常受到艺术及其包蕴思想的熏陶，使自己陶冶其中，教化感悟。

"批评"乃艺术与文学领域所施行的判断活动，而"批评家"作为认知主体，须具备必要知识，以对特定领域内文艺作品的优劣与价值作出确当判断。"判断"这一具有特殊意义的术语最早可溯及活跃于公元前300年至公元前146年的亚历山大学派（Alexandrian Scholars）[1]。该学派从五个方面对书籍展开研究：材料编排、语音校正、句法解析、说明注解以及对相关作品优劣和作者身份的判断。因此，"判断"原本是书

---

[1] 该学派深受柏拉图哲学思想影响，在经典的阐释上注重寓意解经，不同于安提阿学派从字面和历史意义上的解释。——译者

籍研究领域的术语。时至今日，在谈及"批评"和"批评家"时，通常指的便是这种文学判断。而如果要对非书籍类艺术作品进行评判，须在"批评"之前加一限定词，如"艺术批评""戏剧批评"，限定词名目视具体情况而定。本书沿用"批评"和"批评家"二词，取其广义，包含了最初书籍判断的专门意义，但也不尽于此。

正如某些道德原则（即使非普遍，也至少为全体文明人士大致认同）是我们控制自身行为所遵循的依据，同理，某些广泛存在的批评原则（即使非普遍，但有理有据）可引导我们作出审美喜好上的决定。道德原则教会我们克己自制，既能愉悦自身，也能福幸他者。同样，批评原则教会我们正确思考文艺作品，使我们能够从这些作品以及作品所呈现的物质存在和生活事实中获得最大乐趣。然而，如果说道德（也称正确生活的艺术）涵盖了人类存在的整个领域，那么批评只涉及其中的某个方面。因此，我们首要考虑的是艺术的性质和范围，换言之，我们必须对艺术是什么，以及艺术在人类生活中的作用形成一个明确的概念。

为厘清这一概念，我们将首先回顾几种艺术及其由各自理念而衍生的作品，然后将之归纳并提炼出一般概念。

起初，艺术作品被分为两类——"美的"艺术（"Fine" Arts）和"次要"（或"机械"）艺术（"Lesser" or "Mechanical" Arts）。美的艺术包括建筑、雕塑、绘画、音乐和诗歌。[1] 次要艺术指由铁匠、木匠、木工、石匠、陶工、织工、玻璃匠、油漆工等制造的产品。这两种艺术的区别在于，一般而言，前者旨在提升人的精神享受，而后者意图满足人的物

---

[1] 除此以外，我们或许还可以加上戏剧这门综合艺术、演说艺术以及失传的舞蹈艺术。

质需求。二者都是人类发展的表现，美的艺术重在关注道德和智力的成长，而次要艺术主要关切身体与物质的满足。在这两类艺术的典型形式之间，还存在其他艺术形式，比如在木头或铜上雕刻、在瓷器或玻璃上绘画、在墙面设计装饰或在布料上设计图案等，根据所展示艺术价值的高低，它们都可以归于以上两类艺术中的一类。

次要艺术的起源和意图很简单，也易于理解。它源于人类追求衣食住行等基本需求的自然欲望，并随着文明的发展而发展。次要艺术的意图也很明确，其底层逻辑便是实用（utility），这一逻辑化身为原则，分别检验了不同作品的价值。该原则影响深远，所以次要艺术常被恰如其分地称为"有用的"艺术。无论是一所房子、一把椅子，还是一个金属或黏土制成的器皿，其典型价值都是实现其既定的实用性。而它们的形式之美无非就是这种价值的瞬间显现。次要艺术的作品大多[1]通过这种价值显现，满足视觉享受和心理慰藉；如若没有这种价值显现，任何装饰或装饰效果都毫无意义，所装饰对象的美不增反减。

因此，关于次要艺术，无需赘言；而关于美的艺术，必须予以审慎思考，因为后者的性质更为精妙和复杂。迄今为止，批评家们对于其确切起源和准确意图尚未达成完全一致的看法。当我们考虑文学价值的检验标准时，必须注意这种意见分歧对诗歌艺术的重要意义。因此，后文提及的"艺术作品"和"艺术"特指"美的艺术作品"和"美的艺术"。

艺术有两种有效分类方式。第一种分为"眼"的艺术和"耳"的艺术，取决于是通过视觉还是听觉进入思想。因此，建筑、雕塑和绘画便

1　这里说"大多"，是因为金属抛光后的色泽本身就是美的元素。

与音乐和诗歌形成鲜明的艺术对比。第二种分类基于艺术形式在实现各自目的的过程中对物质基础的依赖程度。据此原则，黑格尔[1]按尊贵程度，把建筑排在末流，而将诗歌奉为至高。建筑之所以被置于最末，是因为在这种艺术表现形式中，物质基础极为突显，而正是建筑师在材料的组建中所表达出的意图，将建造用的大堆石头和砖块提升到了艺术作品的高度。比建筑高一个层级的是雕塑，它的基础也完全是物质的，但雕塑家可以化腐朽为神奇，赋予大理石或金属一种这些材料本身所不具有的意义。雕塑再往上是绘画，它的物质基础相对较弱，因为它将物质空间的第三维度排斥在画布的平面之外，即仅有长和宽。但画家在画布的平面上，创造出与物质对象相似的形象，即有着同样的质地、形式和色彩。然后是音乐，其唯一的物质基础是声音。声音化为音符，被音乐家巧妙组合，从而表达出不同的情感，甚至可以使听者脑海中浮现出真情实感。最上层是诗歌，它与物质材料相距甚远，其唯一媒介（除了韵律元素外）便是符号——词或词的组合，它们能唤起感悟，直击心灵。

如上所述，这两种分类是有效的，它们突出了如下三个方面。首先，艺术创作需要一个物质基础，无论是建筑艺术中的石头砖块，还是诗歌艺术中的文字符号。其次，它们进入思想的主要途径是视觉和（程度其次的）听觉。最后，这些物质基础和两种主要途径都只是艺术家与观者进行思想沟通的手段，这一点尤为重要。因此，从大教堂到十四行诗，举凡艺术作品都具有象征意义；也即，它们超越官能感知，具有一

---

[1] 黑格尔（1770—1831），德国古典美学理论的重要代表，著有《美学》一书，提出"美就是理念的感性显现"。——译者

种思想所赋予和感知得到的特质。至此，或许可以把这些事实归纳为一个大致的概念，并大胆地给艺术下个定义：**艺术是现实在精神层面的呈现**。

为了理解此定义的含义与重要性，我们将分别审视每种艺术，思考其（1）物质基础；（2）把物质基础置于感官认知之下的方法；（3）在此种艺术中，现实进入脑海而后在精神层面的显露程度。

建筑艺术的物质基础是最粗糙的，包括石头、砖块、金属和木材，与其他材料一起用于建筑物建造。由于这种媒介完全是物质的，所以建筑师的作品对眼睛的影响，与任何其他外部物体对眼睛的影响完全相同。阳光、明暗、色彩、氛围、场地或自然位置和环境的影响都可以为建筑师所用，他们无须像其他艺术家那样借助视觉技巧进入思想[1]。原因有二：一是他们并不展现生命或运动；二是他们的作品与其他没有生命的外部物体具有完全相同的特性，如坚实、有形和有色。然而，建筑师创造的作品，虽然是真实存在的，但也是现实在精神层面的呈现。换言之，建筑作品也是思想的表达。哥特式[2]大教堂是最为人熟知之例，它不仅是人们做礼拜的场所，本身也具有崇拜的神圣性，因为其外在形式和特征表达了人类对永生的渴望。这种思想同样体现在众多的尖塔、直插云霄的尖顶以及支撑起高耸屋顶的束柱之上。这种建筑展现的是精神层面上的礼拜场所，即大教堂的设计与建造反映了建筑师对基督教礼拜圣地的理

---

1 除非我们考虑希腊建筑师在建造某些庙宇时所采用的"视觉矫正"。
2 哥特式艺术（Art gothique），12 至 16 世纪初期盛行于欧洲的一种以新型建筑为主的艺术，包括雕塑、绘画和工艺美术。哥特式建筑的基本构件是尖拱和肋架拱顶，造成一种向上升华、天国神秘的幻觉。——译者

念，但由于物质（或感官上）的部分太过突显，乃至喧宾夺主，观者可能会对建筑作品印象深刻，感到赏心悦目，但却丝毫没有意识到建筑师通过作品各部分想要传达的意图。

雕塑艺术的物质基础是石头或金属，经千雕万琢而塑造成生命体或非生命体形态。雕塑家可以支配除动态之外的所有现实属性；因为其作品坚实、有形、有色（如果他选择色彩的话），足以呈现现实中的人和物。因此，只有雕刻动态人物时，他们才需要使用技巧来欺骗观者的眼睛。但是，由于缺乏动态属性，他们本可以自由表现的外部现实受到了一种

《米洛斯的维纳斯》

自然限制；这种限制的存在，使雕塑艺术的特别之处体现在其最适当的表现对象都静默着，包括单独全身像、单独半身像或小群体雕塑。雕塑家以极少的装饰和极简的方式来表现人物，同时也因为他们很难用石头或金属等坚硬介质来表现织物衣料，所以最完美的人物塑像往往是半裸或全裸的。然而，现实的精神层面在雕塑家的作品中比在建筑师的作品中更为突出；因为雕塑家赋予其用以创作的石头或金属雕像以生命的外观，并展现对生命物种最完美形式的构想，将其呈现在每一件作品中。因此，静默的形体美是雕塑艺术的特殊主题。

第一章　艺术本质之哲思

俄国著名风景画家希施金素描作品

绘画的物质基础由画布、木板或其他平面组成,在此之上绘制线条和涂画人工色彩,以展现空间感和外物原色。但就比例来说,由于这些物质基础比雕塑家的少,画家需要更多的技巧使这些线条和色彩为视觉所感知,因为他必须要在一个平面上通过线条和色彩来展现立体物及其真实色彩。若只用线条来表现立体感,画家必须用到透视法,也就是说,必须在画布上同样的位置画出物体不同角度的线条轮廓,因为观者只能从单一视角来观看这些物体。同样,为了表现与观者距离不同的对象所呈现的真实色彩,画家须将人造色彩放置在一个统一的平面上,正确给出每个物体的色彩明暗度。画家必须使色彩的明暗程度与实际对象的色彩相称,从而使人造色彩产生视觉上的距离差异。这样,画家运用透视法绘制线条,适当划分色彩明暗度,使平面图像在视觉上呈现一处风景或一处室内景观。此外,绘画比雕塑更突出现实的精神层面,当然更远超建筑。因为在任何情况下,无论绘画的主题是历史事件还是自然风景,画作都是画家对这一事件或场景的观念呈现,而非仅通过画作来还原已知事件的外在细节或精确地展现自然风光。换言之,画家将现实的再现予以理想化:他们不仅复制或模仿,还诠释和甄选。和其他艺术家一样,画家展现了现实的精神层面,其作品不仅关注感官,而且关注观者的思想和理解。

至此,我们一直讨论的是"眼"的艺术,尚未涉及"耳"的艺术,即音乐和诗歌。音乐和诗歌的物质基础都不突显,因此作品所展现的现实的精神层面就显得更为重要。

音乐家使用的唯一物质基础就是声音,包括人类的嗓音,还包括在漫长岁月中被发明并完善的乐器发出的声音。声音或单独呈现,或与文字结合;根据和声和作曲规则,声音被排列成音符,并被分隔出音程。无论音乐家如何借助诗歌艺术、使用多少文字,音乐最典型的媒介还是声音——难以名状的声音。这种典型媒介被认为是表达思想的一种手段,其明显特征就是极度的不确定性和模糊性;与模糊性相对应的是音乐的特有价值,它能够在广阔的思维领域中驰骋,与人类普遍灵魂的原始方面进行对话。因此,音乐不仅吸引着幼稚孩童和粗野蛮人,也吸引着博学大儒与文明之士。而音乐家除了遵循作曲和演奏的规则,还使用技巧通过听觉来进入思想。他可以展现真实存在,但只能在音乐这种艺术形式的限制之下。有一个例子可以很好地说明他是如何受到这些条件限制的。法国批评家维克托·库辛（Victor Cousin）向我们说明，海顿[1]在意识到音乐艺术的表现力有其自身的局限后，是如何呈现出恶劣天气的真实场景的。

"让最聪明的交响乐作曲家展现一场暴风雨，最容易的方式莫过于模仿呼啸的风声和轰隆的雷声。闪电瞬间撕破夜幕，暴风雨露出骇人的一面，暗藏汹涌的波涛，时而前进上升，掀起滔天巨浪，时而倒退下沉，似跌进无底深渊……但是，如何对声音组合排列，才能使听众眼前浮现出这样的景象呢？如果听者事先不知情，那他永远也猜不到音乐的主题，我敢说听者肯定分不清音乐所表现的是暴风雨还是战争。尽管有科学的技巧和天才的资质加持，声音还是无法呈现形式。明智的话，音乐应当拒绝参加这场无望的竞赛，不去描述波浪的起伏和其他类似的形式。相反，它应发挥自己的独特优势。运用声音，音乐能够让我们的灵魂感受到暴风雨的各种场景，使我们内心深处接连涌现出不同的情感。正是因此，我们说，海顿和画家旗鼓相当，甚至要技高一筹，因为他的音乐比绘画更为深刻地撼动了灵魂。"[2]

关于诗歌，我只需说一些必要的东西就可以结束本章对艺术的简要回顾，因为后续多个章节会对这门特殊艺术的各个方面进行详细讨论。在所有的艺术中，诗歌的物质基础最少。抛开韵律、韵脚和头韵所包含

---

[1] 海顿（1732—1809），奥地利作曲家。维也纳古典乐派代表人物之一，被誉为"交响乐之父"和"弦乐四重奏之父"。——译者

[2] 《论真、善、美》，第九讲，第195—196页（第27版）。

的乐音[1],诗歌运用视觉或听觉,只是将一些文字符号传递给心灵。传递文字符号无需任何技巧,因为眼睛或耳朵会自然感知。但是,现实生活及外部自然景象的精神层面,要通过理念或理念的组合呈现出来,而诗歌中的文字符号正是这些理念的表达媒介,这是非常重要的。诗歌直面心灵,因为诗人创作的源素材,就是理念或脑海中的画面,没有任何媒介能像语言那样强烈地影响想象力。在表达现实方面,诗人受到诗歌艺术自身的条件限制,只能呈现外部存在的精神层面。

---

1 震动发音有明显规则的、能分辨出明显音高并能进行模仿的声音就是乐音,如乐器演奏的声音和广播中的音乐都是乐音,而某些噪音在通过采样和处理之后,也能成为乐音。音强、音调和音色构成乐音三要素。——译者

沃尔夫将军之死（油画，本杰明·韦斯特绘）

第二章 文学智慧之洞察

感知现实的客观和主观途径——文学有助于主观世界观的形成——关于一场战役的绘画和文字描述之间的比较——文学的性质和题材——书籍如何助益于人的主观存在

人之主体从客观和主观两方面了解世界，即了解除人自身以外的所有现实。在主体生命的每一刻，除却睡眠，都在以这两种不同方式感知周边世界。使人产生情感的总体感受，部分来自于物质存在（包括生命体与非生命体形式），也就是说，与世界真实深入的接触，在任何时候都会影响人的感官；部分来自于脑海中不断重现的精神图像，它们有时与物质存在有关，有时又与其完全脱离。因此，看待世界的两种观念都在展示着现实，只不过前者以客观为主，后者以主观为要。

如果主体反省某一时刻，就能意识到，个体通过心灵所获得的世界观显然更为宏大，因为借助记忆和理性（或二者相互作用），我们能随意唤起外部客观存在的形象或观念。就在我写作的此刻，通过自我感官即时获得的"视界观"，仅限于所在房间的四面墙，以及偶尔透过敞开的窗户看到的建筑物、树木和路人。但是，如果把注意力从这些物体上移开，进行反思，本我思想就可延伸且漫游于任何国家、任何时代的事物与存在。事实上，自我往往借助自身或他者的经历来认知世界。因为在主观世界观中，自我不再局限于自身的即时感觉，还可鉴往知来。其中，借鉴他者之经验感觉尤为重要。不同年龄和种族的人，其思想和经验被记录在建筑物、艺术作品与习俗中，尤其是对其观点及行为的书面记载中，后者以书籍或手稿的形式保存下来。在所有这些思想经验的间接来源中，迄今为止最有效且影响深远的是最后一种，可以用"文学"这一术语概括。所有的艺术都是在精神层面再现外部现实，但是除了诗歌这一文学的最高形式之外，其他艺术都是利用现实的客观层面来协助呈现精神层面。但是文学，除了（已经提到过的）乐音元素外，并不需要这种帮助；因为文学——作为文学本身——只关心对世界的主观看法。

为了更清楚地表达我的意思，现举一简例，比方一场战役，我会尽量指出画家和历史学家如何以不同的方式将这一事件呈现在人们脑海中。我家墙上挂着一幅画，画家以客观的视角描绘了战场上的情景。这让我觉得如果我在关键时刻身处观战的较佳位置，就能明晰战场上的一切。他向我展示了密集人群、刀光剑影、烽火硝烟、指挥官及其参谋、其他重要人物、躺在地上的死者和伤员。如果基于这一特定时刻，从这个单一角度仔细观察这幅画，我还会看到一些精确的细节，比如各种军服的颜色和样式，以及各军队的部署等。但这些细节只能通过肉眼感知。当我转身离开这幅画，我会这样总结："现在，如果我置身现场，我会明了战役的模样。"然后我转向书架，拿下一卷历史书，里面记录了同一场战役。在阅读过程中，我发现历史学家向我描述的是完全不同的一类事实。他最先关心的是事件的主观层面，因此，他的观点不局限于某个单一看法或某一特定时刻。它涵盖了一系列事实，它们构成这场战役作为一次事件的重要性。他描述了战役发生的地点、各方战斗人员的数量和国籍、战斗的现时结果和远期影响、各方指挥官的姓名、他们的计划以及在执行计划时所展现的战略战术，还有许多其他细节。此外，他向我展示了这场战役与之前或之后的其他事件的相互关联。然而，即使我已经获知所有细节，也了解了历史学家对各军队的看法，但我并没有得到像画家留给我的那样生动的印象。不过，这种生动印象的持续时间也仅限于我观看这幅画的时候。于我而言，回忆起历史学家的描述要容易得多，它使得我在头脑中形成对战役的概念，虽然它更为耗时，但一旦获得，就更具完整性和永久性。因为他告诉我的事实，就是我基于对世界的主观看法所能掌握的一切，它们很容易储存在头脑中，随时能被记忆唤醒，组成一幅精神图像——也即独立于感官的"想法"。对比这两种方式所产生的不同结果，可以用一句话来描述：当我看完画转身离开时，我会惊呼："我看到了这场战役"；而当我合上书时，我会说："我了解了这场战役，因为历史学家已经把发生的一切都告诉我了。"

因此，作家用文字符号再现的不是事件的外在，不是官能感知的事物外表，而是人与这些事件的关系以及事物在他脑海中留下的印象。他呈现的不是城镇建筑、国事议会、兵戎相见、川谷河流，而是这些事件和场景在其本人以及他人脑海中产生的意志功能、言语辞话和思想观念。

因此，广义而言，文学就是记录伟大思想家对各种外在现实的印象，以及他们进行的思考。文学主题涵盖了人类生命与活动的全部范畴，以及客观自然的所有表现形式。因为文学作品不仅再现了现实生活中的事件和人物的言行，还记载了基于对人类生活状况的观察而推导出的规则。同样，它不仅向我们展示了某一特定时代下，某些国家的人们对什么感兴趣，而且还展示了通过对自然过程的长期观察而逐渐形成的一般规律。所以文学在人类生活中起着非常重要的作用。它是感觉的第二大来源，对综合事实（个人和种族经验的共同结果）作出了巨大贡献，塑造了我们每个人对整个世界的主观看法。

要了解人的主观存在对书籍材料的依赖程度，我们需停下来思考一下文学于我们的意义何在。通过文学，我们可以与柏拉图、佛陀、蒙田、艾迪生等伟大的逝者对话；[1]通过文学，我们可以行走在巴比伦、雅典、罗马、亚历山大的街道上；通过文学，我们可以看到早已化为尘埃的丰碑；通过文学，我们可以重现远古时代的生活，进而以比较的眼光衡量今人所取得的进步；通过文学，我们从亚里士多德[2]那里体悟智慧，从欧几里得[3]那里学习几何，从查士丁尼[4]那里习得律法，从克莱斯特[5]和圣保罗[6]那里了解伦理；通过文学，一方水土如地貌、居民、气候、物产等可为人熟知。更重要的是，通过文学，大师们创造性地开拓了属于自己的领域，

---

1 柏拉图（前427—前347），古希腊哲学家，与其师苏格拉底和其徒亚里士多德合称"西方三圣贤"或"希腊三哲"。柏拉图的著作多以对话录形式记录，较为轻视诗歌的作用；佛陀（Buddha），狭义而言，指历史上的释迦牟尼；蒙田（1533—1592），文艺复兴时期法国思想家、散文作家，著有《随笔集》3卷；艾迪生（1672—1719），英国散文作家，曾与好友斯梯尔合编两份著名刊物《闲话报》（*Tatler*）和《旁观者》（*Spectator*）。——译者

2 亚里士多德（前384—前322），古希腊哲学家，其著述涉猎多个学科，在物理学、心理学、生物学、历史学、修辞学等领域都作出了重要贡献。所作《诗学》是西方文明第一部系统的美学和艺术理论作品，主要谈及悲剧、喜剧和史诗。亚氏在考究艺术后，认为艺术的基本原则在于：艺术的本质是模仿，即反映现实；艺术的类型决定现实如何在诗中得以反映。——译者

3 欧几里得（约前330—前275），古希腊数学家。著有《几何原本》13卷，此书反映的理性思维精神，对后来数学和科学发展的影响巨大。——译者

4 查士丁尼（483—565），东罗马帝国皇帝（527—565在位）。他收复了许多失地、重建圣索菲亚大教堂并编撰《查士丁尼法典》，被称为"查士丁尼大帝"。——译者

5 克莱斯特（1777—1811），德国诗人、戏剧家、小说家。其"编年史式"的小说叙事对人类社会结构、观念、情感经验以及人类关系有非常精准的文学描写。——译者

6 使徒保罗，俗称圣保罗，是使徒时代（公元1世纪）向世界传播基督福音的重要人物之一。——译者

以供天才之子自由驰骋。如荷马[1]为我们创造了爱琴海上阳光普照的岛屿和紫色的海洋；但丁[2]描绘了一个黑暗而神秘的地狱；弥尔顿[3]给了我们一个伊甸园；莎士比亚[4]笔下的伊丽莎白时期的英国，与历史真实相比，风景色彩更加明亮，人物形象更为逼真；莫里哀[5]描绘的法国，较之于大君主时代（The Grand Monarque）的法国更加自然和生动。通过文学，奥德修斯、安提戈涅、比阿特丽斯、哈姆雷特、塔尔图夫[6]和其他伟大灵魂的精神后裔，能够与摩西、亚历山大、恺撒、圣女贞德和亨利八世[7]并肩生活。

---

1 荷马（约前9世纪—前8世纪），古希腊诗人，专事行吟的盲歌手。相传著名史诗《伊利亚特》和《奥德赛》为他所作。——译者

2 但丁（1265—1321），著名的中世纪意大利诗人，现代意大利语的奠基者，也是欧洲文艺复兴时代的开拓人。其史诗《神曲》留名后世，是欧洲最伟大的诗人和全世界最伟大的作家之一。——译者

3 约翰·弥尔顿（1608—1674），英国诗人、思想家，因其史诗《失乐园》和反对书报审查制的《论出版自由》而闻名于后世。——译者

4 莎士比亚（1564—1616），英国文学史上最杰出的戏剧家，也是西方文艺史上最杰出的作家之一。其流传后世的作品包括38部戏剧、154首十四行诗、2首长叙事诗和其他诗歌。——译者

5 莫里哀（1622—1673），17世纪法国喜剧作家、演员、戏剧活动家，其名作有《伪君子》《吝啬鬼》《唐璜》等，被认为是西方文学史上最伟大的喜剧作家之一。——译者

6 "奥德修斯"是史诗《奥德赛》中的人物，传说中希腊西部伊萨卡岛之王，曾参加特洛伊战争；"安提戈涅"是希腊神话中忒拜国王俄狄浦斯的女儿，剧作家索福克勒斯和欧里庇得斯都曾以安提戈涅为主角进行创作；"比阿特丽斯"是一位意大利女性，通常被认为是但丁作品创作的主要灵感来源；王子"哈姆雷特"是同名剧作《哈姆雷特》中的主角，其叔父谋害了国王父亲，篡取王位，娶了国王遗孀。哈姆雷特因此为父王之死向叔父复仇；塔尔图夫是莫里哀同名喜剧《塔尔图夫》中被伪装成道德和宗教信仰的伪君子角色，该剧于1664年首次演出。——译者

7 摩西是在《圣经·旧约》的《出埃及记》等书中所记载的、公元前13世纪时犹太人的民族领袖，犹太教徒认为他是犹太教的创始人；亚历山大大帝是古希腊著名王室阿吉德王朝成员，能征善战，未有败绩，被认为是历史上最伟大的将军之一；恺撒是罗马共和国末期的军事统帅、政治家，拉丁文散文作者，制定了《儒略历》；贞德是法国的军事家、天主教圣人、民族英雄，在英法百年战争中带领法兰西王国军队对抗英格兰王国军队的入侵，最后被捕并被处以火刑；亨利八世是英格兰都铎王朝第二任国王，推行宗教改革，成为英格兰最高宗教领袖，另外还积极鼓励人文主义研究。——译者

总之,文学使我们熟悉人的品性与物的特征,好比熟悉自己的至爱与至亲。

在我们思考文学对世界的重要贡献之前,必须注意一点:主观观念作用于客观认识。我们通过自己先前的感觉和文学作品获得对世界的认识,这增加了我们理解客观世界的能力,并强化了我们从欣赏艺术作品或欣赏大自然的面貌中所获得的乐趣。只有通过看待世界的主观方面,我们才能正确地认识客观世界。这就是为什么我在第一章中提到,我们追求批判性洞察力的目标之一,是我们不仅能够欣赏艺术作品,而且能够欣赏这些作品所代表的外部现实。这也恰恰是歌德所认为的真理的基础,如他所说,一个旅行者从罗马带走的任何东西都是他首先带进罗马的。

总之,文学就是人类的智慧结晶。智慧保存着个体以前的感觉、经验和已获得知识的记录,正是根据这一记录,个体才能解释每一种新的感觉和体验。同理,整个人类都有其在文学上的历史记录,只有根据这一记录,才能理解它目前的情况。如果没有文学智慧的合作,感官信息对个体来说是模糊的和没有价值的;如果没有文学所赋予的经验积累,人类生命的意义将被降级为一个纯粹的动物式存在。

柏拉图与亚里士多德（《雅典学院》油画局部，拉斐尔绘）

第三章 古典文学之批评

两类书籍，分别给出生活的事实和生活的"图景"——非创造性文学采用科学的方法，创造性文学采用艺术的方法——文学作品中三个卓越的元素：题材、风格、审美愉悦——柏拉图的批评——艺术与道德相互依存的原则——他对"真实"的检验——他没有区分逻辑的真实和艺术的真实——这导致了他对希腊诗歌的批判——亚里士多德的名作《诗学》——他将一切艺术视为模仿的过程——他对悲剧组成要素的分析——他将科学中的真实和艺术中的真实区分开来，从而纠正了柏拉图对创造性文学方法的错误认识——他解释诗歌如何引发人们的情感共鸣——亚历山大和古罗马的批评尽人皆知，我们对人情物事之了解如此广泛，在很大程度上要归功于文学，而非通过感官直接作用所得。的确，在我们的生活中，或者至少在我们若干个性的形成过程中，书籍所起的作用是如此重要，以至于通识教育的主要内容就包括掌握经典。换言之，书籍是一种公认的向世人宣介思想的媒介。虽然所有的文学作品都有助于我们形成主观世界观，但从书籍对我们的作用来看，仍然存在两种较大区别。就某些书籍而言，其贡献的价值在于它们所包含的主要事实；而就另外一些书籍而言，事实是次要的，其主要价值在于这些事实是以何种方式呈现在读者脑海中的。两种类别间没有明确的界线。但可以概括性地认为，前者记叙的是生活的事实，而后者呈现的是生活的"图景（pictures）"。

让我用一两个例子来说明这种不同。譬如洛克的《人类理解论》[1]

---

[1] 《人类理解论》是英国哲学家约翰·洛克最著名的作品，成书于1690年，其中讨论了人类知识与理解的基础。该书认为人在出生时的心智犹如一块白板（tabula rasa），随后由经验所得的知识填满。——译者

和吉本的《罗马帝国衰亡史》[1]这样的作品，显然必须归于强调事实的书籍类别。而乔治·艾略特[2]的小说应该归类到陈述事实比事实本身更重要的书籍中，比如她向我们全面而真实地描绘了英格兰中部地区（Midland Counties）的生活图景。同样，在《一个非洲庄园的故事》[3]或《十字路口的戴安娜》[4]中，我们可以看到南非的乡村生活图景。只有在后一部作品中，中心人物的个性才会如此引人注目，与其说这本书是一张图片，不如说是一幅肖像画，画中是一个美丽而任性的女人，她被环境和天赋所诱惑。在这里，我们有两种截然不同的要素：题材与风格（matter and manner），根据它们在作品中各自呈现的程度，可以将创意文学作品与一般文学作品区分开来。

至此，我们已然明确了这种区别对文学批评有着非常重要的影响。正如第一章所述，文学批评是一种对文学作品的优劣和价值作出确当判断的科学。因此，非创意文学主要（非全部）采用了科学的方法；而创意文学主要（非全部）采用了艺术的方法。所以，我们一开始就面临这样的情况：在书籍中寻求两种截然不同的价值观，每一种都必须用一种独立、独特的标准来衡量。在文学中，如果创造性因素很少或者完全没有，

---

[1] 该书是英国历史学家爱德华·吉本关于罗马帝国的历史巨著，涵盖从公元98年到1590年罗马帝国的全部历史。——译者

[2] 乔治·艾略特（1819—1880）是一位英国小说家，作品包括《弗洛斯河上的磨坊》（1860）和《米德尔马契》（1871—1872）等。——译者

[3] 本书作者奥丽芙·旭莱纳是19世纪非洲最卓越的作家之一，讲述了三个孩子在荒凉的非洲草原上的生活与成长，其中对南非草原的描述真实而残忍。书中再现了维多利亚时代英国殖民下的南非社会生活图景，反映了19世纪后半叶一代人反抗神权统治的觉醒与幻灭。——译者

[4] 本书是乔治·梅瑞狄斯1885年出版的一本小说，描写了一个聪明而强势的女人被困于悲惨婚姻中的故事。——译者

那么，知识学者、哲学家和领域内的专家就是最合格的批评家；但对于创意文学，情况就不同了。在这里，专业知识是次要的，事实乃众所周知的，处理方式是最重要的，呈现方法是艺术性的，因此，艺术家就是理想的批评家。

这两种截然不同的品质或价值不仅可以在分属于这两种主要文学类别的作品中找到，而且两种品质还以不同比例混合在一起，巧妙地结合，出现在科学、哲学、历史、传记、散文、小说和诗歌中。此外，所有创意文学和一般性文学不仅仅是科学，其中都包含着一种更深层次的品质或价值。我目前还没有谈论过，但它却是非常真实和重要的。这是诗歌与其姊妹艺术所共有的一种品质，即给人愉悦——审美愉悦——的品质。这种愉悦不是来自对正确行为的自觉，也不是来自对物质利益的期望，而是一种纯粹自足和无私的享受感。因此，在文学作品中，三个不同且独特的优秀元素的存在是可以在不同程度上辨别出来的，即题材、风格和审美愉悦。三者或其一都以不同的程度和不同的组合出现，既出现在不同类别的书籍中，又出现在同一类别的不同作品中。这样看来，伟人们从不同的角度看待书籍，提出用不同的标准来衡量其价值，或者批评家们对某一部文学作品褒贬不一，也就不足为奇了。

然而，正是由于这些尝试性的探究和不确定的摸索，我们今天才能确定某些原则的有效确当性。为了理解这些原则，有必要了解几个探究的性质，这些努力对批评的发展作出了最大的贡献。

最早致力于文学研究的伟大作家是柏拉图。他是该领域的佼佼者，而且对道德问题有极大的兴趣。这也就不难理解他最注重的是文学的题材，而相对忽视风格和审美愉悦，而后面这两点现在被认为与前者几乎是同等重要的。柏拉图认为，衡量一部文学作品的价值，以及一般艺术作品的价值，唯一的标准是它所传达的信息能否真实地反映外部现实。基于艺术与道德相互依存的原则，他似乎把文艺作品仅仅看作是传递道德真理的工具。这一原则在柏拉图的哲学体系中占有十分重要的地位，所以我用他自己的话来加以说明。

"好言辞、好音调、好风格、好节奏都来自好的精神状态，所谓好的精神状态并不是指我们用以委婉地称呼那些没有头脑的忠厚老实人的精神状态，而是指用来称呼那些智力好、品格好的人的真正良好的精神状态……

"绘画肯定充满这些特点，其他类似工艺如纺织、刺绣、建筑、家具制作、动物身体以及植物树木等的自然姿态，也都充满了这些品质。因为在这些事物里都有优美与丑恶。坏风格、坏节奏、坏音调，类乎坏言辞、坏品格。反之，美好的表现与明智、美好的品格相合相近。

"我们必须寻找一些艺人巨匠，用其大才美德，开辟一条道路，使我们的年轻人由此而进，如入健康之乡；眼睛所看到的，耳朵所听到的，艺术作品，随处都是；使他们如坐春风，得沾化雨，潜移默化，不知不觉之间受到熏陶，从童年时，就和优美、理智融合为一。"[1]

柏拉图从这一观念出发，运用批评眼光看待文学和艺术，来确定一部文学作品在多大程度上对生活事实进行了确凿且完备的传达。通过"真实性原则"的检验，他发现当时流行的希腊文学缺乏道德感，尤其

---

[1] 译文引自郭斌和、张竹明译本，商务印书馆，1986年，第109—110页。本书《理想国》引文均出自这一译本。——译者

是荷马和赫西奥德[1]的诗歌、品达[2]的抒情诗和雅典剧作家的杰作。他认为，"诗人和故事作者，在最紧要点上，在关于人的问题上说法有错误。他们举出许多人来说明不正直的人很快乐，正直的人很苦痛；还说不正直是有利可图的，只要不被发觉就行；正直是对人有利而对己有害的。"除了根据希腊创意文学题材的特点而一概指责其不道德之外，他发现，同样的检验方法其运用本身也是有缺陷的。正是在这后一种批评中，时代对他的局限性最为明显。柏拉图并没有意识到，文学本质上只与主观的世界观有关，这既是一种缺陷，也是文学的最高美德——诗人或创意文学的作家通过自己的描述再现的真实存在，它不是现实，而是现实的精神层面。柏拉图因此陷入荒谬的境地，他认为描写真实对象的作家——即用文字符号再现该对象的精神形象的作家——在真实再现的尺度上比用线条和颜色复制对象的艺术家要低级。更为甚者，柏拉图自己举例说，这些作家甚至比那些基于实物床榻进行描绘和制图的工匠还要低端。换句话说，即使像柏拉图这样敏锐的思想家，也还没有弄清楚感官的真实和思想的真实，或者逻辑的真实和艺术的真实之间的区别。因此，他谴责创意文学中的思想图景是不真实的，因此也毫无指导意义。

这种不真实的缺陷直接源于创意文学的创作方法，而柏拉图又加上了另一重缺陷，这种缺陷非直接却也源于其创作方法。为了更好地描绘

---

[1] 赫西奥德（约前8世纪），古希腊诗人。略晚于荷马。代表作长诗《工作与时日》为劝诫之作，内容涉及善与恶，人类的历史、劳动、农事知识等，诗中夹杂不少神话传说。——译者

[2] 品达（约前518—前438），古希腊抒情诗人。其合唱歌对后世欧洲文学有很大影响，在17世纪古典主义时期被认为是"崇高的颂歌"的典范。——译者

生活图景，诗人们——柏拉图常提到的雅典的悲剧作家们——不得不选择设定和再现行为恶劣、狂热滥情的人物，而非举止得当、端庄持重的形象。因为"我们那个不冷静的部分给模仿提供了大量各式各样的材料。而那个理智的平静的精神状态，因为它几乎是永远不变的，所以是不容易模仿的，模仿起来也是不容易看懂的"。[1] 所以柏拉图认为阅读创意文学可能会助长人性中的情感元素，并损害人的理智。柏拉图写道："舞台演出时诗人是在满足和迎合我们心灵的那个（在我们自己遭到不幸时被强行压抑的，）本性渴望痛哭流涕以求发泄的部分。而我们天性最优秀的那个部分，因未能受到理性甚或习惯应有的教育，放松了对哭诉的监督。理由是，它是在看别人的苦难，而赞美和怜悯别人——一个宣扬自己的美德而又表演出极端苦难的人——是没什么可耻的。此外，它（心灵的理性部分）认为自己得到的这个快乐全然是好事，它是一定不会同意因反对全部的诗歌而让这种快乐一起失去的。因为没有多少人能想到，替别人设身处地的感受将不可避免地影响我们为自己的感受，在那种场合养肥了的怜悯之情，到了我们自己受苦时就不容易被制服了。"[2]

现在看来，一方面，柏拉图的批评，既可以被认为是对创意文艺作品所需的必要条件的精妙见解，又是对艺术再现的本质和效果的完全误解。无论是艺术和道德相互依存的核心原则，还是提议将"真实性"作为检验艺术家和诗人作品价值的核心标准，都完全符合最优秀的现代思想。另一方面，通过仔细分析心理过程，我们完全了解了科学研究和艺

---

1 引自郭斌和、张竹明译本，第407页。
2 同上书，第409页。

术创作之间的方法区别，而诗人和小说家展现的生活图景的本质真实，以及情感诉求的意义与价值（我们称之为"共情"）都已被人们接受。柏拉图的批评提供了一个重要的例子，让我们看到不断增加心理学知识的重要性，这也是当今时代的特征。柏拉图因缺乏心理知识而无视隽美，夸大罅隙，最后竟对希腊文学作品大加挞伐，而这些杰作现在已经获得整个文明世界的赞赏。

亚里士多德是继柏拉图之后关注艺术和文学产出过程的又一伟大思想家，他的优势在于能够站在巨人的肩膀上继续前行。同时，身为写作手法的大师，他通过全面而复杂的体系，阐释如何处理人类活动和自然的所有表现，这些艺术过程及其产出的作品形成了特立独行的研究门类。他运用该研究方法探究美的艺术，并撰写名作《诗学》。这部作品篇幅简短、内容不成体系且缺乏完整性，当时的人们对书中蕴含的思想似乎也是一知半解，但它却是所有现代文学批评的基础。因此，了解该作品的主要结论，是理解批评原则的先决条件。正如我所说，这些批评原则现已获得认可，下面我们来详细探讨。

亚里士多德把所有艺术创作和创意文学产出的过程看作是模仿或再现。他追溯了这些艺术和创意文学作品的来源，认为它们是人类活动的表现形式，是一种模仿的原始冲动。换言之，作品的来源与人类活动的习得过程类似，孩子们最初也是受模仿冲动驱使而"学会"父母的语言和行为。亚里士多德还发现这些人类活动最终的目标或目的就是给人愉悦。他把悲剧看作是诗学最成熟的形式，又将整个创意文学表述为"诗学"，并分析了诗学主旨的组成要素；在分析过程中，他区分出了在创意文学中或多或少能够找到的特征要素，且认为作品的优点和价值都取决于这些基本要素。他考察各个单独的要素，探究各要素之间的关系，讨论各要素和它们所组成的作品之间的关系。他提出悲剧的六要素，分别是：情节（Plot，即事件网络）；人物品格（Character，即所刻画人物的鲜明特性）；语言（Diction，即体现人物思想和言语的文学表达）；剧中人物的情感（Sentiment，即支配人物活动的精神基础）；戏剧场景（Stage-representation）和剧中唱段（Musical Accompaniment）。在此分析过程中，有两点必须注意。第一，通过悲剧这一形式来研究文学，亚里士多德引入了两个要素（即戏剧场景和剧中唱段），但这两个根本不属于恰当的文学创作要素。第二，这种研究文学作品的方法侧重于外在层面。亚氏建议用特征测试来衡量一个作品的价值，也即提出这个问题："从其所属的文学形式和艺术的主要目的（给人愉悦）两方面考虑，这部作品是以尽可能完美的方式组织的吗？"亚里士多德继续分析，讨论了文学作品中的次级要素，比如情节的建构、它的"发展"与"结局"，以及"插曲"的安排，这些术语的含义一直未变；他还区分和对比了悲剧、喜剧和史诗这三种诗学形式各自的特点。

进行这种形式上的文学批评时，亚里士多德无非是告诉我们不要用写悲剧的方式写史诗，也不要用写史诗的方式写抒情诗。随着印刷术的发明，我们得以更广泛地研究各类文学作品的外部特征，这种研究传递出的信息及其遵循的规则似乎是肤浅且毫无意义的。但我们发现，了解这些形式上的特征依然有用，它有助于探寻优秀文学中更重要的元素。实际上，当代文学批评最初就是运用这些形式上的规则来研究当代文学。17世纪的批评家运用这些规则时，意识到其不足之处，从而极大地推动了文学批评的发展。我们将在后续章节就此进行扼要探讨。

但亚里士多德做的却远不止于此。他顺带纠正了对创造性文学方法本质的误解，正是这一误解导致柏拉图犯了严重的错误。在纠偏过程中，亚里士多德阐明了某些艺术原则。这些原则如同柏拉图提出的艺术与道德相互依存的原则一样永久有效。至于柏拉图对失真的谴责，亚里士多德回应说，不能因为创意文学所呈现的生活图景与生活事实不相一致，就断言其失真，因为真实性在文学作品中的界定与其在科学中不同。柏拉图沉浸于文学的事实层面，认为文学是一种信息来源，从而混淆了创意文学和一般性文学的区别。亚里士多德表示，不能用同一套标准来衡量这两种文学的实在性或真实性。如历史就是典型的事实至上的文学作品，而以诗歌为代表的文学作品，比起事实本身，更加注重的是如何处理事实。

亚里士多德写道："诗人的职责不在于描述已经发生的事，而在于描述可能发生的事，即根据可然或必然的原则可能发生的事。历史学家和诗人的区别不在于是否用格律文写作（希罗多德的作品可以被改写成格律文，但仍然是一种历史，用不用格律不会改变这一点），而在于前者记述已经发生的事，后者描述可能发生的事。所以，诗是一种比历史更富哲学性、更严肃的艺术，因为诗倾向于表现带普遍性的事，而历史却倾向于记载具体事件。"[1]

亚里士多德这些精辟的论述全面地界定了创造性文学的创作方法，并将创造性文学与其他文学类型区分开来。

同样，亚里士多德也精辟地回应了柏拉图的第二项谴责。柏拉图说，

---

[1] 《诗学》，第 1451^b 页。译文引自黄中梅译注，《诗学》，商务印书馆，1996 年，第 81 页。

这种创造性文学如要取得成功，必得要制造戏剧性的效果，助长了人性中情感的部分，却损害了高尚和理智。亚里士多德在文中写道，悲剧旨在引发人们的恐惧和同情。他借助一个医学例子来回应柏拉图的谴责。诗歌会勾起人们的情感，而不是一味地去促发情感，这一过程会祛除多余的情感元素，从而净化[1]人性。观看过舞台上的悲剧表演后，观众会感到激动，他们的道德情感得以释放，就像我们服用泻药后身体倍感舒畅一样。

他写道："悲剧是对一个严肃、完整、有一定长度的行动的模仿，它的媒介是经过'装饰'的语言，以不同的形式分别被用于剧的不同部分。它的模仿方式是借助人物的行动，而不是叙述，通过引发怜悯和恐惧使这些情感得到疏泄。"[2]

因此，亚里士多德证明并解释了共情的价值和意义。事实上，如果我们反思一下，就能发现我们的一些日常经历和这位伟大希腊思想家的言论有契合之处。回忆一下观看完一场悲剧从影院走出来，或者平和地看完一本极具感染力的优秀小说后的感觉，我们可能会记得自己有一种明显释然的感受。在观看电影或阅读小说的几个小时里，我们与戏剧或小说中的虚构人物产生共鸣，沉浸其中，全然忘记了自己的烦恼和忧愁。如果那时候用语言来表达这种感觉，我们可能会这样说：好吧，毕竟我

---

[1] 传统的理解强调这个词原本的医学含义，即净化指的是用泻药一类的东西帮人疏解某些淤积的体液。根据这种解释，悲剧的作用就是帮人们疏解灵魂之中过分淤积和压抑的情感。后人更开发出净化概念的伦理解读，即净化并不是一个单纯的情感发泄问题，而是与悲剧作为模仿艺术的本质密切相关，并且有着更重要的伦理意涵。——译者

[2] 《诗学》，第1449b页。译文引自黄中梅译注，《诗学》，商务印书馆，1996年，第63页。

的麻烦还是没有这些虚构人物面临的那么严重。通过对比我们自己的生活和他人的生活，我们会与自己的命运和解，也许还能更好地理解人类生命整体的意义。

柏拉图和亚里士多德两位伟大思想家的观点，代表着古典时期的文学研究中最真实且影响最深远的思想。之后的古希腊和古罗马的作家也都在研究这一主题，但他们并没有对柏拉图和亚里士多德确立的广泛原则予以任何增补。文学批评狭义上是指研究伟大作家的外部特征，比如写作风格、语言朴实还是华丽、方言的使用等，同时观照作者身份和不同作品风格的整体性。亚历山大文学中心的希腊学者尤其热衷于这样的文学批评。我们已经注意到[1]，文学批评从狭义上来说源自这些生活在公元前300年至前150年间的学者们的作品。实际上，古典时代只理解了狭义的文学批评。即便是名作《论崇高》[2]的作者（一般认为是生活在公元3世纪的朗基努斯），他虽然补充了优秀文学作品次要的层面，也没能给出足够的论据让我们相信他已经明白了这些广义且影响深远的原则所蕴含的深意。这些原则是柏拉图和亚里士多德的批评观点的真正价值，而且，正如我所说的，它们体现和表达了古典时期文学批评思想的精华。关于这些原则的论述必然不完整也不明确，然而，这正是彼时最辉煌时代的思想和当代思想相联系的节点。而且，正是基于这些不完整、不明确的表述，文学批评才能够在许多个世纪之后仍然能够再次向前推进。

---

1 第一章第4页。

2 《论崇高》是罗马帝国时期传下的一部古希腊文艺理论著作。该作品表达了一种让主观意识者受到震撼从而产生庄严感或敬畏感的审美经验。——译者当然，诸多作家为古罗马伟大文学的形成作出了贡献，其中有些人转到了对文学形式和创作方法的研究上。但西塞罗[1]和昆体良[2]——两位最重要的人物——也仅仅重申了柏拉图和亚里士多德有关文学与艺术显性特征的论述；罗马诗人贺拉斯[3]在他的《诗艺》中提出的批评见解，要么直接引用亚里士多德的论述，要么阐述显而易见的常识。贺拉斯的语言十分简洁流畅，符合我们对这位伟大诗人的期待；但在文学批评这一主题下，它们既不具有也不佯装具有任何原创性贡献与价值。

---

1 西塞罗（前106—前43），古罗马政治家、雄辩家、哲学家。其作品的文学成就极高，被誉为拉丁语的典范。其言说风格雄伟、论文机智、散文流畅，并通过翻译，为罗马人介绍了诸多希腊哲学作品。有学者认为，文艺复兴本质上是对西塞罗的复兴。——译者

2 昆体良（约35—95），古罗马教育家、演说家、修辞家。著有《雄辩家的培训》以及《长篇雄辩术》《短篇雄辩术》等，其著作在文艺复兴时期被广泛运用。——译者

3 贺拉斯（前65—前8），古罗马诗人。代表作《诗艺》主张写诗须以古希腊诗歌为典范，讲求规律，尤其要"寓教于乐"。——译者

约瑟夫·艾迪生（Joseph Addsion, 1672—1719）

第四章 现代文学之批评

柏拉图和亚里士多德的作品——现代批评始于亚里士多德对 16 和 17 世纪文学的形式批评的应用——法国"古典"戏剧——批评家应用亚里士多德的规则时经常曲解他的意思——艾迪生将这种形式批评应用于研究《失乐园》——弥尔顿作品的优缺点通过这一批评手段得以显现——艾迪生《想象之愉悦》系列文章对这一批评科学的贡献——他将新的心理学知识用于文学研究——认定唤起想象力是诗歌的重要特征——思想中再现的"图像"主要源于视觉——想象在诗人头脑中的运作过程——唤起读者想象的本质——它的重要性

在考察某些现代批评家各自取得的进展之前，总结归纳柏拉图和亚里士多德的研究成果是有益的。

柏拉图首先提出艺术与道德相互依存的原则。不仅伟大的艺术家或诗人必须是品德高尚者（good man），而且艺术的高雅和鄙俗往往影响着社会道德风尚的好与坏。另外一个同等重要的原则是："真实性"，指艺术或文学的表现与其所基于的真实基本对应，在此意义上，"真实性"是艺术作品或创意文学作品的最高价值。

亚里士多德对文艺批评的贡献更大，具体表现在以下几个方面：

定义诗歌（或创意文学）和艺术，并将二者特征的形成过程追溯至模仿的原始本能；

探寻创意文学的本质特征，并将其定义为对普遍性或典型性的呈现，而非描述特定或真实的事实。换言之，如果现实的理想化是艺术家思想形成的特征，那么，创意文学的本质可视为主观表述的真实；

将创意文学与一般性文学区别开来，且需要分别使用艺术方法和科学方法来衡量二者的真实性；

为运用共情或者展现想象中的痛苦找到正当理由；并解释其特殊目的和方法。

此外，亚里士多德提出了分析一种典型的创意文学形式[1]的构成要素，以及这些不同要素如情节、人物品格等在一套形式规则系统中的运用。与这种方法相呼应，亚氏还提出将对称或结构性完美作为卓越艺术的衡量标准，这是对创意文学价值的检验，也是对柏拉图提出的标准的回应。

现代批评始于最后这种形式的应用，我们现在认为它是亚里士多德有关艺术和文学理论中价值最小的部分。文艺复兴之后，欧洲的创意文学获得长足发展，迎来思考与创作共进的时代。在17、18世纪，人们怀揣新的热情和更为有效的理论工具，重新开始了对自然与文学的研究。当时，人们审视新的文学作品时，再次将注意力转向如何批评这一主题。自然地，开始衡量现代作品价值的作家再次将目光投向亚里士多德提出的规则，因为《诗学》虽成书于两千多年前，但它包含了批评体系的所有研究途径。人们同时推测，这些基于荷马史诗和雅典戏剧家作品形成的规则，在用于分析现代作品时会存在不足，因为现代作品的形式已发生改变，反映出现代社会状况的变化。奇怪的是，人们却将这一点忽略了，事实的确如此。在17、18世纪的某些时期，批评主要涉及《诗学》阐述的形式规则，批评家的工作是将这些规则或多或少地严格应用于当代文学作品。尤其在当时作为欧洲思想和风格中心的法国，人们认为一部优秀戏剧作品的诞生完全建立在古典模式的基础上。圣茨伯里（Saintsbury）先生写道："法国戏剧家和戏剧批评家追随，或自认为追随古希腊先贤，

---

1 即前文所谈的"悲剧"。——译者

采用了某些固定的规则，认为诗人必须遵循此规则进行创作，就像惠斯特纸牌玩家要遵循游戏规则一样。"[1] 法国伟大诗人高乃依和拉辛[2]的"古典"戏剧便体现出这种人为规则系统的影响。德莫吉特[3]认为，"它是高乃依所服膺严格形式统一的源头，也是拉辛轻松却负轭的肇端。这就是为何少数人物总是受制于情节需要；为何某个单一而完整的动作快速且不间断地进行；为何出现许多宽阔废弃的门廊，对话的人物在那里相遇，地点模糊，没有人物，没有姓名，它是一个理想行为的场面，并仔细清除掉了所有庸俗的情节。我们可以说，这种时间与地点的统一与其说是一种统一，不如说是一种虚无。这种非物质的精神活动，像思想一样，似乎是独立存在的，既不占据时间，也不占据空间。"

现在看来，如此应用亚里士多德的规则，既无知又错误。称其为无知，是因为这些批评家所习得的诗学知识大多是二手的，经常曲解亚里士多德的意思；而他们采用的模式往往根本不是希腊模式，而是那些伪古典模式，塞涅卡[4]的戏剧就是公认的例子。称其为错误，是因为希腊作品的创作条件与现代世界完全不同。然而在法国，这是可能的，因为法国的大师们在写作时，故意着眼于那些古典和伪古典的模式，而这些模

---

[1] 引自他撰写的《法国文学史》。

[2] 高乃依（1606—1684），17世纪上半叶法国古典主义悲剧的代表人物，与莫里哀、拉辛并称法国古典戏剧三杰。主要作品有《西拿》《贺拉斯》等；让·拉辛（Racine, 1639—1699）的戏剧创作以悲剧为主，主要作品有《费德尔》《阿达利》等。——译者

[3] 德莫吉特（1808—1894）是一位法国文学家。——译者

[4] 塞涅卡（约前4—65），古罗马哲学家、戏剧家，晚期斯多葛学派主要代表之一。其主张提到道德、智慧，保持精神上的安宁是人唯一的任务，倡导禁欲主义，要求人们放弃现实生活和欲望，等待神的启示和精神上的解脱。有悲剧《美狄亚》《俄狄浦斯》等九种传世。——译者

式正是形式批评的基础。但在英国情况就不同了。英国最伟大的大师，伊丽莎白和斯图亚特时期的诗人，反对伪古典主义模式的奴役：他们从振兴民族生活的源泉中汲取灵感。随着希腊和罗马失传文献的恢复、科学知识的扩展、美洲新大陆和通往东方海洋之路的发现，思想得到了充盈，再加上国家扩张时期产生的能量，这足以使他们产生一种创作冲动，这种冲动不再受限于任何先前发展起来的诗歌形式。

然而，在法国文艺批评原则占统治地位时期，公认的批评信条的影响是如此之大，以至于艾迪生在证实弥尔顿的伟大才华时，不得不说明《失乐园》符合亚里士多德式的检验标准。正是这种应用——这种将一加仑的内容度量成一品脱的尝试，让他发现，无论某个时代的文学多么光辉灿烂，建立在单一时代文学研究基础上的批评规则体系都会存在不足。他同时发现了一种新的诗歌唤起想象（poetical appeal）原则，并提出新的价值检验方法，而创意文学的新形式（其实是所有形式）都可以通过它来衡量价值。在他对《失乐园》的批评中，艾迪生主要但不完全局限于亚里士多德经典的应用和解释。尤其在《想象之愉悦》（*Essays on the Pleasures of the Imagination*）系列文章中，他采用了笛卡儿、霍布斯和洛克著作中体现思想形成过程的新知识；[1] 正是在这种新的心理知识的帮助下，他讨论并应用了艺术唤起想象的原则，这标志着古典与现代文艺批

---

1 笛卡儿（1596—1650），法国哲学家，主要著作有《形而上学的沉思》《哲学原理》《论世界》等。霍布斯（1588—1679），英国哲学家，建立了近代第一个机械唯物主义体系，主要著作有《利维坦》《对笛卡儿〈形而上学的沉思〉的第三组诘难》。洛克（1632—1704），英国哲学家，继承并发展了培根和霍布斯的思想，建立并论证了唯物主义经验论的"知识起源于感觉"的学说。主要著作有《人类理解论》等。——译者

评的根本区别。

首先，作为这种形式批评方法的典型例子，我们将简要回顾一下艾迪生对《失乐园》的批评，然后分析其新的诗歌唤起想象原则的特点和意义。

艾迪生在《旁观者》十八篇论文的最后一篇中，向我们展示了他对《失乐园》的批评框架。其中四篇论文分别从寓言（或情节）、人物品格、情感和语言四个方面来考察这部史诗，即亚里士多德分析史诗中悲剧的四个组成要素。有两篇论文是关于"作者在每一个标题下可能招致的责难"，其余的十二篇则是依次考察这首诗的十二卷；在这一考察中，他指出了属于每卷的"特殊之美"，并说明了"美之构成"。作为批评检验结果，他宣布了大体上赞同的裁决，也指出了其中的不足之处。

他认为，总的来说弥尔顿在以上各方面都很出色。但另一方面，他发现《失乐园》的"情节"有两个缺陷。第一个是"事件是不愉快的"；亚里士多德认为悲剧的情节应该以灾难告终，并确立史诗应该以快乐结尾的一般规则。第二个是它包含了太多的"离题"。同样，他发现弥尔顿的"人物品格"也有缺陷。这一缺陷在于引入了"两个具有阴暗和虚构性质的角色，即罪与死神"。他笔下的这些寓言性人物不适合写入史诗，因为"他们并没有附带可能性的衡量标准，该标准在这类作品中是必不可少的"。在提出这种批评时，他将罪与死神区别于撒旦，因为从所有的意图和目的上说，撒旦都符合人的形象品格。他又抱怨说，弥尔顿在探讨"自由意志与宿命、历史学、天文学、地理学等内容"时，原本"不需要卖弄学问"，这么做损害了弥尔顿的"情感"表达。

这些例子足以说明，试图运用形式规则来评估一部创意文学作品价值时所得到的结果。引用这些例子旨在说明此种方法不可取，而非作为艾迪生批评的样本。因此，有必要立刻补充一点，那就是艾迪生将这些缺点比作"耀眼太阳的暗黑斑点"，他用了两倍的篇幅来愉快地讨论《失乐园》之美，认为它比所有其他同类的著作都更为精美。在欣赏作品的过程中，他探寻并强调了包含于这部伟大英国史诗中的卓越特征的大部分。特别是他确信弥尔顿的主要品质是其崇高性，之后的所有评论家都同意该观点。

"弥尔顿的主要才华，实际上也是他的卓越之处，在于他思想的崇高性。现代人中还有其他人能在诗歌的其他方面与他相提并论，但就伟大的思想情感而言，他战胜了所有现代和古代的诗人（荷马除外）。他在第一、二、六卷中展现的伟大思想，是人类的想象力所能达到的高度极限。"[1]

在《想象之愉悦》中，艾迪生对批评科学作出了巨大贡献。这一贡献体现在衡量创意文学价值的提议之上，这个提议的确切性质可以扼要概括为：唤起想象力。

为此，我们有必要回顾一下前文。亚里士多德阐明，不能像柏拉图那样用真实的标准来检验诗歌的价值，他指出这样一个事实：创意文学作品作为艺术作品，以不同于非创意或科学文献的方式表现外部现实。他深思熟虑后指出，这种表现不是少了，而是更真实；因为在艺术方法下，再现的是现实的最基本方面。艾迪生运用其所处时代的新思想精神，特别是将联想学说应用于文学研究，注意到艺术作品的再现，无论是雕

---

[1]《旁观者》，第279期。

像、绘画，还是创意文学作品，都是通过再现现实的基本方面——而非与之相对应的现实的原始材料（可以这么说）——来作用于观者的思想；换句话说，凭借艺术家体现在情感属性中的想象力，他们更迅速、更生动地在人们的头脑中唤起图像。他从这一观察中得出结论，即唤起想象力的品质是衡量作品独特价值的最好途径。

追溯艾迪生得出这个结论的步骤很有趣。但首先必须注意到，他很清楚，"想象的能力"只不过是一个简便的术语，用来描述整体思想活动的一个方面。他说："我们把灵魂分成几种能力和官能，但灵魂本身没有这种区分，因为它是作为一个整体来进行记忆、理解、决策或想象的。"

在开始检验想象或幻想的效果时，他指出，视觉首先为头脑提供了随后在思想中再现的"图像"，并简要地描述了这些感官印象所遵循的心理过程。

"正是这种感觉，"他写道，"为想象提供了思想，而想象或幻想（我将混用二者）则带来愉悦，我这里的意思是，这种愉悦来自于实物，无论我们是亲眼见到它，还是借由绘画、雕像、描述或任何其他方式在头脑中唤起它的图像。我们确实不能幻想出从未进入视野中的图像，但我们有能力保留、改变和合成那些我们曾经获得的图像，使之成为各种各样的画面和视觉，并最符合我们的想象；一个因禁于地牢里的人通过这种能力娱乐自我，他能想象出比整个大自然都更加美丽的景色。"[1]

随后，他把这些想象愉悦分为两种——初级想象愉悦和次级想象愉

---

1 《旁观者》，第411期。

悦。初级想象愉悦来自于"眼前的物体";次级想象愉悦来自于"可视物体的观念,即物体实际上并不在眼前,而是被召唤到我们的记忆中,或者形成对事物的令人愉快的幻觉,这些幻觉要么是不存在的,要么是虚构的"。此外,他发现,自然作品更容易产生初级想象愉悦,而艺术作品更容易产生次级想象愉悦。因此,与艺术和文学有关的是次级想象愉悦;它不是由真实的物体引起,而是由这些物体的观念引起的。但在这里,他再次区分了"眼"的艺术和"耳"的艺术分别产生的两种表现形式。建筑、雕塑和绘画具有物理形态,能够被肉眼感知,但音乐和创意文学唯一的物质基础是音符或单词,或是代表发音的文字符号。

在所有类似情况下,他都把想象力的次级愉悦溯及"思想的行为","这一行为将从原始物体中产生的想法与从表现原始物体的雕像、图画、描述或声音中获得的想法进行比较"。

创意文学中的思想是"由文字提出的",想象力在这里起双重作用。

首先,想象力会在诗人内心发挥作用,即:

"人的思想渴求比物质本身更完美的东西,而自然景象永远不能使人达到愉悦的最高境界;或者换句话说,相比于肉眼所见,想象力能把事物变得更加'伟大、神奇或美丽',而依然觉察所见之物的缺陷;因此,诗人要承担这样的责任,按照自己的观念,在描述现实时修补并完善自然,以满足想象;并在描述幻象时,增加比自然本身更多的美感。

他不必关注自然之景从一季到另一季的缓慢进展,也无须观察植物和花卉的连续生长。他可以把一切春秋美景纳入画笔之下,乃至用四季的景象来衬托,使之更为宜人怡心。他的月季树、忍冬和素馨可以同时盛放,他的花坛也可以同时覆盖着百合花、紫罗兰和不凋花。他笔下的土壤并不局限于任何特定的植物，无论橡树还是桃金娘[1]都适合在其中生长，并适应各种气候的产物。橘子树可以肆意生长；没药[2]散见于树篱中；若他认为应当有一片香料林，便很快用足够的光照来助其生长。倘若这一切还不能营造出一幅令人愉悦的景象，那么他还可以创造出几种新的花卉品种，它们的香味和色彩要比自然界花园里的任何一种花卉都更浓郁、更绚烂。他笔下的鸟群品种繁多、相处和谐，树林亦如他所想，葱葱郁郁。营造远景和近景对他而言都毫不费力。他可以从半英里高的悬崖上，像从二十码高的悬崖上一样，轻易抛出一条瀑布。他可以选择各种风，可以让河流蜿蜒曲折，这是最令读者感到愉悦的想象。总而言之，他掌握着塑造大自然的能力，只要不过分改造使之显得过于荒谬，便可随心所欲地赋予其魅力。"[3]

其次，创意文学拥有一种独特力量，能够唤起听众或读者的想象力，即："语言文字，但凡选择得当，其力量是如此之大，以至于一个描述往往能给我们带来比事物本身更生动的思想想法。读者会发现，借助于文字，他在想象中能将一个场景描绘得更加色彩斑斓、鲜明生动，远胜实际景象。如此一来，诗人似乎更好地描绘了大自然；他吸纳了自然本有的景象，又赋予它更加充满活力的细节，增强其美感，从而使之充满生气，以至于物体本身的意象与描绘的意象相比，显得苍白无力。其原因可能是，在观察任何物体时，我们在想象中所描绘的东西仅限于肉眼

---

1 原文 Mirtles 应为 Myrtles，属于印刷错误。——译者
2 原文 Myrr 应为 Myrrh，属于印刷错误。——译者
3 《旁观者》，第418期。

所见；但在诗人的描述中，他随心所欲地为我们提供自由观察的视角，并展现我们过去未曾见过的新内容，或者我们第一次看的时候，并没有注意到它们。当我们观察任何物体时，我们对于这个物体的看法，也许是由两三个简单的概念组成的。但当诗人呈现它时，他要么给我们一个更复杂的观念，要么促使我们产生一些易于引发想象力的概念。"[1]

想象力这一要素能够衡量创意文学的价值，因此它非常重要。艾迪生写道，"影响想象力的能力"是诗歌的"生命所在和完美的最高形式"。因此，我们在这里有一个价值检验标准，它足够灵活，能够用于创意文学的各种形式和各个发展阶段，它考虑的是"愉悦"这一要素，"愉悦"是创意文学三个特征品质中的最后一个，另外两个是"题材"和"风格"。在文学研究中运用心理学知识，是现代文艺批评的特色，之后所有的批评家们都有意无意地采用了艾迪生制定并阐释的原则：唤起想象力。

---

1 《旁观者》，第416期。

拉奥孔(大理石群雕作品)

第五章 如何唤起想象力

文艺作品的三个检验标准：真实、对称和唤起想象力——莱辛和库辛——《拉奥孔》——绘画与诗歌的艺术手法对比——诗歌，在时间上使用清晰的声音，描摹动作；绘画，在空间上同时使用形式和颜色，描摹人体——荷马如何让我们感受到海伦的美——不适宜用诗歌来表现的主题——库辛勾画关于美和艺术之完整理论的框架图——他对于理想化过程的阐述——这在诗歌或创意文学中得到最自由的发挥艾迪生将17世纪的心理学成果应用于文学与艺术研究，才使得我们今天有了文艺作品三个基本检验标准：真实、对称和唤起想象力，它们分别对应创造性文学的三个主要方面：题材、风格和给予愉悦的能力（感染力）。不过，在我们开始探讨当代作家对这些检验标准的应用，以及由于个人思想差异而赋予检验标准不同程度的重要性所带来的相关问题之前，确实有必要看一看两位现代批评家的作品——出版于1766年的莱辛[1]的《拉奥孔》[2]和发表于1818年、出版于1853年的维克托·库辛的讲演录《论真、善、美》[3]。

这两位作者都认识到，艺术的魅力主要是想象，其次是理解和感觉，

---

1 莱辛（1729—1781），德国启蒙思想家、文艺理论家和剧作家。其美学论著《拉奥孔——论绘画和诗的界限》《汉堡剧评》奠定了德国现实主义文艺理论的基础。——译者

2 拉奥孔，希腊神话中特洛伊的祭师。曾警告特洛伊人勿中木马计，因此触怒天神，和两个儿子同被巨蟒缠死。拉奥孔的大理石雕塑成为莱辛于1766年所著《拉奥孔》一书的中心议题。——译者

3 《论真、善、美》(Du Vrai, du Beau et du Bien)是法国教育家、哲学家、历史学家库辛的名作，分别由认识论、伦理学和美学三方面来研究人的精神所具有的感性、意志和理性三种功能。——译者

但他们审视艺术魅力本质的角度却刚好相反。莱辛从客观角度认为，如果诗人和画家能够分别通过不同的表现手段来展现艺术魅力，那么他们应该努力去再现现实的各个方面和多种要素；另一方面，库辛则从主观的角度，追溯了艺术家（或诗人）将感官提供的原材料转化为思想或形式的过程，这种思想或形式若能使用与其艺术相适应的媒介来表达，将会最有力地唤起观众的想象力。简言之，莱辛向我们展示了艺术家在表现现实的时候，应该如何修饰原型的材质属性以适应其艺术局限性；而库辛所谈的则是"思想"——或者说现实的精神层面（也就是艺术所要表达的特殊对象）——是如何在艺术家的头脑中形成的。

　　莱辛探索的方式是有趣的，它也是对亚里士多德在《诗学》中的形式或外部特征批评的进一步发展。在开始讨论著名的雕塑作品《拉奥孔》[1]（莱辛的著作标题取自该雕塑作品的标题）的创作日期时，莱辛注意到，该作品与维吉尔在《埃涅阿斯纪（下）》[2]中对拉奥孔及其两个儿子之死的描写极为相似。

　　于是，他认为，在所有历史证据之外，拉奥孔群雕的日期可以通过艺术分析来确定：因为如果诗人复制了艺术家的作品，自然会省略一些不适合用文字再现意境的细节；同样，如果艺术家复制了诗人的作品，也会省略诗中不适合雕塑家用石头再现的某些细节。莱辛分析并比较了这两种作品的细节，最后断定是艺术家复制了诗人的作品，因为与维吉

---

[1] 参见章首插画。
[2] 该史诗是诗人维吉尔于公元前29—前19年所创，叙述了埃涅阿斯在特洛伊陷落之后辗转来到意大利，最终成为罗马人祖先的故事。——译者

尔的描述相比，雕塑家仅仅是因为媒介的特性而被迫使用不同的处理方式。莱辛特别指出，当维吉尔描述拉奥孔哀号时，雕塑家却赋予他一种高贵而平静的表情。莱辛认为这符合我们的期待，因为大理石根本无法表现维吉尔所描述的痛苦：

  同时，他尖锐的哀号声直冲云霄：
  那声音如同一头受伤的公牛，
  甩掉脖子上插偏了的斧头，从祭坛逃走时的嚎叫。

  尝试表现这种痛苦只会带来荒谬或可怕的怪相，因为雕塑应当以静态表现形体美。而如果这个群雕作品完成在先，维吉尔看到了它，然后用文字来描述群雕所展现的拉奥孔之死，他必然会描写拉奥孔庄严隐忍的表情，因为用文字描述这种崇高的忍耐与描述痛苦的哀号一样容易。

  通过比较，莱辛分别详述了作为"视觉艺术"代表的绘画和作为"听觉艺术"代表的诗歌的表现方法。在讨论过程中，他非常仔细地分析了这两种典型艺术所选用的表现现实的方法。

  莱辛指出，诗歌"在时间上使用连续发出的声音"，而绘画则"在空间上同时使用形式和颜色"。最适合画家的现实是"一种可见的、静止的动作（或一组物体），其不同部分是在空间中并列展开的"；最适合诗人的现实是"一种可见的、渐进的动作，其不同部分是按时间顺序相继发生的"。因此，画家只能间接描摹动作，即通过描绘人体来暗示动作。同样，诗人只能间接描绘人体，向我们述说这些人体（不管是有生命或无生命的）的动作或行为效果。因此，画家在表现一个动作时，必须选择该动作的某个瞬间，它最能暗示过去发生的事以及接下来要发生的事；而诗人描述人体时，必须选择人体的某个属性，以激活大脑中人体最生动的画面。举个简单的例子来解释这个严密的论证。拿一个普通的物体来说吧，比如一条船。画家通过在画布上使用尽可能多的形式和颜色来呈现该物体，以满足观者单一角度的欣赏。而诗人会给这条船加上一个能召唤其意象的修饰词——"快船"。这只是一个非常简单的例子，但是如果加上梅瑞狄斯[1]先生在《十字路口的戴安娜》中说的一番话，我想将有助于解释莱辛的观点。

梅瑞狄斯写道："创作之笔是一门艺术，旨在唤起内心的憧憬，而非一支描绘舞台幕布之笔，仅呈现肉眼所见；我们自由飞翔的思想无法容纳冗长的描述，这就是为什么诗人用单词或短语激发想象力，描绘出永恒的图景。莎士比亚和但丁仅用一行字或最多两行字便能展现画面。"不过，最好的例子是荷马的创作手法，他使我们感受到海伦之美，但并不直接告诉我们海伦脸颊的颜色或她的嘴、鼻子和眼睛的形状，也就是说，他没有接连列举构成她面部和形态美的几个要素，而是描述了特洛伊城最年长、最睿智的男人们看到海伦之后的反应。这些长者是最不容易被女人的美貌所影响的男人，但当他们看到海伦优雅的仪态、曼妙的身姿，便忘记了她所犯的错误，以及她给国家带来的苦难：

难怪特洛伊人和全副武装的亚加亚人容忍邪恶如此之久，

---

1 梅瑞狄斯（1828—1909），英国作家。写有小说20余部，揭露贵族社会中的丑恶现象。——译者

全因这个女人——她看上去就像不死的女神。[1]

适用于人类之美的事物，同样适用于自然之美，因此，描述风景这一主题对诗人而言不适合。并非说诗人不能描述这样的场景，而是他要做到这一点，要靠文字或语言这种媒介，使人在脑海中唤起所有可能的想法。但是，创意文学的作家，其目的与历史学家或哲学家不同。他是一位艺术家，必须采用艺术方法；就是说，他的描述必须能够唤起想象力，而不仅仅是促进理解。尽管莱辛没有刻意使用唤起想象力的心理学原则——我已经说过，他是从外部或形式的角度来研究不同的艺术——但他令人钦佩地阐述了如何将该原则应用于研究创意文学的表现形式。

他写道："既然语言符号是我们自己所采用的符号，通过它们，我们全然可以完整地表达主体各部分的全貌，其效果如同我们能够在自然界中感知到该主体的各部分一样。但这通常是言语及其符号的属性，该属性并非专门为诗歌的目的服务。诗人的目标不仅是要易于理解，他的表现手法也远不只是清晰明了（这对于故事作者来说已经足够了）。诗人希望在我们心中唤起生动的思想，这样，当它们在我们的脑海中闪现时，我们相信自己正在体验真实而客观的印象，它们是思想中客观之原型的产物，在我们展开想象的这一刻，我们不再意识到诗人为此目的所借助的媒介，即他的文字。这一原则形成了诗画阐释的基础。"[2]

库辛的研究与莱辛的研究形成了直接的对比，前者是对后者的有力

---

1 《伊利亚特》第三卷，第156—158页。
2 《拉奥孔》第十七卷，作者译文见于《批评原则》一书。

补充。莱辛的分析是基于亚里士多德的观点，而那位法国批评家的宽泛结论却是基于柏拉图的哲学思想。库辛说，他的目标是"至少提供一个关于美和艺术的常规且完整的理论框架图"。为此，他依次考虑：（1）主观之美，或感知美的能力；（2）客观之美，或分别使某个动作、思想、人物和实物变美的品质；（3）艺术之本质，或者说再现真实存在之美的过程；（4）不同艺术各自的方法和目的，或艺术如何分类。库辛以精确的文字和哲学的洞察力来探讨美的各个方面，但他对批评科学最重要的贡献，在于其对理想化过程的精辟阐述——如我们所见，理想化过程与艾迪生关于诗人头脑中想象运作的论述完全相同，如今被认为是艺术家思维的独特过程。

库辛说，"我们渴望再次看到并从身心两方面感受自然之美，这些美使我们在现实生活中感到愉悦；因此，我们努力再现的**不是它本身的模样，而是它在我们想象中呈现的样子。因此，对于人类来说，创作之作品是具有原创性和适切性的作品，即艺术作品。**"[1] 艺术家进行创作，既不像我们所说的如上帝造物，也不只是模仿。他在现实世界中寻找素材，但以一种变化的形式对这些素材进行再创造。这种形式的变化是理想化过程的结果。库辛写道，"真正的艺术家对自然有着深厚的情感与热爱，但对自然界事物的喜爱程度不一。"艺术家再创造的是关于现实的"观念"，这是他要表现的主题，是经过选择和省略双重加工后在脑海中形成的观念。如果艺术家表现的是某个行为、某个人物或某个物体，那就无所谓了；在形成这一观念的所有情况下，艺术家都忽略了原型中存在的缺陷，

---

[1] 《论真、善、美》第八讲。

并增加了原型所不具备的优点。简言之,他把他的主题理想化了。因此,理想化是"人类对自然的无意识批判"[1],它是一种理想化的现实,而不是现实本身,艺术家用适合于自身的艺术媒介对现实进行再创造。用库辛的话来说,艺术的目的是借助形体之美来表现道德之美。"对艺术来说,后者只是前者的象征。在自然界中,道德之美经常是模糊的;但艺术使它清晰地呈现出来,大自然很少产生这种效果。大自然还有另一种方法来愉悦我们,以生命的形式赋予想象力和视觉最大的魅力,我再次声明,这种生命形式至高无上、无与伦比;艺术在更高的层次触动了我们,因为艺术将呈现道德美作为其首要目的,所以它更直接地吸引了最深层的情感之源。艺术可以比自然更令人伤感,而共情是最高阶之美的标志和量度。"[2]

在所有的艺术形式中,诗歌或创意文学使得理想化过程可以最自由地发挥作用。首先,其媒介是语言,而语言是各种艺术所使用的媒介中最灵活的一种。其次,语言作为思想的实际媒介,使艺术家能够最直接地与观者进行心灵交流。

库辛写道,"言语是诗歌的工具;诗歌按照自己的目的对其进行塑造,将其理想化,以表达理想之美。诗歌赋予言语以韵律的魅力和庄严,诗歌将其变成了既非声音也非音乐的东西,但却含有两者的本质,它既是物质的又是精神的;一种完成的、清晰且精确的东西,好比最鲜明的轮廓和形式;一种如色彩一般活生生的东西;一种像声音一样悲悯且无

---

[1] 《批评原则》。
[2] 《论真、善、美》第八讲。

限的东西。一个词本身，尤其是经过诗歌选择和美化的词，是最具活力且最具普世性的。如同雕塑和绘画，诗歌凭借自己创造的这个法宝，反映了感官世界的种种形象；如同绘画和音乐，诗歌以各种变化来呈现情感。其节奏变化多端，音乐根本无法企及；其转替快速迅捷，绘画也难以望其项背。而它虽变化快速却又像雕塑一样平静；不仅如此，它还表达了所有其他艺术无法企及的东西，那就是思想。我所说的思想，它无声、无色，亦无性；我所说的思想，它崇高至尚，任意翱翔，是最精炼的抽象概念。"[1]

---

1 《论真、善、美》第九讲。译文见于《批评原则》一书。

马修·阿诺德（Mathew Arnold, 1822—1888）

第六章

当代文学之批评

伟人在评价同代人作品时展现出盲目性——专业批评的失败——新闻批评的特点——华兹华斯认为以既有模式判断新作品是无效的——马修·阿诺德是当代英国批评的最高典范——强调作家与其所处时代之间的联系——称诗歌为"对生活的批评"——解释诗歌真实要高于科学真实——阐述诗歌具有本质上的道德性——拉斯金和威廉·莫里斯先生坚持艺术与道德相互依存的原则——"为艺术而艺术"的信条——斯温伯恩先生阐述这一信条——偏离传统标准和不符合道德原则,区分两者的困难——时人常常指责新作家"晦涩"和"不道德"——"艺术应是自由的"这一信条的价值——遵从特定艺术的法则并非充分的检验标准——必须认识到品味的存在——罗斯金先生的教导——罗斯金和斯温伯恩的观点前后并不一致——两人的观点都只是局部正确尽管伟大的思想家们一直专注于思考文学创作过程及其与一般艺术表现过程之间的关系，但直到今天，文学中任何明确的判断原则似乎最终都是从众多模糊的思想中浮现出来的，围绕批评这一主题的思想迄今已有数百年的历史。我说"今天"，是因为那些伟大的（有时是最伟大的）人们在评价其同代人的作品，尤其是当代作家的作品时，展现出盲目性，这使文学修习者颇感惊讶。拿出我们称之为18、19世纪的"专业"评论家们的裁决——他们的目的通常是直白地"毁灭"——我们会看到一些"破坏性"的批评言辞，伏尔泰[1]宣称《哈姆雷特》是一部粗鲁又野蛮的作品，像是某个喝醉了的野蛮人想象出来的；歌德[2]认为但丁的《神曲》三部曲中，"《地狱》是可憎的、《炼狱》是令人怀疑的、《天堂》是招人厌烦的"；

---

[1] 伏尔泰（1694—1778），法国启蒙时代思想家、作家、哲学家，启蒙运动公认的领袖和导师，"法兰西思想之父"。其论说以讽刺见长，常常抨击天主教教会的教条和当时的法国教育制度。——译者
[2] 歌德（1749—1832），德国戏剧家、诗人、自然科学家、文艺理论家，是世界文学领域出类拔萃的光辉人物之一，倡导世界主义文学思想。——译者

拜伦[1]对整个英国抒情诗界的魅力无动于衷，马修·阿诺德[2]对古代和中世纪大师的美丽与力量极度敏感，但却忽视了同时代最伟大的天才——丁尼生、勃朗宁、斯温伯恩、罗塞蒂和威廉·莫里斯。[3]在这种专业的批评中——本世纪初蓬勃发展的伟大评论便效法于此——倡导者们惊人的错误和恶毒的语句暴露出其人性的卑下，令人感到羞耻。许多文学期刊和华兹华斯[4]诗集[5]的《序言补论》（*Essay Supplementary*）都详尽地说明了此事。多顿先生近期在《文学诠释》（*Interpretation of Literature*）中的文章[6]收集并展示了一些最异乎寻常的例子，借以说明在完成一项不可能的任务时，即便是伟大的作家也会显得乖戾和愚笨。

如今，这种试图用形式或技术检验来衡量文学作品（无论是当代的或过去的）价值的做法，虽说还没有真正绝迹，但已经受到全盘质疑。这样的检测方法，即使应用它们的评论家对其完全理解，也只能测量出只有少数人才可以察觉的优点或缺陷，而完全没有触及那些广泛而占据

---

1 拜伦（1788—1824），英国诗人、革命家，独领风骚的浪漫主义文学泰斗。代表作有讽刺长诗《唐璜》。——译者

2 马修·阿诺德（1822—1888），英国近代诗人、评论家。其著名诗作《多佛海滩》主要表现维多利亚时代的信仰危机。另著有《评论一集》《评论二集》《评荷马史诗译本》等。——译者

3 丁尼生（1809—1892）是华兹华斯之后的英国桂冠诗人；勃朗宁（1806—1861）是英国维多利亚时代最受尊敬的诗人之一；斯温伯恩（1837—1909）是英国维多利亚时代最后一位重要诗人，崇尚希腊文化，对后世诗人影响深远；罗塞蒂（1828—1882）是英国画家、诗人、插图画家、翻译家，前拉斐尔派的创始人之一；莫里斯（1834—1896）是一位小说家和诗人，也是英国社会主义运动的早期发起者之一。——译者

4 华兹华斯（1770—1850），英国浪漫主义诗人，湖畔派代表，1843年被封为桂冠诗人。著有《抒情歌谣集》、长诗《序曲》《漫游》等。——译者

5 1815年版的《序曲》。

6 《当代评论》，1886年。

主流的品质，这些品质吸引着普罗大众，并获得普遍认可，这是最高价值的标志和体现。在期刊的普通批评中，仍然保留着尝试对新文学作品进行裁决的做法；尽管这样的批评往往是公正和开明的，但众所周知，这些评论或声明的作者并没有作出有约束力的决断。事实上，不论批评家的资历有多深，如果将作家排除在外，他们所作的批评往往是肤浅的。因此，期刊的普通"评论"中所体现的批评是无效的，我们可不予理会。尽管如此，文学研究在英国从未像今天这样盛行，并取得如此丰硕的成果。但是，在思考并理解当代英国批评的动机和原则之前，我们最好简述一下最杰出的批评家作品中体现的重要成果。

华兹华斯在抗议专业批评家的假设时，对所有批评系统的内在缺陷提出指责：这些批评系统完全或主要基于既有模式形成的知识，来衡量创意文学的新作品。这种形式上的和技术上的批评所衡量的外部品质是完全独立于原创性元素而存在的；其失败正是由于没有考虑到这种未知的量。他因自己的作品受到的不公正和冷漠对待感到痛心，并写道：

"在对诗歌作品命运的评论中，如果有一种结论比其他更使我们信服，那就是，所有伟大且具有独创性的作家都有一项任务，即创造出一种让人欣赏的风格；过去如此，将来也会如此……天赋异禀且富有原创精神的前辈们有义务为后来者铺平道路，因为他已经（或即将）与他们产生同鸣共振；但是，对于他独有的特色，他必须清除障碍并走出自己的路，就像汉尼拔翻越阿尔卑斯山一样。"[1]

他还非常清楚地说明了为什么仅凭形式检验——如情节的架构、韵

---

1 《序言补充》。

律的完善、措辞的纯正或优雅，以及专业评论家作出赞成或谴责之裁决所依据的标准——我们无法作出有约束力的裁决。一部作品可以在技术或形式上达到完美，但却缺乏给予愉悦的品质，而这种品质正是作品要流传后世所必备的。相反，一部在技术上不甚完美的作品却可能在很大程度上拥有这种品质。正如我们所见，给予愉悦这一品质的基础就是唤起想象的能力。诗人借助这种能力获得更大的创作自由，它构成了诗意地呈现生活事实的更高价值。但是诗人意在唤起的不是批评家的想象，而是普通读者的想象，他们拥有的并非专业知识，而是日常智慧。的确，技巧水平远不能作为衡量诗歌优劣程度的绝对基础，事实上，技巧发展到一定程度反而可能妨碍人们对作品的欣赏或接受。他说："诗人的创作只有一个限制，那就是，他的作品须给人带来愉悦。人们——作为人本身，而不是作为律师、医生、水手、天文学家或自然哲学家——期待从诗人那里获得愉悦。除了这个限制，诗人和事物形象相间无物；而传记作家和历史学家与之却千隔万阻。"[1]

换句话说，通过唤起读者想象来给予愉悦的力量，是创意文学应当具备的基本品质。唯有这种品质，才能满足人类的一般感知。它也是任何技术检验都衡量不出的品质。

在马修·阿诺德的批评著作中，我们发现了当代英国批评的最高典范。其《评论集》（*Essays in Criticism*）两卷书的研究对象为英国和外国的作家，与其他同类著作相比，更能体现我所说的这种精神的变化。书中针对作家个体的研究有着明确的处理、清晰的表达、丰富的例证等

---

[1]《观察》，《抒情歌谣集》（第二版）的附文。

特点，我虽力有不逮，无法概述，但有一点我可以明确，批评家马修·阿诺德似乎给自己设定了一个宏伟目标，即收集所有有用的事实，阐释作家的特殊个性、其创作的特殊动机，以及追溯这些条件与其作品优缺点之间的联系。简言之，就是向读者提供初步的信息，使其能辨别、欣赏作者的作品。

然而，在对特定作者的研究过程中，马修·阿诺德间接地阐明了某些普遍适用的原则。

（1）他强调并界定了作家与其所处时代的密切联系，指出在每一部创意文学作品中，都可以看到两个不同的因素：作家的个性和作家所处时代的精神文化氛围。在其诗歌评论中，他以格雷（Gray）为例说明：倘若培育天才的土壤不够肥沃，那么天才必定难结果实。

他在书中写道，"格雷拥有真正诗人的思想和灵魂品质，但却与他所处的时代格格不入。他以高深的学问来滋养诗人的精神品质，却不能充分地发挥和享受它们；友好的氛围是缺失的，他也无法获得同时代人的同情。如果与弥尔顿或彭斯[1]同年出生，他将会成为另一个人，大放异彩。若是出生在1608年（弥尔顿出生之年），他将受益于伊丽莎白时代更自由、更富有诗意的英国精神；若是出生在1759年（彭斯出生之年），他将受益于欧洲的思想革新，其最伟大的历史表现就是法国大革命。"[2]

（2）他从哲学层面概括道：在所有对现实的诗性表现中，诗学是"对

---

[1] 彭斯（1759—1769），苏格兰诗人。诗作《自由树》颂扬法国大革命；《苏格兰人》歌颂反抗英格兰侵略的民族英雄，号召人民争取自由。——译者
[2] 《评论二集》。

生活的批评"。也就是说，诗人或小说家通过创造理想的生活图景，提供一个理想生活的标准，以和现实生活的事实进行对比。由于这种现实与理想的反差有助于我们理解人类存在的普遍目的和状况，所以他把诗性思维的特殊性定义为"阐释力"。不仅如此，他还准确地把诗歌的真实与科学的真实区分开来。他告诉我们诗歌何以凭借这种阐释力成为华兹华斯所说的"一切知识的气息和精神升华"，原因是它可以感染整体之人，包括一个人的情绪、感觉以及理性。如果我们将这种阐释力理解并定义为唤起想象力的主观方面——或诗歌在听者或读者头脑中造成的影响，我们在下文便可细致分析诗歌感染力的影响。它在所有艺术形式中，拥有最高等的阐释力。

"诗歌的伟大力量在于其阐释力，我所指的不是用白纸黑字解释宇宙之谜的力量，而是对事物的处理能力，能够唤醒我们内心对万物的美妙而亲密的感觉，深切感受到物我合一的默契。对身外之物的感知被唤醒时，我们感觉自己与事物的本质交融，不再被其表相迷惑和压迫，而是知晓其秘密并与之和谐相处。这种感觉使我们平静和满足，这是其他任何感觉都无法企及的。诚然，诗歌还有另一种方式阐释生活，但它运用阐释力达到极致的两种方式之一，就是在我们心中唤起这种感知。我不会追问它是否虚幻，或是否能被证明是虚幻的，或它是否完全使我们掌握事物的真实本质；我要说的是，诗歌能唤醒我们内心的感知，这是诗歌最具穿透力的力量之一。科学解释并不似诗歌那般能让我们对物体产生亲密的感受，它们只吸引特定的官能，而不是整体之人。让我们感受到真正意义上的动物、水或植物的，不是生物学家林奈、物理学家卡文迪许或自然博物学家居维叶，而是莎士比亚"携三月之风先燕子而至的水仙花"[1];是华兹华斯"听到报春的杜鹃歌声打破了最遥远的赫布里底群岛海上的宁静"[2];是济慈[3]笔下的"流水,如牧师一般,为苦海中的人类进行洗礼";是夏多布里昂[4]"密林朦胧的树冠";是塞纳库尔[5]的山间白桦树:"我喜爱它白色、光滑、龟裂的树皮;喜爱它粗野的枝丫;喜爱它弯下腰的枝干;树叶的摇曳及飘零;喜爱大自然的简单和荒漠的姿态。"[6]

(3)在一定的范围内,诗歌到达最高境界就必须运用这种阐释力唤起想象(阿诺德称之为"富于想象的理性")。此时,诗歌中大师们的腔调就表现为"高度严肃、绝对真诚"。

"对于最高的诗学成就来说,其不仅仅要求把思想有力地应用于生活;也要求它在符合诗歌真实和美感法则的限制条件下得到运用。这两种法则是必要条件,诗人对这些问题的处理是高度严肃的,这种严肃性来自于绝对的真诚。"[7]这样的诗歌必须具有本质上的道德性,也就是说,它必须满足道德原则所体现的人类的普遍意识。

"因此,重要的是要牢牢把握一点:诗歌归根结底是对生活的批评;诗人的伟大之处在于,他将思想有力且完美地应用于生活,并用于回答'如何生活'之问。人们常常用狭隘和虚伪的方式对待道德;道德与它

---

1 出自莎士比亚《冬天的故事》第四幕第四场。——译者
2 出自华兹华斯《孤独的刈麦女》。——译者
3 出自约翰·济慈《明亮的星》。——译者
4 夏多布里昂(1768—1848),法国作家、政治家、外交家,浪漫主义文学先驱之一。——译者
5 塞纳库尔(1770—1846),法国散文家和哲学家,著有书信体小说《奥伯曼》。——译者
6 《评论一集》。
7 《评论二集》。

所在时代的思想和信仰体系紧密相关；它被学究和专业商人玩弄于股掌之上；有些人对它感到厌烦。有时，我们会被反抗道德的诗歌吸引；比如奥马尔·凯亚姆[1]的格言：'让我们在酒馆找补浪费在清真寺的时光。'又或者，我们被漠视道德的诗歌吸引，其内容天马行空，但形式精美考究。无论是哪种情况，我们都在自欺，而停止自欺的最好办法，就是让我们的思想于那伟大的、无穷尽的'生活'一词中憩息，直到我们真正领悟它的意义。在诗歌中，反抗现代观念就是反抗生活，对道德漠不关心就是对生活漠不关心。"[2]

"美的艺术"领域的罗斯金[3]先生和"次要艺术"领域的威廉·莫里斯认为，我们应当果断地运用艺术与道德相互依存的原则。罗斯金对于建筑和绘画作品均有批评，其特征在他自己的笔下阐述得最为充分，他写道："我书中有关艺术的文章，其独特之处是把一切归根于人类的激情或人类的希望。"在下面这段文字中，道德与诗歌成就之间不可分割的联系，得到了最为有力的阐明。

"同样，所有人类之歌都是艺术的完整表达，它以正当的理由来歌颂高尚之士的乐与悲。'美的艺术'其可能性来自正当理由和纯洁情感之间的精确配比。这种最高到最低的精细度是艺术的精妙之处，是道德纯洁性和情感庄严度的指标。所有的艺术都是如此。因此，一个国家的

---

1 奥马尔·凯亚姆（1048—1131），波斯诗人、天文学家、数学家，留有诗集《柔巴依集》（又译《鲁拜集》）。19世纪，英国作家爱德华·菲茨杰拉德将其译为英文，从此《柔巴依集》不再仅是历史笔记，而作为著名诗集为整个世界所接受。——译者
2 《评论二集》。
3 罗斯金（1819—1900）是英国维多利亚时代主要的艺术评论家之一。——译者

艺术，只要它存在，对其进行的细致审视便能反映出该国的道德状态，这不会有假，也没有例外。"[1]

此外，罗斯金（与马修·阿诺德一样）更为细致地阐述了唤起想象力原则。诗歌和艺术能够通过唤起想象力在人们心中有力地激发思想，这种思想必定与该种族最优秀的传统相契合。

"因此，我并不是说，给人最多快乐的艺术就是最伟大的艺术，因为有些艺术的目的是教育而不是给予愉悦；也不是说，带给我们最多教诲的艺术是最伟大的艺术，因为有些艺术的目的是给予愉悦而不是教育；也不是说，模仿得最好的艺术是最伟大的艺术，因为有些艺术的目的是创新而不是模仿。但可以说，艺术的最伟大之处，在于它能尽一切方法向观者传达最伟大的思想。我称一个思想伟大，是因为它能为更具思维能力的头脑所接受，且在这个过程中使其得到进一步的锻炼和提升。如果这是艺术伟大与否的判定标准，那么伟大艺术家的定义自然随之而来，即在其作品中体现了最多最伟大思想的艺术家。"[2]

另一方面，当代作家强调艺术"自由"这一重要原则。

"为艺术而艺术"是他们的旗帜。斯温伯恩先生就完美地阐述了这个原则——他本人以完美的诗句在当代诗坛负有盛名。

"如果不遵循艺术创作的绝对规范，艺术作品便毫无价值或生命力可言，最重要的是，以其遵从的艺术法则来判断，它并非优秀的作品。"对于诗歌，他如此写道：

---

[1]《艺术讲座》第三卷。
[2]《现代画家》第一卷。

"一首诗的价值与其道德意义或道德设计全然无关；相比于用最宽宏大量的谩骂抨击暴政（热爱国家和自由的巴乌斯和赛特的作品中可能会出现），维吉尔对恺撒的赞歌和德莱顿对斯图亚特的赞歌更可取。"[1]

他还写道：

"在所有伟大的诗人身上，都有一种炽热的和谐，以及对精神生活的热情，它引导而不抑制优雅的行为，并赋予其作品魅力与力量：柔美而不虚弱，有力却不粗犷。他们本能地追求完美，不允许思想或文字出现缺陷或错误。他们自然地拥有正义之心，决不允许道德畸形或瑕疵的存在，并且在他们的作品中完全找不到努力避免罅隙或追求完美的痕迹。"[2]

尽管斯温伯恩所说的原则很难以极端的形式履行，但它在强调艺术的独立性时仍具价值。创意文学和一般艺术往往从宗教和爱国主义中获得灵感，但它们决不能与宗教和爱国主义混为一谈。再者，真实的检验标准要求诗人所写的东西必须与人类的普遍意识相协调，但诗歌或其他创意文学作品，不能因其观点与个别评论家或与大多数同胞的观点相悖，而被视为非艺术性的作品。当然，我们很难界定并区分哪些与当时或当地的情感或行为规范相背离，哪些与道德原则不相符，并因此永远无法与人类的一般感知相符。由于对这两种情况界定的困难，加之没有对艺术的独立性给予应有的尊重，伟大作家的作品总是被时人指责"晦涩"和"不道德"。举一两个例子来说明这种现实的困难，以及背离传统或民族情感在本质上不同于偏离人类的一般感知。在那个时

---

[1]《文论》。
[2] 同上。

代的爱丁堡评论家眼中，柯勒律治[1]的《克里斯塔贝尔》（*Cristabel*）只是"一通胡言乱语"。华兹华斯的《不朽颂》（*Ode on Intimations of Immortality*）是整卷书中"最难以辨认和无法理解的部分"。他们还建议雪莱出版其诗歌的"生词汇编"。而现在被认为是最荡涤人心的骚塞[2]和华兹华斯的作品当时也被认为有损于社会道德，只因湖畔派（Lake School）在卢梭[3]的作品中找到灵感，他们的名声也因卢梭诟病社会组织而受到影响。《卫报》（*the Guardian*）谴责查尔斯·金斯利的《酵母》（*Yeast*）[4]，称"作者赞同当下最糟糕的风气，他用冠冕堂皇的哲学话语来掩饰放荡的道德，这应当受到明确的谴责"。这样的例子数不胜数，它们足以表明，创意文学的修习者在对新作家作出不利的批评之前，应该认真思考以上因素。因为创意文学的艺术价值，不单单基于对艺术自由的认可，也涉及道德价值，因为它是推动进步的力量之一。勃朗宁夫人[5]在《奥罗拉·丽》（*Aurora Leigh*）一书中也充分描述了她"对生活和艺术的最高信念"。她认为诗人们是"如今唯一对上帝说真话的人"：

---

1 柯勒律治（1772—1834），英国诗人、文评家，浪漫主义文学奠基人之一。——译者

2 骚塞（1774—1843），英国作家，湖畔派诗人之一，于1813年被封为桂冠诗人。——译者

3 让－雅克·卢梭（1712—1778），法国启蒙思想家、哲学家、教育学家、文学家。1762年因发表《社会契约论》《爱弥儿》遭迫害而流亡瑞士。他的思想影响了法国大革命。在美学上，他提出风俗败坏艺术，艺术败坏风俗的观点，但他的创作实践与"返归自然"的口号，对之后的感伤主义和浪漫主义影响极大。——译者

4 查尔斯·金斯利（1819—1875），英国文学家、学者与神学家，擅长儿童文学创作。所著长篇小说《酵母》和《阿尔顿·洛克》描写雇农和手工业者的困苦处境。——译者

5 勃朗宁夫人（1806—1861），英国女诗人。诗人罗伯特·勃朗宁之妻。她的故事长诗《奥罗拉·丽》混合了诗歌和小说的风格，讲述了主人公奥罗拉从小女孩成长为一位女性艺术家的历程。——译者

"唯一为本质真实发声之人,

而非相对真实、比较真实

和短暂真实;唯一身披

阳光之裙之人,穿过灰色幽暗的习俗;

唯一众生之导师,引导人类

从死亡之墙上的投影中

找到人类真正的高度

高耸、庄严——那是作为人的价值。"

她不仅反对传统的专横,也同样充满激情地呼吁反对专业批评家的暴虐:

"凡能写出好诗之人,

只注重艺术。他不是为你

或为我写诗——也不是为伦敦或爱丁堡写诗;

即使是最好的批评家,他也不会忍受他们

踏入他那自由思想的阳光和自我陶醉的概念之中

不会对神圣的界限有一英寸的偏离。

如果大众的美德

像恶习一样被玷污,那么被赞美或采用的艺术,

是否能保持其光彩与纯粹?

避开这样的奴役吧。诗人写的诗,

他写的诗;如果合适,人类便接受它,

> 这是一种成功：如果不合适，这篇诗歌
>
> 将不断辗转，不断辗转的诗歌，
>
> 终会被后世之人所获，他们大声哭喊，充满同情，
>
> 因为他们的先辈如此愚笨，
>
> 这也是诗人的一种成功。"

但是，尽管这一信条非常重要，但在捍卫它时，斯温伯恩的观点有些极端，他认为，"以一部艺术作品所遵从的艺术法则来判断，它如非优秀的作品，便毫无价值或生命力可言。"首先，如果一部作品要被人接受，它必须通过对自然和人类生活的理想再现，让人产生愉悦感。而要做到这一点，遵从艺术法则只是必要条件，而非充分条件。如果研究一下作品使人产生愉悦感的实际情况，我们会找到与斯温伯恩观点相反的心理学依据，即检验作品价值的最高标准是，符合人类的一般感知。接触艺术作品所带来的愉悦不仅来自外部刺激——例如吸引感官和唤起想象力的一幅图画或一首诗，也取决于受众的思想反应。在后者中，即在一个整体之人的思想中，发挥作用的是社会媒介或作为整体的当代思想。因此，如果艺术家想要给予愉悦，他必须组织材料，表现作品主题，并符合当代思想所体现的情感，或不与之相抵牾。事实上，该论点可作进一步探讨。可以这样说，调整艺术规则，使之符合人类思想的需要，是艺术家的主要功绩。

或者，可以从另一个角度来探讨这个问题。对于一首诗、一幅画或一曲音乐，专业人士看到的是这个作品的一个方面，而普通人看到的是另一个方面。在人群数量上，后者一定比前者多。在专业艺术性的问题

上征求普通大众的意见是荒谬的，但在具体艺术作品的总体效果问题上，必须征求他们的意见。因为通常来说，诗或画并不仅仅是为诗人和艺术家创作，而是为全世界创作。众所周知，公众确实有权决定艺术品的价值，事实上他们也确实对作品的成败作出裁决。因此，鉴赏力或判断力不是某个阶级或职业的特权，而是所有人的权力。它是真正的检验，而不是只有少数人才了解的特定艺术的规则。诚然，"鉴赏力"和道德标准一样，在不同的时期会有所不同，在不同的社会也存在差异。但即便存在这些变化，它仍然有充分一致的基础，构成一种永久有效的鉴赏力。如果我们承认这种鉴赏力的存在，并认同真正的检验标准是"符合人类的一般感知"，那么就必须考虑一件艺术作品对整个世界的影响。其影响无论好坏，都是一个不可忽视的因素。

现在，让我们转向罗斯金先生的教导；他在《现代画家》(*Modern Painter*)一书中说道："我所说的每条绘画的原则都可以追溯到某一重要的或者精神上的事实。在我论建筑的著作中，基于不同流派对普通人生活所产生的影响，我最终会更偏爱某一流派。这个问题是被其他研究建筑的作家完完全全遗忘或轻视的。"根据罗斯金先生的看法，艺术作品的影响好坏是一个攸关其卓越品质且极其重要的因素。和柏拉图一样，该理念是他整个艺术理论的基础。因此，他将其用于指导艺术的各个分支。在绘画方面，他说："虚荣或自私的人不可能画出高贵的作品……仅凭聪颖的头脑或特殊的天赋，是永远不会成为艺术家的。"在建筑方面，基于其理念，他认为哥特式风格是最好的。"从某个角度看，哥特式建筑不仅是最好的也是唯一合理的建筑，因为它完全可以做到雅俗共赏。屋顶的坡度、束柱的高度、拱门的宽度或地面的布局都不确定，它可以收缩成一座塔楼，扩展成一个大厅，盘绕成一段楼梯，或耸立成一个塔尖，其优雅永存、能量无穷……"。同时，正如我们所见，他认为最伟大的艺术家是"在其所有作品中体现出最多最伟大思想的艺术家"。此外，他还严谨地将该理念应用于个人。在现实主义绘画流派的讲座上，他承认罗塞蒂是"建立英国现代浪漫主义学派的主要思想力量"。但他认为，霍尔曼·亨特[1]信奉基督教真理，因此他"远比罗塞蒂更伟大、更幸福"。"对罗塞蒂而言，《旧约》和《新约》只是伟大的诗歌，他基于圣经而作的画，如同《亚瑟之死》（Morte d'Arthur）和《新生》（Vita Nuova）那样，并不相信它们与当下生活和人类事务有多大关联。但对于霍尔曼·亨特而言，一旦全神贯注于《新约》的故事，就变成像血统纯正、虔诚不二的老清教徒或老天主教徒那样，这些故事不仅是现实，不仅是最伟大的现实，也是唯一的现实。它是如此绝对……以至于在表现宗教元素较弱的主题时，他的力量也被削弱了。那些对其他人来说最容易做的事，他反而做得最差。"[2]

因此，我们可以宣称，罗斯金先生所论道德与艺术的关系，与斯温伯恩先生的观点恰恰相反。"……相比于对国家和自由的热爱所激发的对暴政最宽宏大量的抨击，维吉尔对恺撒的赞歌和德莱顿对斯图亚特的赞歌更可取。"然而探讨这个话题的困难之处在于，两位批评大师的观点前后并不一致。罗斯金先生写想象力时，他以与斯温伯恩先生同样明

---

[1] 霍尔曼·亨特（1827—1910），英国画家，与罗塞蒂一样，是前拉斐尔派的创始人之一。——译者
[2] 《艺术讲座》第二卷，第9页。

确的措辞宣称：艺术家的独特能力是至高无上的，而主题内容是次要的。"它并无道理可言；它既不是通过代数，也不是通过积分学来起作用，而是通过尖锐的、海笋一般的思想之舌，其作用和味道深入人心；不管主题的内容或精神是什么……，诗人或画家的每一个伟大构想都是基于这种想象的能力。"[1]而斯温伯恩先生对某首诗进行批评时，发现了它在某些社会及道德观念中的缺陷，这些缺陷冒犯了他；因此他写道，"《奥罗拉·丽》中闪过的基督化社会主义和野蛮恺撒主义的邪恶影子，损毁并削弱了它纯粹的和高贵的魅力。"[2]

他们二人的观点都包含了一部分真理，但不是全部真理。罗斯金认为，是否传递了"最多最伟大思想"的检验标准适用于艺术作品外在的或客观的方面——艺术作为一个整体被视为"借由实体之美诠释或表达道德之美"[3]；但它不适用于艺术作品内部的或主观的方面——当艺术作品是艺术家思想的表达，是"想法转变为创作"[4]。斯温伯恩关于是否"遵从特定艺术规则"的检验只适用于艺术作品的外在方面。艺术家在形成自己的想法时，应当遵循"伟大思想"的检验；在执行自己的想法时，应当以"艺术规则"为指导。一方面，当然，他不可能完全独立于大众之外，将艺术的卓越作为唯一目标；另一方面，无论道德价值多么独特，也永远不足以赋予其作品艺术的独特魅力。

---

[1] 《现代画家》。
[2] 《维克多·雨果研究》。
[3] 库辛。
[4] 同上。

第六章　当代文学之批评

乔治·艾略特（George Eliot, 1819—1880）

第七章

文学判断之运用

批评思想的发展——区分批评的"规则"与"原则"——当代批评家更多地去"阐释"而非"评估"——"真实"是文学价值的最高检验标准——但这里的真实是本质的真实，在不同的文学形式中性质不同——这种真实即观念真实的例子。对称原则——要求合适的创作形式——对素材进行适当的选择和安排——理想化原则——检视"现实主义"和"现实的"这两个词——对这一原则的最重要应用是"诗性正义"学说——培根对此原则的阐述——悲剧被排除在外——它的原因——理想化原则的使用限度——理想化原则必须受制于真实原则——仅仅知道这些原则是不够的——运用这些原则的方法就是进行比较——艾迪生和阿诺德——通过研究大师们的作品，我们的文艺"品味"得以形成——运用比较的例子："乔治·艾略特"和梅瑞狄斯先生的作品前文章节已举例说明古往今来诸多伟大思想家审视文学的不同观点。这些例证至少在某种程度上向我们表明，在公认为人类遗产的文学作品中，以及在尚未获得认可的新作品中，如何运用批评去寻觅某些主要文艺品质。

广义而言，通过对比不同时期批评家的著述，可以发现，文艺批评的发展与其说是认识新品质，不如说是对最早认识到的品质作出更全面的理解与更准确的界定，从而可以应用新的或更适当的文艺检验方法来发现这些基本品质。我们已经注意到，文学整体上具有三个特质：题材、风格和审美愉悦。题材是指包含"思想性"，即有助于世界观的形成；风格是指呈现"思想"所运用的文学手法要与作品的文学形式相适应；如果文学作品的目的是给予愉悦，它必须具有艺术作品的特有力量，即必须"唤起我们的想象"，或让我们产生"对事物的亲密感"，这使得诗意的真实比科学的真实更有说服力——更容易为大脑所接受。

现在，当人们开始将文学（及艺术）视为可以发挥更高能力的独立、独特领域时，就发现了所有这些品质。例如，柏拉图意识到它们的存在，并选择将传递思想并且是最优秀的思想,作为文学整体最基本和最重要的品质。但他提出衡量这一品质存在的检验标准却是,创意文学对于现实的再现在多大程度上接近于现实的最原始状态。然而,对现实最原始状态的描述也可以在那些非创意文学类型中找到。换句话说,柏拉图建议通过一个只适用于"模仿"的检验标准来衡量文艺"表现"的真实。或者,如亚里士多德所指出的,他并未区分诗人与历史学家试图表现的现实——即未区分感觉真实和理性真实。亚里士多德还意识到,创意文学作品向大脑传递信息的方式不同于历史或哲学作品,并认为衡量这种特有品质的方法,是观察公认有价值的诗歌作品的不同创作形式。但我们现在理所当然地认为,一个虚构文学作家,无论写诗歌或散文,都会采用适当而且必要的创作形式。我们主要(而不完全)关注其作品的整体效果,并且如果我们发现其创作具有唤起想象力的基本品质,便不再费神去考虑他在达到这一最高目的的过程中,在材料组织上是否严格遵循了任何业已存在的模式。

如果我们把那些涉及情节结构、韵律、语言或措辞等次要因素的规范称为"规则",把那些涉及基本品质的规范称为"原则",并将"规则"与"原则"区分开,我们就能够指出批评精神发生的变化,即它越来越倾向于无视"规则",并更多地关注"原则"。因为,尽管运用"规则"可以揭示在各时代重要性不一的优点和缺点,但"原则"与某些普遍重要的品质相关——也即,与人类思维中某些基本特征的品质相关。由于对这种品质的欣赏不会随着人类生活条件的改变而发生变化,因此,批评的有效性取决于是否有能力区分"原则"所涵盖的不变因素和"规则"所涵盖的变化因素。

这种变化的影响表现在当代批评家对已确立声誉的作品和那些价值尚未确定的新作品的检验方式上。如果他关注前者,便会更多地去"阐释"而非"评估"。他不再探寻作品的缺陷或失败之处,而是忙于发现和解释"原则"这一检验方式在作品中所揭示的品质,或者即便他探寻了,其出发点也是比对价值,以获得更强烈的宽慰。他更关心读者,而不是作者;因为他的主要目的是让我们了解作者所处的特殊社会和物质环境及其个人禀赋,进而展示这些决定性条件如何反映在其作品特征中。这样,批评家们将信息提供给我们,使我们理解作者的动机与观点,并让我们自己去评估。简言之,应用于这类作品的批评已经变成文学阐释。而在审视当代作品时,批评家们面临更艰难的任务。他充其量只能提供一个临时性的裁决,而为了形成这个裁决,他要运用旨在衡量题材、风格及唤起想象力特征的检验标准,并忽视技巧的、非永久品质的"规则"。当然,在这里,毫无疑问,遵循公认的语法和韵律规则是必须的。一般而言,违反这些规则的作品将被排除在文学范畴之外,因此也进入不了批评家的视野。我说"一般而言",是因为我们必须记住,这些规则本身是基于观察伟大作家们的创作实践而制定,其有效性来源于文学用法。因此,我们必须认识到,规则的运用有一定的自由度,因为是文学用法造就了它们,同样也能拓展它们;而且有时文字的规则被打破,但规则的精神依然得到遵守。正因这一特例,当代批评家越来越倾向于把对新作品的初步判断建立在某些"原则"之上,这些原则意在揭示一些品质的存在或缺失,历史经验已教会我们在人类天才的过往成就中识别并欣赏这些品质。由于我们既要阅读当代文学作品,也要阅读名著,因此了解这些"原则"十分必要,它能让我们在日常选择和欣赏书籍时作出一定的判断。当代作品有独立于(严格意义上的)文学价值之外的价值和吸引力。它们完美地展示我们周围的生命运动,反思并探讨问题,这些问题与我们每个人都有直接的利害关系;它们在当下充满活力,仿佛就是我们身边一位邻居的所思所想。除非假设英语文学的源泉突然枯竭,否则,当代文学作品中定会诞生未来的杰作。

让我们看看,能否把已经学到的原则总结为足够清晰的、具有实践价值的陈述,从而指导我们形成对作品的判断。

第一条原则——就历史演变顺序和重要性来说,排在首位的——是真实原则。这一原则使我们期待并要求文学作品具备一种基本的对应关系,即作品传递给我们大脑的信息对应其陈述的外部现实或生活事实。这是有效级别最高的原则,因为它用于检验所有品质中最重要的品质,即艺术或文学作品要符合人类的一般感知,它也因此被认为是对人类知识遗产的永久贡献。一般来说,文学作品的最高价值是为世界贡献一种新思想,而创意文学作品的最高价值在于唤起想象,进而令人愉悦地产生这种思想。而真实是文学价值的最终检验标准。如果我们必须在题材和风格之间作出选择,我们宁愿失去后者。因为一部与生活事实不相符合的作品,或一部违背人类普遍和基本信仰的作品,无论其纯粹的艺术品质有多么伟大,都是毫无价值的。

但文学所要求的真实是"本质"的真实。也就是说,在不同的文学形式中,书的内容与其陈述的现实之间的对应性是不同的。为了确定这种对应性的存在,真实的检验必须以不同程度恰当地应用在不同文学形式当中。我们期望从哲学家、历史学家或传记作者那里获得的真实是真正的事实,就如法庭上目击证人提供的证据那样"确凿不移,唯有真实",

是对被压制或被掩盖之必要事实的完整陈述。他们应当完全坦率地展示信息来源，提供准确的时间、数据以及事件发生的顺序或事实的编排，并在证据发生冲突时保持观点的绝对公正。从散文家、描写作家和旅行家那里，我们要求的是不那么严格的事实再现，它们是作家形成观点或描绘人物和地点的基础。在这里，个人因素更加凸显，理想化的过程使事实的呈现从简单的描述转化为表现。也即，与其说他告诉我们的是其所见或所学，不如说是自然景物或与他人的接触在他心中产生的思想或感情。他很可能通过自由运用理想主义的艺术方法，给我们描绘出更为逼真的人物举止以及更为真切的自然图景。在描绘过程中，他会选择某些特征进行突出处理，削弱甚至忽略一些细节，因为这些细节可能会弱化描绘对象在我们脑海中造成的整体效果。

　　需要再次强调，在创意文学中，无论是小说还是诗歌，我们都需要真实。这是艺术性真实，因为诗人和小说家塑造的人物和事件都是典型的，而不是实际的。诗人（或小说家）描绘的场景和勾勒的人物都没有现成的原型。原型，包括其表现，都是思想的创造；小说里的真实就是观念的真实。也就是说，作者个人的普遍经验必须对应团体的或种族的普遍经验。例如，"米德尔马契"不是纽尼顿，"玛吉·塔利弗"也不是少女时期的玛丽·安·埃文斯，[1]但如果我们想知道英国中部小镇的生活情况，或了解"乔治·艾略特"曾经是什么样的女孩，最好的方式就是阅读小说里关于米德尔马契和玛吉·塔利弗的描述。以上都是个人的普遍经验产出

1　英国女作家乔治·艾略特原名玛丽·安·埃文斯，纽尼顿是她的家乡。"米德尔马契"是她的同名小说中一个虚构的地名，"玛吉·塔利弗"是她另一部小说《弗洛斯河上的磨坊》中的女主人公。

观念真实的例子。因为所有人都会发现，"乔治·艾略特"的描写和特征与普遍现实和事实之间存在本质的对应，其描写正是基于现实。创造若是融合了个人经验和体现在种族精神传统中的普遍经验，那么这种创造的本质真实会更高级也更持久。倘若我们想"了解"爱情激情所产生的无上的献身精神，我们不会想到某个熟人的订婚或结婚，而是想到"罗密欧与朱丽叶"的故事；我们理解女性对理想责任的奉献，是基于索福克勒斯的"安提戈涅"的行为；我们理解骑士职责，是基于《国王田园诗》（*Idylls of the King*）里的亚瑟。伟大的诗学大师们作品里的观念真实，在某种意义上优于历史或传记真实，也优于对现实的文字记录。它之所以优越，是因为其包含的概念是基于多个时代和多个国度的普遍经验，事实上，它是种族经验的缩影。因此，亚里士多德曾说："与历史相比，诗歌具有更广泛的真实和更崇高的目标；因为诗歌探讨普遍真实，而历史探讨具体真实。"又或者，如华兹华斯所言，"诗是一切知识的菁华"。

无论是散文还是诗歌，我们所要求的创意文学作品的观念真实，其本质是诗人或小说家的观点、情感与人类一般感知之间的一致性。由于人类对最重要之事的一般感知体现在社会规律的准则中，遵守这些准则被称为"道德"，因此最高级、最优秀的创意作品与道德之间的联系绝对不是虚假的。不同国家或不同社会的道德在某些方面存在差异，西方的道德观与东方的道德观有明显不同。尽管如此，仍有某些原则——作为原则之原则——被所有文明社会普遍接受。一本小说或一首诗歌如果表现出不道德的人（在这个意义上）比道德的人更快乐，那它就不具备创意文学的观念真实，因为作者在其创作中体现的经验并不符合道德准则所表达的种族的普遍经验。因此，这些作品会受到真实原则的谴责。

道德是某一特定团体或一般社会的经验总和，作品中的内容若与之冲突，将会受到真实性这一最高检验标准的谴责。

第二条原则是对称原则，即某个作品的外部品质与它试图达到的特殊目的相适应。该原则应用于一般艺术时，通常要求艺术家在任何情况下，都要选择他的艺术形式能够最佳表现的某些现实属性，也要求艺术家限制自己，运用恰当的方法再现这些属性。从这一外部观点看，对称被分解为"组合"，或正确的选择和正确的使用材料。该原则应用于文学时，具有双重意义。首先，它适用于文学整体；其次，除去这种普适性，在某种特殊意义上，它也适用于运用艺术表现方法的创意文学。在第一种情况下，它要求文学作品的外部品质，例如作品的长度和形式（散文或诗歌，叙事，对话，或叙事与对话结合），需符合作品各自处理的主题需要。这是相对简单又明确的要求。举两个极端的例子——需要陈述大量事实的历史学家，会自然地选择叙事形式，用轻松的散文写作，不受韵律的拘束，也不受结构长度的限制；而当诗人想表达某个思想时，他会自然地选择有严格限制的诗歌形式，如十四行诗，这样他便能将文学之美灌注在字里行间，其思想也如镶嵌在精致底座之上的珠宝一样闪耀。从这个意义上说，对称原则适用于文学整体，无论其目的或形式有多么简单。即使对于一本历史或科学手册，写作时也必须考虑编排；也就是说，主题应作为一个整体予以呈现，事实要按照应有的顺序予以排列，重点内容要突出，次要内容需置于从属位置。

在第二种意义上，对称原则只适用于创意文学，因为只有这类文学才使用艺术手法来表现现实。对称原则要求作品的创作形式符合其所属的诗歌文学形式的外在要求，而且要求作者尊重创作媒介对他的限制。

简言之，这种创作媒介即文字符号，包括书面的和口头的，它们通过在视觉或听觉上的排列组合来表达时间的属性。因此，对称原则要求作家应选择性地表现现实世界的某些特定方面，而非全部现实。因此，如果一首诗要想具有对称性，首先，它必须只表现客观或主观现实的某些方面；其次，在对话、叙述、描述和独白等一些诗歌要素中，文字仅限于指代这些要素各自所指的具体事物、行为、精神状态或物质现实场景。这种情况下，文字不再是传递思想的手段，而是一种展现思想画卷的方法，即激发读者想象力的手段。亚里士多德在《诗学》中对这一规则作了大体勾勒，阐明艺术家所使用的媒介限制并控制了艺术家的文字。莱辛对此做了深入详细的补充，他研究了"眼睛"（视觉）和"耳朵"（听觉）这两种对比鲜明的艺术表现方式。我已经指出，亚里士多德把对称原则作为衡量创意文学作品价值的主要标准，并把悲剧视为创意文学的最高发展形式，因此他自然坚持情节至上的原则。无论是舞台剧还是小说，只有在情节的建构中，艺术家才有了最广阔的语言空间，来表现作品的优劣。所以亚里士多德站在对称原则的角度写道："可以说，情节是悲剧的核心与灵魂，而人物品格在重要性上次之。"亚里士多德认为，情节的构建包括两部分，一是选择合适的素材，二是将素材进行有效安排。而素材的有效安排依靠对中心事件的凸显，并使"插曲"在恰当地从属于这个中心事件的同时，又能够直接作用于其中。亚里士多德研究的是作品整体的对称性，或者说恰当配置，而莱辛则告诉我们如何将其运用到作品的各个部分。莱辛不教我们如何建构情节，而告诉我们如何运用对称原则去描写一个人物、一件物体、一个动作又或是一个情景。第五章已经介绍了他相关研究中最精彩的部分，在此不再赘述，但可以用梅瑞狄斯先生的一句名言来概括它，即："创作之笔是一门艺术，旨在唤起内心的憧憬……因为我们自由飞翔的思想无法容纳冗长的描述。莎士比亚和但丁仅用一行字或最多两行字便能展现画面。"另外，沃尔特·贝赞特爵士在其《小说艺术》（*Art of Fiction*）一书中提出的人物刻画法非常有用。这是一部秉持实用精神写就的作品，主要与散文小说相关。

"让读者清晰理解角色的方法有很多。首要且最简单的做法就是描写其古怪的言行举止。这种方法最低级，但确实最简单。另外一个办法是围绕该人物进行长篇叙述，但如此堆砌文字也是个糟糕的选择。只要你稍微读过任何一个名家写的东西，你便会发现好的小说家会在故事开头用两三笔就把人物介绍清楚，然后通过描写该人物的言行来逐步建构其个性特点。而且，反复提醒读者注意人物在对话中的手势、眼神或表情变化实在是缺乏艺术性的表现。在我知道的一些鼎鼎有名的故事情节中，尽管作者在人物的态度、举止和表情描写上惜墨如金，他们笔下的人物依然个性鲜明。这就是艺术创作的最高境界，即在不给出文字的情况下，让读者自己体会人物变换的面容举止和起伏的声线，给读者在剧院里闭眼看剧的感受——闭上眼却依然能感受到舞台上的演员，听到他们的声音。作者要做到这一点，首先须在作品开头先将人物的整体轮廓简单直白地呈现给读者，然后再通过一笔笔的描写慢慢勾勒出人物的脸庞和身形，并最终让人物从起初的简单轮廓发展成有血有肉的个体。"

因此，唯有具备这种对称性的作品——即在这些作品中，材料在整体性和细节上得到恰当配置，以捕捉"飞翔的思想"——才能唤起人们的想象力。也正因此，检验一部作品的对称性也间接成为了发掘和衡量其艺术价值的手段。

第三条是理想化原则。这是一个只适用于创意文学的原则，也就是说，创意文学作品同时也是艺术品，因此，这类文学作品必须具备艺术品该有的品质，我们主观上将这一品质称为"审美愉悦"，客观上，我们将其称作"美感"。理想化原则适用于创意文学作品时，要求作者不仅要呈现现实的精神层面，而且要首先从现实的精神层面进行选择，此种选择要去除读者审美意识的消极方面。正如维克托·库辛所言："艺术在我们身上激发的所有感受都应该受到美感的约束和控制。如果艺术仅仅致力于激发超过一定限度的（尤其是生理上的）悲伤或恐惧，那么它将令人反感，不再具有魅力，且会变得庸俗而使人感到陌生。"只有参照理想化原则，我们才能给"现实主义"和"现实的"这两个用于创意文学（以及一般艺术）的术语赋予确切的内涵。如果作者再现的是现实，而不是现实的精神层面，那么任何创意文学作品都不可能是"现实的"。如果"现实主义"被用作一个贬义词的话，那么它只能用在那些为了理想化地表现现实而忽视写作素材选择的作家身上，当然，这样的作家写出来的作品也早已丧失了"审美愉悦"的品质。然而，文学作品"审美愉悦"的品质显然取决于不同读者的品性，也取决于具体某个作品自身的特点。所以说，当某个作品无法愉悦某个读者时，我们只有在确保该读者拥有常人具备的艺术感和道德感的前提下，才能说这部作品不具备"审美愉悦"的品质。并且，由于"道德感"一词相较于前者被广泛滥用，使其几乎沾染上了"不道德"的含义，所以我们在使用该词时需牢记，其本义和拓展义是截然不同的。广义而言，如果作者（或艺术家）的创作只是机械复制了某个主题或某个主题的某个方面，且削弱或消除了艺术作品凭借"美感"而"产生愉悦"的品质，"道德感"一词的拓展义（即不道德）便可用来描述该作品的特征。

理想化原则最突出的应用是"诗性正义"学说。根据这一学说，除悲剧外，所有创意文学作品的情节都应有一个"愉快的结局"，借此表现出人类根植情感深处的乐观主义精神。这种精神源于一种信仰，即乾坤宇宙是由一位全知全能的神（Being）所主宰。培根清晰而精彩地阐述了理想化原则在创意文学中的应用，为我们提供了这一学说的哲学基础——文学作品中的成功和人物的行动应符合因果报应与神的旨意。

"诗歌……只不过是一种伪装的历史。它可以采用韵文的形式，也可以采用散文的形式。这种伪装的历史的功效在于，当自然不能给予人们满足时，它能让人产生一种虚幻的满足，在这种历史中，自然的世界与人的灵魂相比处于比较低下的位置。因此人的精神世界与物质的世界相比更广大、更仁慈、变化更多。如果真实历史中的行为和事件其庄重的程度无法让人的心灵得到满足，诗歌便虚构出更加伟大和宏伟的行为和事件来；如果真实历史中记述的事件其成功和结果不足以表达人们对善恶是非的评判，诗歌便虚构出更加公正、更加符合天意的事件作为补偿；真实历史叙述的故事平淡无奇，所以诗歌赋予它们更加罕见，更加难以预料、变化多端的特质。因此，诗歌似乎适合并有助于彰显崇高的行为，有助于宣扬道德规范，有助于人们的娱乐。因此，曾有人猜测诗歌活动中有神灵的参与，因为诗歌通过让事物假装服从人们的意愿，从而提升和塑造人们的心灵；而理性只能让人的心灵向事物的本性屈服。我们可以看出，在蒙昧时代和愚昧的地区，没有其他的学问，只有诗歌迎合人们的天性，利用人们好愉悦的特性与音乐相呼应、相配而大行其道。"[1]

我们注意到，悲剧被排除在"诗性正义"学说的应用领域之外，因为这一学说要求创意文学作品的情节必须最终传达给心灵一种满足感。原因是这样的：悲剧是创意文学的特殊形式，其作品效果主要取决于（尽管不完全是）悲情，或者说以尖锐的形式表现人类的苦难。用亚里士多德的定义来说，悲剧的诗性体现在其对"恐惧和悲伤"的集中呈现，而达到这种效果的最有力手段便是让情节以"灾难"告终。因为正是通过描绘一幅没有丝毫希望可以穿透普遍阴郁的最终图景，悲剧艺术家才能激起受众的情感，并最终实现悲剧特殊的感召人性的效果。换言之，尽管以灾难收尾是悲剧的必备要素，但对于其他形式的创意文学来说，它只是附带的。这类收尾方式偶尔才在那些确实有必要把结尾写成灾难的诗歌或小说中出现。在悲剧以外的创意文学形式中，人们天生具有的乐观主义精神都能在一般意义上的散文或诗歌中得以实现。的确，创意文学所特有的艺术美感在一定程度上直接得益于理想化原则在作品中的特色运用。[2]

然而，理想化原则的使用也是有限度的。这一原则受制于真实原则，后者也是检验某个文学作品是否具有创造性的最高及最终标准。但是，在了解这种限制对创意文学创作的影响前，我们有必要知道：创意文学的真实性源自观念，而非逻辑。现实主义作家基于其主观感知描写事物，

---

[1] 《学术的进展》第二卷，第四章。译文引自刘运同译，《学术的进展》，上海人民出版社，2015，第 75—76 页。
[2] 在写完上面的内容之后，有人向我提出悲剧以"灾难"收尾的另一个非艺术性的原因：牺牲，在希腊悲剧中有着宗教动机；当必须为某个罪行作出牺牲或赎罪时，无辜者也难以幸免。

第七章　文学判断之运用

有时尽管其对事物的某些书写会与传统的道德观念相悖，但他也会为自己辩护。有人说，艺术早已走过了童话故事的发展阶段，成年人的艺术应该展现事物的本真。这种论调的合理性也十分有限。这里所言之真实性绝非艺术作品所能展现。在小说或诗歌中探寻科学意义上的真实性是肯定行不通的，科学意义上的真实性应该去政治学或经济学的论文、蓝皮书抑或是犯罪报告中查找。然而，真实原则的确限制了作者对理想化原则的运用。如果一个诗人或小说家一方面将他笔下的人物置于现实环境中，另一方面又让他们不受任何约束地行动，那这样的作品就缺乏真实性，因为其所表达的思想具有本质上的谬误。同样，如果作品中的人物同现实世界的人一样行动，却身处完全理想化的环境中，那作品所呈现的思想就与现实不符。这样的作品既没有科学的真实性，也缺乏艺术的真实性。所以，思想谬误源于伪造的真实，而现实谬误则要归咎于虚妄的思想。简言之，名实不符，生活的整个图景被扭曲了。创意文学绝不能像史书、传记、科学或哲学论文那般展现生活，而真这么做的作品也不会具有创造性和艺术作品特有的美感。另一方面，真实原则从两方面控制着理想化原则的运用。第一，它要求理想化原则贯穿作品始终，否则作品将呈现出一个扭曲的，并因此不真实的思想世界；第二，它要求理想化原则的运用应以广泛而正确的知识为指导，这种知识即为"哲学"术语所指，涉及世间万物。如果没有这种广泛而准确的知识基础来指导艺术家形成自己的精神原创，那他所呈现的人物和场景就不会与精神原创所要阐释的现实有任何相似之处。这种不受真实原则控制的理想化写作常见于散文和小说。用梅瑞狄斯的话说，受此影响的小说艺术已经"把所有人都当成了白痴"。这种小说中的人物都是"奉承的老好人"，是"所有错觉中最危险的一类事物"。只有当小说家学会用真实原则指导他的理想化创作,并在"哲学"知识的指导下抒发自己的灵感,才不至于写出"不会因羞涩而脸红的婴儿,不具备行为能力的成年人"这样的句子。如果有哪个作家能将真实原则同理想化原则在作品中完美结合,那他便是创意文学的大师。

他又说道:"这样我们就能真实地记录现实。诸如玫瑰粉或是肮脏褐之类的虚假描写都将不复存在。在哲学的引导下,愚蠢的竞争终将消失。它们将不再囿于虚无的虚假统治,不再阻碍自然人性的思考,不再扼杀我们灵魂深处发出的呐喊。哲学让我们明白我们并不像玫瑰粉那样美丽,但也不像肮脏褐那样令人作呕;除了我们内心深处那不可改变的荒凉外,我们将看到一个健康而又充满希望的自己,并最终收获快乐。"[1]但是,仅仅知道优秀作品应具备的品质及其创作原则,我们还不能对一部作品的优劣作出评判,我们还必须学会在阅读文学作品时灵活运用这些原则。真实原则是检验作品的叙述是否优秀的标准;对称原则是检验作品的整体布局是否出色的原则;美感是检验理想化原则在作品中是否运用得当的标准。那么我们在评价一部作品时该如何灵活运用这些原则呢?答案只有一个,而且我已经说了很多遍了,即对这些检验所采用的方法和支持这些检验的原理进行比较。假设要评鉴一部作品,我们不仅要寻找真实性,还要理清是哪一类的真实性。换言之,对于非创意文学,要找出其逻辑上的真实性;对于创意文学,要找出其艺术上的真实性。当它是创意文学作品时,我们要弄清楚这部作品在多大程度上具备创造

---

[1]《十字路口的戴安娜》。

性。而要达到这个目的，我们就必须将其同公认的"杰作"或是同类型的名著作比较。这样的工作重复多次后，我们会逐渐对每个类型的佳作所具备的品质了然于胸，并在阅读其他作品时本能地欢迎它们的存在，而厌恶它们的缺席。正如艾迪生所言："所谓文学鉴赏力，即为发掘到某部作品的美而深感愉悦，而为看到它的不足而心生不快。如果有人想知道他是否具有文学鉴赏力，我会让他仔细读读历经时间和空间检验的古典巨作。"[1] 阿诺德也有类似的看法："如果我们想要研究最高级的诗歌特有的韵律及其高度规整的行文，我们须先熟读荷马、但丁、莎士比亚和弥尔顿的作品，用他们的作品武装我们的头脑。我们必须牢记大师们遣词造句的方法，并将其作为评鉴其他诗歌的试金石。"他还补充道："只要能做到灵活运用，哪怕只取文学大师们创作的几行诗歌作为评判标准，我们依然可以不失公允地、客观地评判其他诗歌。"[2]

只有通过研究大师们的作品，我们对文学和艺术的"品味"才得以形成。将我们对大师作品的了解作为"试金石"，或者更准确地说，如道登先生所说的"音叉"，我们可以确定任何新的未被认可之作的总体特征。但是，如果想要对其作进一步的评鉴，我们还必须与同类型作品作更深入和更精确的对比。每一类文学都有一些公认的佳作，每一位名家也有一些作品为个别读者所喜爱，因为总会有读者对个别作品情有独钟。而如果我们想要更进一步地评鉴一部新作，我们就得选择书中某个具体的片段（或者几个片段），并将其与其他作品中类似的描写作比较。

---

1 《旁观者》，第409期。
2 《评论二集》。（《诗歌研究》）

注意，这样的比较要有一个公平的基础。简单来说，如果我们想要弄清楚作家 X 的作品好在什么地方，我们必须将作家 A、B、C 所创作的同类佳作拿来与之进行比较。下面我用散文小说中的一两个例子加以详细说明。

乍一看，要将一个农民和他的家人走向教堂的过程写出艺术效果似乎很难。如果我们想知道诸如此类的片段如何才能写得出彩，我们得读一读《亚当·比德》(*Adam Bede*)[1]第十八章的前半部分。"乔治·艾略特"明白用艺术的优雅与哲学的感知来描绘这样一个平凡的主题是多么困难，在前一章她便已经告诉我们这一点，但她成功了。因此，她在日记里写道，每次给乔治·亨利·刘易斯[2]介绍一位女性形象的时候，他都"非常开心"，对此我们并不感到意外。这就是一个"标准的"段落。如果我们在新作品中遇到类似题材的描述，又想衡量作者的创作功力，那我们只需并置这两个段落，先读一段，再读另一段。或者，再举另一个题材的例子。大多数小说家在把男女主人公带入宣誓爱情的情节时，会避开描述行为和言语的内在困难，这些行为和言语若脱离现实生活中的强烈情感背景，便毫无意义或显得荒诞。所以，他们一般都会让我们自己去想象当时的情景，或者告诉我们，所有发生的事情只与男女主人公有关，并不会照顾读者的兴趣。尽管如此，梅瑞狄斯在《理查德·弗维莱尔的

---

1 乔治·艾略特的《亚当·彼得》出版于 1859 年，小说以乡村生活为背景，围绕木匠亚当·彼得展开。——译者

2 乔治·亨利·刘易斯是维多利亚时代重要的学者、传记作家，曾在生物学、心理学、哲学、文学批评等众多领域作出过突出贡献。——译者

苦难》(The Ordeal of Richard Feverel)[1]的"费迪南和米兰达(Ferdinand and Miranda)"一章中,不仅向我们讲述了理查德和露西"在野花绽放的芳香与美好之中"相遇时说的每一句话,而且还在读者的头脑中营造了一种外在的美感,一种令人心跳加速的情感氛围,使得每一句简短的言语、每一个不经意的动作都意义非凡而又舒适美好。为了充分领会梅瑞狄斯极高的艺术表现,我们可以将这一章与《罗密欧与朱丽叶》中的相应场景进行比较。这种比较有助于我们找到伟大艺术家在文字上采用的一般方法的一致性,同时也可以看出那些因文学媒介、精神以及社会环境不同而随之产生的处理及思维上的差异。

无论是戏剧还是小说,都有同样的一见钟情,都有同样来自父母和亲戚的反对,迫使爱侣们将注意力集中在他们自身——这便是绝对至上的自我主义。在这两种情况下,短暂的幸福过后总是离别,同样,仅仅是因为命运的捉弄,其带来的苦难都是彻底而难以承受的。在《罗密欧与朱丽叶》这部剧作中,朱丽叶代表着伊丽莎白时期的女性,话语直白坦率。在《理查德·弗维莱尔的苦难》这部小说中,露西·德斯伯勒(Lucy Desborough)的感情裹挟着19世纪女主人公的矜持,她的话语断断续续,总是借用典故和扑朔迷离的思绪来传达意思。

"温柔的罗密欧啊!

---

[1] 这是梅瑞狄斯 1859 年完成的第一部长篇小说,有自传的成分在内。小说写的是一位煞费苦心教育孩子的父亲最后徒劳无功,表达了人所受的教育的影响无法胜过自然影响和自身欲望冲动的观点。后世作家和批评家认为这部小说具有现代小说的雏形,"不再走以前到达文学创作目的的种种道路"。——译者

你要是真的爱我，就请你诚意告诉我；

你要是嫌我太容易降心相从，

我也会堆起怒容，装出倔强的神气，拒绝你的好意，

好让你向我婉转求情，否则我是无论如何不会拒绝你的。

俊秀的蒙太古啊，我真的太痴心了，

所以也许你会觉得我的举动有点轻浮；

可是相信我，朋友，总有一天你会知道

我的忠心远胜过那些善于矜持作态的人。"（朱生豪译）

我们把这段坦率的对话与露西承认她爱理查德的对话进行对比。

他握着她的手说道：

"不要走好吗？"

"请让我走吧。"她恳求道，清秀的眉毛皱了起来。

"不要走好吗？"他不自主地将她那白皙的手拉近了他怦怦跳动的心脏。

"得走。"她颤抖着，可怜兮兮地说道。

"别走，好吗？"

"噢，要走！要走！"

"告诉我，你真的想走吗？"

"我没有办法回答。"她沉默了片刻，然后预料到了他要问的话，说了句："是。"

"你真的——真的想走吗？"他向上望着她，睫毛微颤。

她微弱而肯定地回应他深情的挽留。

"你真的想——真的想离开我吗?"说完这句话,他快无法呼吸了。

"我真的必须……"

她最终还是回来了。

"我觉得没跟你再次道谢就走是有失礼貌的,"她说着,又伸出手来。于是,她离开了他,然后……在他的头顶上方,一只声音甜美的天堂鸟凄凄地鸣唱出了他的心声。天堂的慈辉照入他的灵魂。他抚摸着她的手,眼睛片刻不离,却也一语不发;她轻轻地说了句再见,穿过门廊走到了小路上,走进闪着露珠的密林,消失在弧状的光晕里,离开了他的视线。

以上例子都选自我们可能最熟悉的文学分支——散文小说。我希望它们有助于说明,通过类似的比较,一般检验和原则能够在所有文学领域中得到应用。

《罗密欧与朱丽叶》书籍插图

古希腊神话中的九位缪斯女神

第八章 形式方法与风格

诗歌或格律体创意文学——内心对韵律的喜爱——史诗或叙事诗——抒情诗——挽歌——戏剧——阿提卡悲剧中的"报应说"——悲剧的动机,人与环境的冲突——喜剧的动机,展示环境的讽刺性——现代戏剧中文学元素重要性降低——非诗歌类创意文学——小说在19世纪的发展——小说作为思想载体的重要性——历史与传记——散文——古典手法——浪漫手法——风格诗歌，或称格律体创意文学，是艺术价值最高，也是最早出现的文学形式。

文字的排列或多或少具有生动的音乐表现力，我们可以将它们追溯到人类的原始冲动。爱默生便很好地阐述了这种冲动的本质与诗歌的联系。

"我们都喜欢格律和押韵，它们是音乐的一种周而复始的表现。婴儿在保姆哼唱的摇篮曲中酣然入睡，水手们喊着船歌更加地干劲十足，士兵们在鼓号齐鸣下士气高涨，勇猛杀敌。韵律起源于脉搏的跳动，而歌曲和诗行的长度是由我们的肺活量决定的。如果你哼唱或者用口哨吹着耳熟能详的英国韵律，不管是十音节四行诗，八音节交替六音节，还是其他节奏，你很容易会相信这些韵律都是天然的，它来自人跳动的脉搏，因此它不是一个民族特有的，而是属于整个人类的。我想你也会在这些节奏中找到它英勇、哀怨抑或悲壮的魅力，并能马上找到可以恰当填补这些空缺节奏的词语。年轻人喜欢韵律、鼓点、曲调，喜欢事物成双成对或交替呈现，而且在更高的程度上，我们知道音乐还能对我们的脾性产生即时的力量,它可以改变我们的情绪,并将它自身的情绪传递给我们。捕获了这些与身心合拍的旋律,人性情感便会力争找到适当的文字来填充它们,或者把音乐与思想相结合,就像婚姻一样,我们相信天作之合,每一种思想都有适合它的旋律或韵律,但我们找到它的几率很小,因为只有天才才能铸就这桩良缘。"[1]

希腊人归纳出了诗(即诗体诗)的最佳分类方式。在这一分类体系下主要有几种形式:史诗或叙事诗、抒情诗、挽歌和戏剧。

第一种是**史诗**,也可以称为讲故事的诗(词;词诗),它是格律诗中最长的创作形式。除了诗人以自己的身份讲述故事之外(也就是向读者或者最早的听众讲述故事,抑或是在音乐的伴奏下吟唱),它还有大量的对话元素,在这些对话中,诗人会通过他笔下的人物来讲述故事。与戏剧相比,史诗有两个优点。首先,情节的周期可以无限制地延长,除了主要情节能覆盖更多时间外,它还可以加入更多的插叙或者附属故事,以及处理周期更长的插叙。其次,诗人还可以引入更多令人惊叹的元素,因为它所呈现的演员或事件无需视觉的审查,和我们观看舞台表演不同。换句话说,与戏剧相比,诗人在史诗中可以更自由地发挥想象力,而且事实上,许多伟大史诗的主题显然都是超常态的,许多人物和事件也是超自然的。另一方面,这种诗歌形式的创作具有本质上的困难,其成功案例极为罕见。它的形式磅礴浩大,需要大量思想而且是最崇高的思想才能赋予它以尊严,需要真正强大的灵感来源才能赋予它以生命。准确地说,它需要总结一个时代的思想,或者表达一个民族的愿望,这

---

[1]《诗歌与想象》。

就是为什么伟大的史诗屈指可数了：印度史诗《罗摩衍那》和《摩诃婆罗多》[1]、《伊利亚特》和《奥德赛》[2]、卢克莱修的《物性论》[3]、《埃涅阿斯纪》、《尼伯龙根之歌》[4]、《地狱》和《失乐园》。在这些作品中，有一些是多人的心血，而有些甚至是几代人的创作结晶。

抒情诗（七弦琴；歌词），顾名思义是指最初用七弦琴或其他乐器伴奏的诗。我们从这个词语便可知，它承载着在强烈情绪或灵感冲动下创作的歌曲中的所有情感爆发。雪莱的抒情诗《致云雀》（*To a Skylark*）[5]的最后一节就阐释了这种诗的特点，即个性与主题的完全融合。

你从大地一跃而起，

往上飞翔又飞翔，

有如一团火云，在蓝天

---

1 《罗摩衍那》和《摩诃婆罗多》并称为印度两大史诗，对印度文学影响很大。前者叙述王子罗摩因庶母排挤被放逐，妻子悉多被魔王劫掳，后得群猴帮助，夫妻团聚，恢复王位。后者描写般度和俱庐两族争夺王位的斗争，反映印度奴隶社会的生活，并涉及当时哲学、宗教和法律问题。——译者

2 《伊利亚特》与《奥德赛》并称为古希腊两大史诗，相传为荷马所作。前者主要叙述特洛伊战争最后一年的故事。后者延续了前者的故事情节，讲述了希腊英雄奥德修斯在特洛伊陷落后返乡。——译者

3 《物性论》是古罗马卢克莱修的哲学诗篇。全书以诗的语言全面系统地阐述并发展了德谟克利特与伊壁鸠鲁的原子说与无神论思想，是现存古希腊罗马唯物主义原子说唯一完整的一部著作。——译者

4 《尼伯龙根之歌》为德意志民间史诗。全诗分上下两部，主要根据神话和历史传说，结合当时人们的生活和思想感情创作而成。上部记述王子西格弗里德的英雄事迹和遇害经过，下部写他妻子克里姆希尔德为夫复仇的故事。——译者

5 《致云雀》为英国诗人雪莱的抒情诗代表作之一。诗歌运用浪漫主义的手法，热情地赞颂了云雀。云雀是欢乐、光明、美丽的象征。下面的译文为查良铮译本。——译者

平展着你的翅膀,

你不歇地边唱边飞,边飞边唱。

★ ★ ★ ★ ★ ★

只要把你熟知的欢欣

教一半与我歌唱,

从我的唇边就会流出

一种和谐的热狂,

那世人就将听我,像我听你一样。

挽歌(一种哀歌)谱写于深切的情感之下,但是心境截然不同。它是反思性而非冲动性的,所以它的特点是肃穆,而且往往风格沉郁。格雷的《墓园挽歌》[1]就是一个耳熟能详的佳例。

门第的炫耀,有权有势的煊赫,

凡是美和财富所能赋予的好处,

前头都等待着不可避免的时刻:

光荣的道路无非是引导到坟墓。

★ ★ ★ ★ ★ ★

也许这一块地方,尽管荒芜,

就埋着曾经充满过灵焰的一颗心;

---

1 《墓园挽歌》这首诗是有关人生短暂的沉思。作者格雷是英国18世纪的重要诗人,也是英国新古典主义后期的重要诗人。他因此诗而闻名,被称为"墓园派"。下面的译文为卞之琳译本。——译者

第八章 形式方法与风格

一双手，本可以执掌到帝国的王笏

或者出神入化地拨响了七弦琴。

可是"知识"从不曾对他们展开

它世代积累而琳琅满目的书卷；

"贫寒"压制了他们高贵的襟怀，

冻结了他们从灵府涌出的流泉。

戏剧诗（戏剧、舞台剧）是指为舞台表演所作的诗，或是以这种形式写成的诗。由于每一句台词都是由扮演不同角色的多个演员说出，所以这类诗中没有直接的叙述和反映。我之所以认为它没有"直接的"叙述和反映，是因为这两个要素在一定程度上都通过各种途径保留下来。例如，在希腊戏剧中，讲故事的史诗元素部分是通过"信使"（一个在戏剧即时行动之外对事件进行长篇叙述的角色）保留下来的。同时，合唱团也提供了"思考"的元素，他们的作用是在歌声和吟唱中表达对舞台上所呈现事件的感受和思考，就像诗人会在抒情诗或挽歌中直抒胸臆一样。因此，希腊戏剧作为一种文学创作，是史诗与抒情诗形式的结合。在现代戏剧中，叙事性和反映性的因素都被削减了，但情节和对话（或对话所表现的情节）等基本要素却得到了相应的扩大和发展。戏剧文学大体上分为悲剧和喜剧两大类。悲剧的典型动机是展示人在与环境的冲突中落败。在"阿提卡悲剧"（Attic Tragedy）[1]中，显然不该发生的灾难压倒了恪守道德的平凡人，解释的论据则是"报应说"或者继承诅咒，

---

1 雅典所处的地理位置叫"阿提卡"，因而雅典悲剧又称"阿提卡悲剧"。——译者

继承诅咒就是说这个人本身并不该受到惩罚，但却要因其父辈的罪孽而受到惩罚。在这一学说中，他们试图以一种与宣告"第二条诫命"[1]相同的方式来解释邪恶的存在，并与犹太教和基督教神学的一般意旨保持一致。在伊丽莎白时代的戏剧中，这种无端的苦难与时代环境有着相当大的联系；而在艾略特的小说中，受实证主义学派领袖的影响，就其哲学基础而言，同样的问题则是与继承的科学原理或父母将生理和心理缺陷传递给子女的观点密切相关。

而喜剧的动机则是从相反的角度来展现这些冲突。对于那些意想不到甚至不该发生的遭遇，只要不太过严重，不至于激烈地引起我们的同情，便能令人产生一种满足感，这种满足感来源于我们将自身的好运与身边的厄运进行对比。当我们看到一个人追赶着被大风吹跑的帽子，或者一个乘客气喘吁吁并激动万分地到达站台，却只看到了驶出的列车和站台外飘留的蒸汽，我们就会开怀大笑，因为这些不幸轻微到不足挂齿，所以我们能够尽情地品味其中的喜剧元素。但是，如果同一个人，不是丢了帽子，而是被一辆公共汽车碾过，那他悲惨的遭遇就会立即引起我们的同情，我们的脑海就会立刻产生一种痛苦和惊恐，而不是欢笑，因为这已经是悲剧而非喜剧了。此外，如果发生意外灾难的是一个邪恶的人，或者是一个具有反社会品质的人，那我们心中也会产生一种满足感，甚至是彻头彻尾的愉悦感，即使那是一场非常悲惨的灾难。但这种灾难

---

1 "第二条诫命"出自《圣经·旧约》"出埃及记"第20章，原文为：不可为自己雕刻偶像，也不可作什么形像仿佛上天、下地，和地底下，水中的百物。不可跪拜那些像，也不可事奉它，因为我耶和华你的神是忌邪的神。恨我的，我必追讨他的罪，自父及子，直到三四代，爱我、守我诫命的，我必向他们发慈爱，直到千代。

如果要有喜剧效果，就绝不能包含身体痛苦的真实景象，因为这种人类苦难的极端景象总是会引起人们的恐惧感，除非观者的本性极其冷酷，或者情况极其异常。因此，喜剧的核心动机就是展示环境的讽刺性，它试图在观者头脑中产生一种完全令人满足的效果。喜剧能向观者展示，他们看到的周围的许多苦难都是应得的——因为喜剧的合法动机之一就是讽刺或展示恶行的丑陋、自以为高人一等的滑稽，以及过度自尊的苦恼。它教导观者把自己的不幸看作是社会总体生活的一部分，用超脱的态度看待自己的不幸，以此来说明最黑暗的事件也有"光明的一面"。

但戏剧，即在剧场呈现的悲剧或喜剧，在文学元素即文字的实际组成之外，还包含了两个元素，我们将对此作进一步探讨。这两个元素是：演员通过语调、行为和手势对文字进行阐释，以及舞台监督通过各种艺术的或科学的资源展现场景。因此，戏剧是一门综合艺术，是由作者、演员和舞台监督合力制造的整体效果。现代戏剧的发展越来越趋向于完善场景道具，文学元素的重要性已逐渐降低。散文作为文学媒介，非常便于使用，散文话语与现实生活实践更为接近，这导致当代戏剧作家普遍抛弃更严格的诗歌形式。然而，尽管还有其他因素影响，但诗人们的杰出戏剧作品主要还是（但不全是）基于严格的诗歌形式。此外，（严格意义上的）诗歌已经趋向于反思性而非戏剧性的作品，散文小说现在也已成为表现理想化之人类行为的伟大文学载体。尽管诗人对戏剧的贡献有所下降，但戏剧本身作为一种综合艺术却在不断进步。它推动了现实主义的发展，表现在文学媒介与日常生活语言的同化，以及演员们"自然感"的增强，因为他们的学习方法更接近现实并且更易于理解。戏剧还高度尊重历史的准确度并充分运用各种工具和道具，在场景调度上逐渐形成完全的"假象"。

非诗歌类创意文学——我们熟悉且占主导地位的形式就是"**小说**"。它如同一幅想象中的画面,描绘一对热恋情侣,信奉爱情至上。在传统的情节中,尽管命运捉弄,或有亲人反对,男女主人公还是终成眷属。下面这行台词便是很好的诠释:

"真爱之途从不会平坦。"

在这类"罗曼史"中,"冒险"的动机与情爱的欲望交织一体,有时前者甚至完全取代了后者。而且气氛往往会变得虚幻,并引入超常态或超自然的事件和人物。如果作者在小说中传达了一个严肃的意义,而这些小说在人物和事件上纯属虚构,那我们得到的就是寓言和讽刺文学。《堂吉诃德》《天路历程》和《格列佛游记》[1]等此类小说都是典型的例子。

除此以外,还有第三类特点非常鲜明的小说,那就是"乡土"小说。在这类小说中,作者如实地描写某个地区的自然风光,或某一群体的显著特点,并用一条情节的细线将其串联起来。这类小说有其自身的价值,相比于照片和绘画,他们在某种程度上是更高层次的虚构。

小说在 19 世纪经历了重大发展,这种发展的总体结果就是小说具有了哲理性。也就是说,高级小说的作家已经学会了把情节的发展和每个

---

1 《堂吉诃德》的作者塞万提斯在序言中声明"这部书只不过是对于骑士文学的一种讽刺",目的在于"把骑士文学地盘完全摧毁";《天路历程》是班扬的一首基督教的寓言诗(Allegory);《格列佛游记》则是斯威夫特创作的一部长篇游记体讽刺小说,首版于 1726 年。——译者

独立人物的演变建立在两个基础之上,即人类思维过程的科学研究所揭示的原则,以及确定的种族和个体演变现象。这样一来,散文小说作家就把种族的概括性经验与他对同代人的个人观察结合了起来。因此,当他从内在和外在角度研究社会时,就能呈现对生活的观察以及对性格和动机的分析,这些观察和分析透彻易懂,所以能吸引不同国家或者几代人的兴趣。

小说经过发展,已经成为一种极其重要的文学载体。从某种程度上说,它通过展现情节中虚构的人物,取代舞台成为了展示生活画面的媒介。一个非常形象的词语——"口袋剧场"——就很好地体现了小说的这一功能。同时,小说的读者群也非常庞大,人们必须承认,它或许是文学中最伟大的教育力量之一。有鉴于此,本世纪一些最伟大的思想家都采用这种文学形式作为他们思想的载体也就不足为奇了。俄国的托尔斯泰伯爵、法国的埃米尔·左拉[1]以及英国的乔治·梅瑞狄斯先生都既是小说家,又是伟大的思想家,他们通过小说这一媒介为本世纪的思想作出了重要贡献。

作为一种文学形式,小说以情节或交织的行动为基础,把历史与哲学的事实、散文的思考和一切诗性文学所必需的创作因素统一了起来。虽然它缺乏音乐和诗词创作那种结构上的完美,但却具有了散文那种更高的精确性,并且完全摆脱了结构性完美所附带的严格限制。

历史与传记。——在阐述"真实"原则时,我已经指出这两大文学

---

1 左拉(1840—1902)是19世纪法国最重要的作家之一,自然主义文学的代表人物,亦是法国自由主义政治运动的重要角色。——译者

分支的独特价值。这类作品若想拥有永久价值，就必须首先具备公正性的品质。这种公正性源自一种天生或后天习得的权衡证据的能力，以及历史学家或传记作家在赖以写作的大量材料中去粗取精的能力。正是凭借这种公正态度和审慎选择，基本事实才得以厘清，余下的就是以最有效的方式向读者呈现拆解出来的事实。为此，他们有必要描述多种社会状态以及主要场景和事件所涉及的多个地点。在后者（地点描述）中，作者应展开实地调研，熟悉这些地点。而如果叙述的事件发生在过去，则可利用历史遗迹、碑文和古物等有价值的辅助手段来获取线索。正是由于以上元素的广泛应用，当代历史学家的上乘佳作才更具活力和画面感。

历史学家讲述的是一个民族的生活，或者说是这个民族某个时期的生活，而传记作家讲述的则是一个人的故事。如果我们考虑到了主题不同会导致处理方式不同这一点，那么可以说传记也需具备与历史作品相同的品质；但是，我们或许能够容许甚至欢迎传记作者流露个人情感，而历史学家这么做却不合适。

散文的特点是具有简洁的外在形式和反思性元素。它从单一的视角处理主题，允许作者流露个性。在处理同一主题时，论文或书籍要求规范和完整，而散文则可以呈现更多作家的个人特征。散文与论文的关系就如同素描写生与完成的画作之间的关系，并且它还具有与自然写生一样的优点。就像写生是对外部自然在画家脑海中留下的直接即时印象的即兴记录，散文也应包含作家脑海里对新的事实形成的印象。散文写作的选择过程更自由，因此它在所有非创意文学形式中，艺术性最高。

古典与浪漫。——在所有这类文学作品的创作中，无论是创意的还是非创意的,我们都会溯及两种相反倾向所造成的影响。第一种倾向是遵循各艺术分支中的大师们在作品里所呈现的模式,而第二种倾向是有意识地希望在一个或多个细节上打破这些模式,从而更接近当代生活的现实。第一种方法——古典主义创作方法的风险是:固守过去的形式和方法,而它们已与现代精神及社会条件不相适应,因此导致作品失去活力。而第二种方法——浪漫主义创作方法的风险是:为了确保效果,牺牲某些过去经验已证明具有永久价值的文学品质。尽管对于当代读者来说,这些作品拥有显见的、可观的价值,与当代的运动和思想也有密切联系,但它们可能不会吸引后代的兴趣,甚至难以被理解。在这两个极端之外,追求任何一种方法都能带来鲜明的独特性,它们会自然地受到不同知识阶层的认可。对于受古典方法传统影响的作家,我们期望在他们的作品中找到更完美的文学表现,并期望它具备一种通过与各个时代的伟大智者和艺术家展开"密切交流"而获得的"气度"。但正因如此,我们才更要在那些遵循浪漫主义方法的作家身上寻找"新事物",这种新事物既是种族进步的原因,也是进步的结果。凭借这些新事物,文学从本质上成为人类生活的一部分。

  风格。——最后,我们谈谈"风格",它是一种既明显存在却又难以捉摸的品质。就像我们与一个人接触时(尤其是初识之时),他的行为举止可能会令我们厌恶或倾慕。同样,我们阅读一部作品时,作者的风格也可能会令我们厌恶或倾慕。此外,我们通过观察一个人的行为举止来对他的性格作出评价,这与在深入了解其行为和思想品质之后形成的更准确、更明晰的认识截然不同。所以,这种对风格的直觉也是独立的存在,与任何对其作品价值深思熟虑的批评意见无关。风格之于作家,如同举止之于个人。因此，说"风格即人"是对的，同样，保守地说"举止造就人"也是没错的。风格并不体现在句子的构造或者词语的选择，甚至不体现在某些典型文学创作方法的使用与否。它不同于这些元素，但同时又反过来影响着它们。它是一种文学创作元素，作家并不直接展现对文学规则的遵守或违反，而是无意识地表现自己的性情、教养或境遇。这就是作者在读者面前展现出来的姿态与风度。

美术通诠

〔英〕倭斯弗 著

严复 译

据上海图书馆藏之《寰球中国学生报》第三至六期。1906年6月（光绪三十二年五月），寰球中国学生会在上海创办《寰球中国学生报》，这是一份学报性质的双月刊。严复、曾子安、李登辉、唐介臣等四人任该刊主编。严复曾在该刊发表多篇论、译文，其中《美术通诠》第一、二、三篇，分别发表于该刊的第三期（1906年12月），第四期（1907年3月）和第五、六期合刊（1907年6月）。

目录

篇一　艺术　　　　119

篇二　文辞　　　　128

篇三　古代鉴别　　135

篇一 艺术

行乎都邑之间，所见者莫不有铸像画图、文史典籍，而文明之国，其所有者尤侈富。即在通衢巷陌，其圆柱方坫，或以铜，或以石，高者耸霄汉，卑者掩映林木间。其接于游人之目者，皆其国男女之肖像也。入其居，悬于墙者，则有画。庋于几阁者，则有壶甒尊彝，及他古器，而书史卷帙，纵横床榻。乃至富家旧族，往往辟堂室斋宇，专以待所搜牢者。图像简册，触目珍异，其美若不胜收者焉。夫饮食衣服，其人生最急者非欤？顾既完既足之余，何为有此？此以见治化已臻、文明既进之民，艺术又其生之所待，使神明之地，不资是诸物者以为养，彼劳精力，费货财，以广罗残缺，收拾细碎者，乌所取耶？是故艺术文章之事起，则有鉴别之学，穷耳目心思之用，以识别艺事文辞之正伪高下，是谓孤力狄实沁（criticism）。而具学识神智，有以别艺事文辞之正伪高下而不谬者，谓之衡鉴家，曰孤力狄克（critic）。考孤力狄克字，源于希腊，其义为判断，为评骘，此当亚烈山大世学者（自景教纪元前三百年至一百四十六年）而已然。当此时，有以五事读书之说。所谓五事者，一曰底哇唆悉斯（διόρθωσις），第其次序；次曰安那奴悉斯（ἀνάγνωσις），审其轻重；三曰特格尼（τέχνη），观其会通；四曰额锡吉悉斯（ἐξήγησις），详其疏义；五曰孤力悉斯（χρίσις），衡其巧拙。所谓孤力悉斯者，即衡鉴家之所有事者，特其事止于别裁文字之业耳。虽然，即今所谓鉴别评骘者，亦施于诗文词之作为多；至施于泛常艺林之事，常于其前特加区别之文，如云"金石识别""词曲品评"，随事为异是已。今不佞此篇，所用衡鉴品评诸语，舍其分别，大抵亦言判断文辞之事，盖所循用者，固最初之义也。

民生有群，因其有群，而复有德行之通义。此虽不必为员舆人类所公仞，而文明之众，有共由者。凡吾人之言行，其善恶以合不合于此为分。惟艺林之鉴别亦然，虽无通法，有其达理。凡吾人娱赏之端，其邪正隆污，以合不合于兹为判。是故知鉴别之理者，不独于文章艺术，有以讲其是而去其非也，且赏会之事，必由此而后有其酦至之感情，不独得其寓焉者也，且有以得其所寓焉者。所寓者何？则世间之物理、人事是已。盖惟知德行之通义者，乃克制言行之正，使近之为一身之荣誉，远之为同类之休嘉。故惟知鉴别之达理者，乃克通赏会之微，使近之有以乐于吾心，远之有以契于物妙。夫德行亦艺术而已，所以遂生正命之艺术也。德行之为艺术也，大而溥，吾之身世云为言动，莫能外之。所谓鉴别者，其艺术所有事，不外于吾生之一部分。兹篇所论，此一部分也。夫为论必首于知物，则开宗明义，当先取此部分之性情界域而明之。明其性情界域者，明艺术之为何物，与其系于吾生者为何若耳。

将欲为此，计莫若先举诸种之艺术，与言所各成之功，而以次论之，庶几有以得其会通之大意。其首先可见者，则艺术可别为二类也，其一谓之美术，其一谓之实艺。美术如营建（Achitecture），如刻塑（Sculpture），如绘画（Painting），如音乐（Music），如诗赋（Poetry）。实艺如匠、冶、梓、庐之所操，乃至圬者、陶人、红女、车工之业。二者之界域，其为分盖微，往往有相入者。但自其大别而言之，则美术所以娱心，而实艺所以适用，维二物皆人群天演之见端。然美术之关于民德、民智尤深，移风易俗，存于神明之地；而实艺小术，则形质养生所不可废，而于人理为粗，所以云其为分微者，盖有艺事于二类，若可两属，视操术者用意之何如。此如金木雕镂之事，瓷器玻璃之刻绘，壁缸门铺之涂饰，屋宇栋梁之斧藻，皆往往适用而兼娱情悦目者矣。

国之有实艺，其原始功用，无难明之理。盖自人有生，而饮食衣服、居处运动，莫不求其美利，恶其卑贱。而实艺遂生之事，乃与其众之声明文物，有偕行并进之机。其程度亦了然可言，大抵以利用安身为宗旨。以宗旨之确切不移，故实艺一涂，古又谓之有用之艺术。论一宫室、一几榻，乃至盘盂车舆之属之优劣，必先自其适用者以为言。若其雕饰之华，形制之可喜，抑其次而不关重轻者矣。且使其物牺利用之实，而徒形制雕饰之求，则文胜质亡，转为其物之累者，有之矣。

是故实艺为物，非不佞此篇所详论者。而所扬搉者，乃专在美术之一科。盖美术为物，其理较繁。自上世以逮于今，鉴别家言，于其原始功用，谛而求之，为论无悉合者，此其家自为说之故，可深长思。不佞于后此论及文章诗赋之篇，当为学者举似，特今所豫告者。此后是书所云艺事，皆指美术而已。

而艺事又有可分者焉：有目治之美术，有耳治之美术，视由客观之外物，以达于主观之人心，所由从之何窍。如营建，如刻塑，如丹青，目治者也；而乐律、诗歌，则耳治者。此易明之分也。或又谓美术可贵，存乎形上，必其事有待于物材弥寡，而后其为术弥尊。故德哲黑格尔列美术为五等，而诗歌最上，营建最下。彼谓营建为术，其有待于五材最著。其所以有闳壮深靓之观、悦神赏心之用者，固即在部署物材之得宜。且其成物，虽不尽以适用为期，而适用要为不可忽之一事，以言美术，风斯下矣。进于营建者为刻塑。刻塑之术，所重者形，而形固待质而后显，虽土木金石，所托以呈者非所论，而外之不能，特于证术，其所关者为至少耳，故为进也。进于刻塑者为丹青。丹青减刻塑之三量为两量，故有待于物材者愈寡。一切空闲浑体之形相，皆遇之于平面之中，此目治美术之极致也。入于耳治，如有音乐。音乐所待之外物，惟律吕音声而已。宫商引和，清浊相生，而人心之情，得其代表，不独有以达其情也，且有起人心之情，以与之相应。再进而为美术之极境者，则为词赋诗歌。乃于外物绝然无待，而所用以达于人心者，舍文字语言而外，一无所需。而其异于常用语言者，有节文韵律而已。（复案：中国翰札实为美术之一，此西之所无，而中之所独有者。）

由是观之，则美术之实，有可言者矣：一凡为美术，皆必有所托以为达者。自营建瓦石之最粗，至诗词韵律之微眇，使非有托，无以为功。二其感人之用，必借径于官骸，而大抵在目之为视，与耳之为听。三其有所托以为达，与有所由以为通。言其大用，期诸感人而已。其感惟何？盖操美术与观听之者，两心之相接也。是故艺林之事，自宫殿楼观之巍巍，至于短什小词之娓娓，以言其物，皆托寓也。托寓云何？官与其物接，其所见所闻者为一物，而所见所闻之外，别有物焉，与吾心为感通也。

惟此为美术同具之公德。夫既知其物之公德，则美术界说可试言之。美术者何？曰托意写诚，是为美术。又曰美术者，以意象写物之真相者也。

欲证界说所赅之义，则试取世间美术，一一为之分论。约而举之，大抵所可论者有三：一其所托之物质也，二其为接于耳目之涂术也，三其意境之显晦也。

营建所托之物质，乃其最粗。略言所用，石也，砖也，木也，铁也，及其他所常用者，是其物为最常之五材。是以梓匠之所成物，其接于视官与一切之外物差相若。若夫阴阳帅雪，藻绘陆离，天宇之清澄，山川原隰之雄秀而平远，虽皆营建者所得以借资，顾其事无关于巧术，非若他端目治美术，欲使观者移情，恒有所寓之巧智也。（案：营建之事，希腊古法常讲视差 optical corrections，而光学降而益精，尤巨功所必讲，不可谓无巧智也。）盖其故有二：非以象生物动作之事，一也；其成功之坚浑形色，假于所用之材而未尝变之，二也。虽然设为所成之物皆真相，而无有意境之事，寓于其间，则大不可。试观闳丽之工，游者为之神动，当有以悟相感之所由然，何则？建者意有所寓而呈故也。今更取世俗所习见者而言之，则如欧洲诸国都邑之峨特教寺，为国民事天祷祈之所，此非姑取一居而为之也。见如此之居，必事天祷祈之所用，而人心超凡度世，去溷浊求长存之意，皆可即其形制而见之。员宇岌业而拔地，神尖峥嵘而刺天，凡此皆营建之家意法之所寓也。虽然，意寓之矣，而以其有待物材之众，往往意为物掩，而所寓者，有时而不传。

刻塑以金石土木为所托之物材，施其范铸镌镘之功，而得其所拟似者。物之真相，一切任其指挥，所不能者，独动相耳。坚浑之体，窅眹之形，盖无一焉不可以极似，甚至物之容色，亦有术焉，以肖其真。是故刻塑所难，在乎生动。其术之所穷在是，而巧智之寓，即于是为多。虽然，自动相为刻塑天设之限，故其为术，多取分形之物而施之，如人畜之全体，豪杰之面首，或数人之集，坐立倚卧，皆静相也。又其传者多简易不繁之像，有本干无枝叶者。盖刻塑之功，施如金石，以金石肖衣裳襞积之物，其事为难，即成不可以久，是以古贤传作，多偏袒赤裸之像也。然使自所托之意言之，则寓于刻塑者，过于营建之术远矣。彼之所求肖者，固有生之人物，而仪观筋骨，常极其意所为至美者以为之。故刻塑之极功，止于静形之至美，此可证以希腊上古以来所传之石像也。

丹青为术，其所托者，缣素而已。或一切之平面，于其上可作诸线，以传空闲之形界；可赋诸色，以表物外之天然色者尽矣。故图绘之事，其有待于物材，较之刻塑为寡。而正以所待物材之寡，其术所寓之巧智为多，能以线色二者肖万物之形神，使观者自得之于目击。盖彼于二量无色之中，纯以意象求呈三量空闲之一切物也。夫以点线写空闲一切物者，非引墨含毫，随手可得者也，必循夫视学之规，其图中之画线，必与观者眼帘之视线，一一相符。至其赋色，又不仅即色立别已也，必循夫光学之例，以辨其色之价值。其天然者，各有远近阴阳之差，而为之浅深浓淡。夫而后平面之物，呈诸视官，得野外之景物，或室中之所有也。且丹青之术，其托意写诚，所以较金石刻塑为多，较土木营建为愈多者，非但以能循视学之理以为线，能以光学之理以为色，而极肖物之能已也。使徒如是而止，则照像摄影之业，固优为之。谓之写诚固矣，而托意之说又何居乎？是知丹青诚不止于有物。譬如画家图一前史之人事，或一山林之景物，其布诸缣素殿壁之间者，大抵其意景中之悬像耳。惟其不背于物则，故曰写诚；亦惟其景生于意中，故曰托意。彼之所为，将不仅描摹仿效其天然者,彼方有所弃择,有所会合,有所写而传之。此图画之功,所以为目视美术之极致,而赏会之微眇,所以于此业为独多也。总之,美术之事,皆写其意中之真像,使观听者不徒受之于耳目之官,且必交以神明,喻于情感最深之地。下此者,皆不足与美术也。

右所言皆目治之美术。乃今可言其耳治者,则音乐诗歌是也。夫其术既为耳治,其所托之物质自少,而非显然可见如前三术者。亦惟其托质之少,其意境之事愈多。夫乐律之所托,使必取其形下而言之,则独音声而已。其音声之所由生,出于歌者,唇喉腭舌可也;出于金革丝竹,与一切之可假以鸣者,自邃古制作,以至于今之乐器,亦可也。而是之为声,或其独用,或与歌词之言语引和,有八音十二律之相生,而又节为章奏,是则律吕之学,而工师谱乐者之所为也。使其协律按节之事,无所求助于诗歌,凡其所调,亦仅音声而已。(按:西人独以人语为有节之声,至于余声,皆无节者。)夫恃无节之声,以达其感情思理,斯其浑而不画,杳而难即,又可知也。愿[1]即以其物浑灏悠杳,不囿方隅,而乐之至德,于是乎在。盖惟如是而后有以取人心于至广之域,动其最初之天,而接于万类之所同然者。是故乐之感人,童少壮老,顽艳文野,平等无殊,有时且以及禽兽。呜呼!乐之为道,是其所以神者非欤?虽然,彼善为乐者,不仅调六律、正五音至于无相夺伦已也,其由耳窍以达于人心也,且有其术,能肖物情,写群动,使闻者自得之于想像之表。虽音界不足以传形,声变不可以赋色,是则外缘所限,无以施肖写之极功,而巧者舍短用长,恒有以达其祈向。此观法国鉴别家孤山维陀(Victor Cousin)

---

1 原文为"願",形误,似为"顒(顾)"。

论乐师海敦（Haydn）之精能，可以悟已。

孤山氏之言曰：今假有令至巧之乐工，以一阕之琴声，写天风海涛之豪壮者，大块噫气之怒号，雷霆砰訇之震骇，求于乐而象之，此至无难者也。独至风云之郁怒，掣电之激射，极晦深黑之中，忽耀六合，而尤惊心动魄者，莫若波涛扬起，高逾邱山，及其抑仗，若沦无底。凡若此者，皆当得之于目。至用音声，虽极其洪会，又乌从而得之？虽有聪听之旁人，使非豫告，不能知也。又使与战阵之乐相接而奏之，其何者为万马之奔腾，何者为雷风之相拃，吾又决其无能办也。故声音之事，虽有科学之极精，天才之至敏，而求以达形相不能。然而彼操术者，不如是拙也。彼方置其不可象而为其可象者，盖怒涛激电，天海之容色，所不可象者也；而精夺神摇，人心之情感，所可象者也。故海敦之为乐也，当其意得神会，方有以夺图绘之能事而胜之，乃知音乐有鼓舞灵魂之能力，其感人常较目治之美术为深也。（按：此段乃孤山《美术论》第九篇语。）

若夫诗歌为美术之极致，其体用性情，谓非数言所能尽，不佞方深论之于全书之中。今兹所言，特以与前四者同列美术，故连类及之，著其阶级而已。则自其易明者而言之，美术之托于物质者，诗歌最少，几无可言也。有格律声韵之为用，藉文字语言之简号，并由视听以达于人心。且视而可识，声入心通，其接于吾官，亦不资于巧术，此其异于他艺事者具如此。独其中所托以传之人事，所写而著之物形，为情为景，为合为分，乃其要素，而不可忽者。是故诗歌为物，所与心灵直接者也。言为心声，字为心画，而诗歌所与心灵接者，即以此心声心画为中尘焉，交于神明，此为最利之器矣。夫托意写诚，是谓美术；而文章之事，方其写诚，无间主客二观，所写者即存意界。是其为物，纯乎形上，其形下几无可言，此其所以为诣极者欤？

【复案】中国翰札，前谓为美术之一宗。观孙虔礼《书谱》，与韩昌黎《送高闲尚人序》而可见。盖目治之美术，而且进于图画者也。孙虔礼言："存真寓赏"，绎其象旨，即写诚托意之谓也。外国书文，所不足为美术者，以其物仅为观念简号而止，不特非喜怒哀乐所可见，且无所寓其巧智焉。自秦汉以来，几三千载，篆隶草章，中国士人，互相陶淬，代有宗工，非无故也。

篇二 文辞

世唯两物，曰我、非我。自我而外，一切万物，皆非我也。以我而交于非我，有二途焉：一曰由其客观，一曰由其主观。有生息息之顷（当其迷罔、醉、睡觉，机暂停者，不在此论），皆由此两观觉察身外之万物，以此观念，萃成觉身。其一部分，由于色界之形质，有有生者，有无生者，交于吾前，受以官窍；其一部分，由于法界之意影，来往心镜之间，有时与色界之物连类而并呈，有时纯为意影，无关形气之事。顾所观主客不同，而自我以观非我则一，盖凡可观者皆非我也。凡物皆有两观，从其在物则为客，从其在心则为主，以客主两观而交于非我，使学者自思之，将见主观之所交，其广远实大过于客观。盖主观之交于非象也，纯以意影。其起伏由于记忆，或由于推籀，或由于记忆、推籀二者之杂施互用而得之。譬如不佞今处一室之中，探翰构思而为此论，此时耳目官骸所径接者，尽于四壁之内而止矣。即不然，窗轩间隙之间，遥见云影天光、人家草树，与夫过眼之动物、触耳之诸籁，又止矣尽矣。乃若主观之界，求之于吾意想之中，则上下贯古今，纵横跨宇合，凡吾生之所经历，与古今人之所闻见者，吾皆得而袭之。盖主观之交物也，非一顷官神感觉之所囿。吾不独回既往之所感觉者，且能回一切人类之所感觉者，不论何世，无分何种，但所感觉思忖者，有其传留，或载诸宫室彝器，或垂之于制作典章，使吾经之，皆吾所有。乃至文字简册之所纪述，则古人之思想云为尤隆富，而皆吾主观之物，其过于客观者，广远何如乎？且由此而言之，吾之所以交于非我者，其取径莫大，且便于人类所纪述而留传者。纪述而留传者，文辞是已。夫界说曰：托意写诚，谓之美术。意，主观也；诚，客观也。是故一切之美术，莫不假客观以达其意境。独有文辞，无所假托于客观，而其所有事者，皆主观之产物也。夫使文辞如是，则诗歌词赋者，文辞之精英也，斯其为物，又可知已。

将欲使前说晓然于学者之心胸，不可不为之设喻。则试取战陈之事，以明美术写物之不同，而前说之理可以见。今使某时某地之战，述诸某氏之史矣。而善画者，又取当时之所闻见，以为之图。而二者皆一代之绝作，则不佞得取其所同异，试为学者一二之。夫画者之所为，固欲写当时客观之真相，图成而张于吾壁，使当战之顷，有人置身于便地，与寓目焉，其所见，当与图合。卒徒山立，其势如云奔而潮至也；旌旄徽帜，有火荼之观；尘漫烟起，将军立马于雪刃霜戟之林；人马死伤，卧地横草。近者分明，远者希微，画之所传，尽于此矣。使客更谛而观之，将察两军甲胄章服之各异也，所争地利，所用陈势之为何等也。约而言之，凡可得于寓目者，莫不载之而已。阅图既竟，客曰：美哉此图，使我若亲见当日之战者！乃今试与抽架上之帙，检某氏之史书，读其所以纪述此战者，则数行未了，将见史之所详，与图之所载，其事类乃各异也。夫图之所载者，客观也。其观物也，得其一地一时之所一览者耳。故一寓目而全象呈焉，而其变尽于一瞬。史之所详者，主观也。其叙事也，必举其因果与始卒而陈之：是役所当之时与地，其交绥者为何国，国所以战之人数，将者何人，其策画之相异，其为战之勇怯，莫不及之。且所以致此役者，前必箸其远因近因、所以从此战者，后必详其远果近果。凡如是者，皆不可阙。而叙议之巧拙明暗，则又如其人而为殊。凡客所得于文者，其异于图具如此。虽然详矣，而求其移神耸观，则读史或较读图远不逮耳。移神耸观之效，必得之于临图之顷，使去其图，此情遂失。而史氏所叙述，虽读者领会全局之意较迟，而掩卷寻思，常若具在，是战史所印成之意影，较之图画为完全而耐久。盖其中所传写之事，实皆可受之以主观，为心量所易纳。且既入之后，提记无难，得以会集组织，成此一宗之意影，而无待于眼、耳、鼻、舌、身也。故一言而尽二术之异同：大抵当观图之竟也，吾曰"吾于此战若亲见之"；当读史之终也，吾曰"吾于此战无遁情矣"。

是故史氏之载笔也，所传写者，非事物之外形也，非其所得于耳目者已也，固将详人与事相推相及之致，与其心之所感于其事者。邑居之闳廓，高会之豪华，战斗之惨澹，乃至山川陵谷之所经，彼之所传，诚不若丹青之刿目，乃若事情曲折之致，言语思想由斯景物发于人心，则舍文字言语之形容，其观念绝于人群可也。呜呼！此人禽之分也。

故文辞者，所以写人心所受于物之感情，与其心所即物而得之思理也。其所写者，概古今人事之变端，统幽明物界之现象；其所传载者，不独人类之言行事功散然粲著者也，且凡人情物理之所会通，所可垂之以为义法者。故吾人所可得于载籍者，非一人所遇于一方一世之事实也，实且有其公理物则，人人所仰观俯察于近身远物之际而会通者。嗟乎！文辞之关于吾人身世，顾不重哉！为人类阅历之所会归，乃所以救知觉于根尘之溢，而恢识量于法界之闳，使我之交于非我者，在在物物，可由于主观，而虚灵之量益著，是则文辞而已矣。

欲知吾生主观之界，所待于文字典籍之无穷，则当察其物所以养吾心而泽吾躬者为何若。自其最易见者言之，则吾居千载之后，古人往矣，而吾尚与其圣神豪俊为神交者，恃有此具耳。若释迦牟尼，如柏拉图，若德蒙恬（De Montaigue），若阿狄孙（Addison），略举一二人，其精爽若陟降于吾左右者，资何物以来格乎？吾又尝游于古巴比伦（Babylon）、雅典（Athens）、罗马（Rome）、亚历山地利（Alexandria）之阛阓矣。又尝亲见其中之城郭□碣[1]，所建造于数千载之前，而久经夷为尘土者。又若亲察其时之人心、风俗、制度、典章，可取以较今日五洲之所实有者，是又从何道而得？斯亚理斯多德之智慧，吾之智慧也；欧几里得之形学，吾之形学也；札思狄粘之法典，耶稣基督与圣波罗之至德，皆吾所转益而多师。凡若此者，设非文字，而孰谓为之？乃若并世同时之事，则数万里犹庭户也。员舆抵跖之山川，与其城邑人民、水土产物，吾之察之，有易于百里外之邻邑者。苟无载籍，能如是乎？且此特就其实有者以言之耳，乃若创意寓言之文字，则所言之境界，其思想之所亲辟者也；所描写之人物，其才情之产子也。希腊之鄂谟（Homer）传我以其意构之伊旃（Aegean），绿水青山，依稀在目。但特（Dante）示我以其神游之

---

1 □，为原本缺字。

九幽（Inferno），穷奇极幻，闻之动心。他若弥勒敦（Milton），则写帝设之大园矣。斯丕尔(Shakespeare)则歌额里查白之英伦矣，其山川之秀丽，其女士之昌丰，令人神往。摩里耶（Molière）赋大路易之法兰西，其文物之明盛，百产之繁富，庶几幸民。凡此皆极意匠之经营，殚钩奇之能事者矣。而其中所张皇之人物，如鄂德苏（Odyssey）、安替恭尼（Antigone）、比阿笛思（Beatrice）、罕谟勒（Hamlet）、达尔托佛（Tartufe）等，皆以作者之大心，产疑神之奇杰，著之书册，与真实之摩西（Moses）、亚烈山大（Alexander）、恺撒（Caesar）、若安达克（Joan d'Arc）、显理第八（Henry VIII）辈，常并存于人意之中。盖之数公者，其虚实真假虽悬，而其经哲匠文心之摹写则一，即今聚吾脑景之中，虽挚交亲戚之伦，无以过也。

此篇所论，乃用主观之涂术，而以我交于非我。而其用此术也，假于文字为最多。虽然，尚有一义，不可不为学人指点者，则我之交于非我也，必先有客观之事，而后主观从之。主观者，客观之意影也。然主观虽受成于客观，而浸假客观，乃又蒙吾主观之影响，而被其范围陶铸之功。盖吾观物之神智，抚景之欢忻，与一切接时生心之赏会，将与吾读书穷理之所积者相长而俱深。是故我之交于非我也，惟善用其主观者，而后有喻客观之微，得客观之实。此不佞于前篇之首，所以云通鉴别之理者，不独于术艺有以讲是而去非，且赏会之事，由此而后有浓至之感情，而物理人事，亦由此有以得其深也。德意志鉴别家解尔第（Goethe）有言：客之游罗马，其有取而去于罗马者，无一物焉，非其所挟而入于罗马者也。嗟乎！彼游宝山而空手者，以其非怀宝而来客耳。解之为言，不亦深切著明也哉？

【复案】十年以来，中国少年争言游学，此佳耗也。顾其往者，无问私家官派，大抵于新旧诸学一无所知之曹。至于彼都，言语未通，普通未学，辄抗心高跂，鄙一切为凡近，而求习专门。往者吾之英德诸使，尝以为言，而上之操选政与下之谋遒往者，皆仍不以为意也。呜呼！此真无所挟而游宝山者也。他日归来，又安得不空手而徒为虚憍饰智者耶？

是故总而论之，文辞者，凡人类之脑海也。盖脑之于人也，取其所得于耳目，所历于身世，所积于问学者而记留之。而其人继此之用其耳目，行其身世，道其问学，则又取向之所记留者，为之向导焉，为之鞮译焉。脑之于一人，其用如此，而文辞载籍之于人类，其为用亦犹之耳。语曰："不知为吏，视已成事。"故惟学于古训者，而后能深观其当前之事理与物情也。夫使人而无脑，抑其脑之甚弱，则虽有耳目之用、运动之机，将有益于其生盖浅。然则使一种一群之民，无文辞载籍之积累，或其积累者微，将其生也，下可同于飞走，上但跻于野蛮，与之言强立，且或不克，而美术云乎哉？

【复案】近今百年，其中国文教极衰，将反之时乎？自帖括之敝，至于末流，世几不知学问文章为何物。本朝龙兴辽沈，惩汉族文胜之弊，有还淳返质之思。往往以染其陋习为戒，矫枉既已过真，而丰沛乡亲，攀鳞附翼；王侯将相，皆无待于读书。洎夫挽近丁戊，枢府党派分争，以恶其仇雠，遂并其出身，以与海内抹杀。夫读书固有种子，而文字亦待薪传。盖奖之而不进者有之矣,未有摧剥践踏而不陵迟退演者也。故即今吾国之现象,往往门子寒畯,名为文人,而通品之目,百人之中,殆无一二。其尤可骇者,殆莫若时下之官场,识字知书,凤毛麟角,更勿问其为通才否也。嗟乎!中国之衰,或者以谓不识西学之故,其果由于不识西学也耶?读者反复于倭氏此篇之说,可以憬然矣,可以潸焉矣!

篇三　古代鉴别

使不佞前二篇之论而有合学者，可知吾人身世之故、智识之开，所恃于耳目之觉察者固多，所赖于文字而后通者，尤为众也。以书史所关于生人之巨，而范才成性系之。故谈教育者，尝谓自修要素，在读破数种定论佳书。所介绍吾心以与世界万物接者，以此为公仞之要术也。虽文字之开瀹才智，皆借径于主观，而主观之中，其所以饷我者，有两途之为异：其一所益我者，在其中所言之事实，其一所益我者，在其写情叙事之文章。大抵吾读一书，二者之益，常兼有之，特轻重多寡异耳。譬之一画，前者其中之景物，后者其中之绚染也；前者一书之质，后者一书之文也。

则试标二三名著以明之。吾英之载籍，如洛克之《知识论》、吉贲之《罗马季世史》，二者几户诵之要书，顾所重者，存乎其质。乃至义律之小说，托物寓意，写吾英内部之风俗情景皆实，独所组织者虚，则所重者以其文矣。他若《南非庄田记》，读之若置身阿非利加田墅间。又若《岐路狄安那》一书所写者，乃旅行之美妇，具至优之天赋，处容易失身之境，而卒之有以自全，则作者所为，谓之"狄安那之传"可也。譬之于画，其肖像乎？非画图也。是故以文质之可分，而创意之文与实录之文，区为二类，而所以介绍心灵于万物者，其用固不可偏废也。

【复案】文字分为创意、实录二种，中国亦然。叙录实事者，固为实录，而发挥真理者，亦实录也。至创意一种，如词曲、小说之属，中国以为"乱雅"，摈不列于著作之林，而西国则绝重之。最古如希腊鄂谟之诗史《伊里叶》，而英之狄斯丕尔，法之摩理耶，德之葛尔第，皆以词曲为一国宗匠。以较吾国之临川实甫诸公，其声价为缙绅所不屑道者，而相异岂直云泥而已？顾文字之事，虽在实录，往往有创意者杂行其中。则如左氏述二百余年之人事以释经，史公罗黄帝以来为藏山传人之实录，而乃一则见谓"浮夸"，一则见谓"钓奇"，则其言之非无文，大可见已。他若屈、宋之骚些，扬、马、班、张之词赋，其惝恍迷离、铺张扬厉者，皆西人之所谓文，而不可谓质，断断如也。

所必分文字为抒实、构虚二大类者，盖一言鉴别，则不可不知有此分也。夫鉴别为一宗之科学，而主于别识艺事文章之正伪高下者也。其别识抒实之文字，与别识构虚之文字，其眼藏大殊。别识抒实之文字，其义法本于格物之名理；别识构虚之文字者，其赏会出于怡情之美术也。二者衡尺大殊，虽应用之时，往往有出此入彼之事，顾其大经不可混尔。此学者所宜明之第一义也。假使一文字中所谓构虚者少，或如形数质力之作，一一皆跖实之谈，则操衡鉴者，最宜格物之士，与夫哲学之家。而观创意构虚之文字不然，以其中所叙次之人情物理，往往为匹夫匹妇所与知，故无待于专门之学识刻深之理解也。而其书品格之高下、感人之浅深，悉视其结构脉理，选列物色，凡所以传叙之者之何若，此美术之事也。故擅此者，必在乎文章之宗匠、骚雅之方家。

【复案】此节所言，中国为分久矣。于其前者谓之学人，于其后者谓之文人，而二者皆知言之选也。前以思理胜，后以感情胜；前之事资于问学，后之事资于才气；前之为物毗于礼，后之为物毗于乐。天之所赋各殊，其优劣之间，不可以相强。明乎教育之术，必即所优之天分而培之。斯其民无弃材，而其为教与学也皆易。及其成德，则皆其国之荣华也。孔子曰："安上治民，莫善于礼；移风易俗，莫善于乐。"斯宾塞尔曰："瀹民智者，必益其思理；厚民德者，必高其感情。"故美术者，教化之极高点也。而吾国之浅人，且以为无用而置之矣。此迻译是篇所为不容缓也。

大抵世间文字，不出此两大类中。顾其入于文字也，往往并见而互有。特所居部分，千变万殊；而组织离合，又经纬万端，各呈意匠，此读书之人所在在可以自见者也。若物理，若哲学，若史乘，若传谱，若论说，若稗官，若辞赋，盖艺文九流，一例蔽之矣。虽然，创意构虚之文字，其质文相宜之外，尚有一物焉，为前说所未及者。盖此类之作，作者以其思想性情，写一宗之事实，故书成，读者不仅得其所写之事实也，且并其思想性情之产物而得之，此吾前说所已及者也。至前说所未及者，亦美术之要素而不可忽，故于文字，其见词曲诗赋为最多，或曰"神韵"，或曰"味趣"。神韵也，味趣也，凡其物之可以怡情悦心者是已。今夫人心之觉，乐也。上焉者，以其躬之言行，常合于理义，而无所愧怍于其私；下焉者，以利禄之及身，而有口体之适，此君子小人之所分喻者也。乃美术文字之移我情也，上之无关于理义，而不可以为私；下之无取于利禄，而不可谓其非自得。方其意会，君子小人得共享之，则神明契赏之事也。是故文之美者，其中常有三物之可言：事实也，文章也，机趣也。此即其所撰著者而言之也。而读者于是得三美焉：曰知物，曰通方，曰得意。艺事之所以可贵者，以此第文辞之事，以流别之分，而操觚者识量思力之相越。故一篇一卷之成，不徒三物之分数不均，其组织合并，机杼大异[1]，虽观者皆为知言之哲，而以鉴别之视点相睽，衡尺各用，则其论一书之声价，亦无定评。呜呼！此艺林之所以多聚讼也。

然而鉴别之达理，则必不可诬也。正惟以古今聚讼之多，其衡论或得似而不真，其立言或有漏而未密，使吾党今日能于众哄之中，得所折中，而立其所必不可叛者耳。夫文章鉴别，乃民智民德之见端，真天演之现象，已经累世之蜕变，由粗及精，原疏泽密。常有鸿哲巨子于此焉，竭其智虑，而进步独多。吾党诚欲闻其所谓达理，而必不可叛者欤？是非考其所累进者，固不可也。请先言古代之鉴别：

古代先民，论文最早者莫若希腊之柏拉图，以其为论文之初祖，而又为善言德行之古贤。故其于文所绝重者，存乎所载之实，于向者所标

---

[1] 杼，原本作"抒"，疑误，据改。

之三物，得其一而忽其余。虽文章机趣为后世言文者所并重，而柏氏未之见也。故其论文也，必以立诚载道为宗。其品格之高卑，声价之轻重，视写物言理所传之诚妄为差。彼谓文章之用，与道德相表里，艺事之所以可贵者，惟其为道德之舆，舆而不载，虽有他美，不足观已。此柏氏论文与鉴别，一是美术之宗旨也。此其说据地之高，固不待论，且与其生平所唱哲学之宗风吻合。今以其说所关于此学之重，故不佞特录其言而著之于此，使学者得考览焉。

柏氏之言曰：美术之为物也，其思想之崇高，音情之茂美，形表之完备，节奏之调谐，凡此皆系于其品格之雅正，质性之温良。夫所谓品格雅正、质性温良者，非世俗所谓中庸，荼然无气、泊然无味者也，必本其中精淑善名贵，以自成其如是之品格者。

故美术品格之高于丹青及一切目治之术最易见。如文采刺绣，如营建土木，乃至凡物有机体成长之可言者，其品格皆可等差。盖如是之物，其形体皆有完美玷缺之可分别。故其物之形体、音情、神韵有不备者，其意趣品格亦当不备。若此数者茂美纯完，见术家之能事，则其中必有道德之深懿、自治之修洁，与之相应，又不知已。盖美术，即所以表其性情品格者也。

是惟有之，而后似之，其能肖造物之美善者，必其人自具美善者也。此鉴别美术之通法也。如吾国之少年然，其居于仁里寿乡者，常易与趋善也。其所目接耳交者，皆天地之淑气。若健人之风扇，于清冷之旁国，稍呼吸之，其血脉自利。若此者，自孩提之年，导于所不知，而常与无妄之神明为合，久之心志与固结而不可离，斯宝爱真理之情笃矣。（案：以上三节，皆引柏氏之言所见于共和论者。）

篇三　古代鉴别

柏氏既以此为鉴别之正法眼藏，故其论文字美术也，以载道立诚之多少为高下。而其时希腊词曲，如鄂谟尔，如伊西渥，如平达尔，洎夫一切雅典宗工之所传，后代所称为绝作，柏氏举以为狄滥之音，无可宝贵。尝言曰：近世之诗笔两家，虽有所流传，实皆于人道最要之端，有所不见。彼之喻人也，则谓为恶者常休，而赴义者多苦。身为不义，但使勿为人知，固常有利。其取与廉平不欺者，于所交者，固有利耳，而于当躬未尝不损也。柏氏于当年创意构虚之文，于其所铺张之情事，所以訾议之者，既如此矣。乃其文章，柏氏亦以为未尽合道，而存菲薄之思。可见人之用思，常为时世之所限，即在圣贤，能违者寡。惟柏氏不悟文章之事，其接物纯由主观，故所指为玷缺者，往往即在文章所独擅之能事。盖词人之文，纯由创意，方其写物，所写者非即物也，乃其心目中之万物，设观不同，为用亦异。柏氏未达此指，乃至谓以文写物，不若以图画写物之真。又以尚虚藻而少实功，故美术之有益人伦，不若实艺之所资者广。此其说即今观之，可谓大谬。而柏氏若以为大中至正之论者，则所谓时世之限人耳。夫立诚，诚不可废。然而诚矣，有官觉之诚，有意念之诚。官觉之诚征于实，为理解所可论；意念之诚集于虚，非理解所可论，此美术所独有之境界也。夫古之思想家如柏氏者，非所谓超诣者欤？而所通者，乃不及此。惟不及此，故常以文词之意影为虚诬。以其虚诬，故其物不足资教育之用。不知创意为文，则所写者固不必由于事实，柏氏非之，误矣。且柏氏所不取于创意之文者不止此。盖词曲之作，以动人为宗。既求动人，故其所写生煊染之人事，不得不取诸僻诡淫哇，而中庸平善者，转以其无可钓奇而置之。夫险躁之人，其入书也，可以资无穷之变幻；而宁静淡泊之士，言有经而行有恒，不独其性情为难写也，即写矣，而难喻，即喻矣，而难以动人。是故创意之文家，宁舍此而取彼也。然而柏氏论文，未与于此秘也。故尝谓徒赏创意之文章，若诗史，若词曲，若传奇，若小说稗官，其弊在移情之日深，而养德之日浅耳。夫宇宙之有缺陷久矣，故吾辈灵魂中之最贵者，处困难烦恼之时，能以理自遣，以知驭情，夷然游于其中，使人所不堪其忧者，而吾有以不改其乐也。乃溺于若前种种之文字者不然。其灵魂之一部，尝欲慷慨悲歌，流涕太息，以自疏其郁久矣。以德育之有验，故常约束之于夷犹冲淡而弗知。乃今所乐观之文字者，若搔痒然，即取其所约束者而振触之者也。而向所谓最贵之德心，以其操之未熟之故，于所遣所驭者，或疏其防范焉。则曰：是文之所写状者，固贤人也，固烈士也，其所遭者，亦至不幸尔。吾今者乃为之哀矜焉，为之赞叹焉，犹人情耳，虽所谓贤人烈士者，露其痛愤无聊之情，然其事在当躬，则为可鄙，而在他人，则为可欣。而不知己之性情，即由此为他人所感者而已变矣。盖德育之事，使见古人所遇之可悲，而为之移情太过者，则他日以己当其冲，欲为坚忍卓绝难矣。此诚累试而验者也。柏氏之言如此，自柏拉图之所以为鉴别者而观之，其得失相半者乎？其得者何？识密鉴洞，迥异常流，知文章美术，欲为不废江河，固必有其所谓真命脉者。此其得也。其失者何？不知文有摭实、蹈虚之殊，于美术之性情作用，全未有知，此其失也。其言德行文章，所为相表里之大要，与夫词章美术，必首以立诚之为基。是其为言，固与近世最精之哲学、美术诸家无不合者。然而近世所发明者，则科学、美术二者，涂术之殊，乃心灵所擘理分肌，求诸人心而见者。词赋稗官之状物肖生，其所谓诚，与科学说理之诚同而有异。又其接于吾心者，纯由神情，而非关理。且其事为教育所重，不可偏[1]废，实与摭实之学理相同。凡此皆近时学界所共见，而柏氏则未之窥也。惟其未窥此秘，故所为鉴别之论有所甚，亦有所亡。见此，然后知三百载近今以还，心灵之学所造为至深也。向使柏氏知此，则何至神品当前，昧然不见，而希腊之宗工鸿制，凌踔古今，即今五洲文明之民所心折神移、号为望尘不及者，而柏氏一言之蔽，以为无实，不足贵乎！

若古代之思想家，则次于柏拉图者，不能不为雅里斯多德屈一指矣，于美术文章之事，体验大精，且生于柏拉图之后，故能即其师之所为者而益进之。其人长于裁制，举凡人类心思耳目手足之所成，彼皆为之规矩准绳焉，以言其离合，故文章美术，为其所论之一大宗矣。所著《美术纲要》，为百代所折中，而诗赋词曲有专论者。虽其为书，简略凌碎而不完，即在当时，殆不为世人所尽喻者，然于后代鉴别一科之学，则昆仑墟、星宿海矣。是故学者欲明近世鉴别家之义法，所至今论定而不可摇者，必先取雅氏之言为之详说而深明之，则于不佞继今所言，可以不烦言解矣。

雅里斯多德之论文章，与夫一切创意之美术也，则为之苞举之说焉。曰美术文章者，所以写生肖物者也（希语曰迈美实斯）。必溯最初之源，则本于人心之灵善为相感。孩提之子，见长者之语言动作，则从而效之，而以是为欣乐。此其能事，所与美术，乃至最精之词曲，同一发源者也。言语之精为文，文之精为诗歌，而脱拉节地者，（案：欧洲词曲大者分为三科：一曰脱拉节地，描摹高义俊伟慨慷，而其中往往有死亡危苦之人事。次曰康密地，

---

[1] 偏，原本作"徧"，疑误，据改。

嬉笑讥呵，意存讽刺，而其文邻于游戏。三曰额毕格，则以诗为史，类中国之弹词。前二种皆以演剧，后一则仅著诗篇而已。此自隆古希腊，当中国商周之代而已然者也。）又诗歌之最为完备者也。（案：此言诗歌，然其意实兼一切创意之文，如小说、传奇、词曲、稗官之类皆综之。）今试取其一而分析之，将见其中所以为原行者，有数物焉，为一切创意之文所同有者。其物之可论三：单举而论之，一也；交互为论，二也；即其一物以视其全体，三也。是数物者，有其多寡，无其存亡，而文章之优劣高下，视此数者。譬如言一词曲，则必有结构，所以组织其中之事变者也；则必有人物，所以抒写其人之性情品格者也；则必有词藻，所以宣露其人物之思想语言者也；则必有情素，所以为其人物言行之原因者也。而终之则台场之部署，音乐之佐侑，是则词曲原行而已矣。雅里斯多德所以析之者如此。

ON THE EXERCISE OF JUDGMENT IN LITERATURE

By

W. BASIL WORSFOLD

CONTENTS

Chapter I Art   148

Chapter II Literature   160

Chapter III The Criticism of the Ancient World   167

Chapter IV Modern Criticism   182

Chapter V How Creative Literature Appeals to the Imagination   195

Chapter VI Contemporary Criticism   204

Chapter VII The Exercise of Judgment in Literature   225

Chapter VIII Forms of Literature—Classical and Romantic   250
    Methods—Style

List of Authorities   264

Chapter I

Art

In nearly all large towns, and especially in the capital cities of civilized nations, there are collections of statues, pictures, and books. Even in the streets we see the forms of men and women, wrought in marble or cast in bronze, placed high upon pedestals to meet the gaze of every one who may pass by them. In nearly every house there are pictures upon the walls, and vases or other ornaments arranged upon shelves, and books lying on the table; and in large houses there are whole chambers set apart solely for collections of pictures and statuary, or lined with rows of books. The mere existence of these objects shows us that Art is an element in the life of civilized man, for we should not care to surround ourselves with such things, unless we wished our minds to be sometimes occupied both with them and with the thoughts which they suggest.

Criticism is the exercise of judgment in the province of Art and Literature, and the Critic is a person who is possessed of the knowledge necessary to enable him to pronounce right judgments upon the merit or worth of such works as come within this province. The term "judgment"—*κρίσις*—was first used in this special sense by the Alexandrian Scholars (300 B.C.–146 B.C.), who approached the study of books under five heads, the arrangement of the matter (*διόρθωσις*), the fixing of accents (*ἀνάγνωσις*), the syntax (*τέχνη*), explanatory comment (*ἐξήγησις*), and "judgment" on the merit and authorship of the work in question (*κρίσις*). It was therefore primarily applied to judgment upon books, and indeed even now when we speak of "criticism" and "critics," we generally refer to such literary judgment; but when we wish to indicate a judgment on works of art other than books, we place a qualifying word before the term, and speak of Art Criticism, or Dramatic Criticism, as the case may be. Here, too, we shall use the words "Criticism" and "Critic" chiefly, though not entirely, in this original and specialized sense of "judgment" and "judges" of books.

Just as there are certain principles of morality, recognized, if not universally, at least very generally by all civilized men, by reference to which we govern our conduct, so are there certain principles of Criticism of wide, if not universal, validity, by reference to which we guide our decisions in matters of taste. A knowledge of these principles, by teaching us to think rightly about works of art and literature, enables us to gain the fullest enjoyment both from these works and from the physical existences, or the facts of life, of which they are representations, in the same way as the principles of morality teach us to control our actions so as to be happy ourselves and contribute to the happiness of our neighbours. But while morality, or the art of right living, covers the whole field of man's existence, criticism is concerned with an element only of that existence; and the first point which we have to consider is, therefore, the nature and extent of this element—in other words we must form some definite notion of what Art is, and of the part which it plays in the life of man.

In order to do this we will first recall the several arts and the works which they respectively produce, and then endeavour to collect the facts so recalled in a general idea.

At the outset we are met by a distinction which separates works of art into two classes—the distinction between the "Fine" Arts and the "Lesser" or "Mechanical" Arts. The Fine Arts are Architecture, Sculpture, Painting, Music, and Poetry.[1] The Lesser Arts are those of the smith, the carpenter, the cabinet-maker, the mason, the potter, the weaver, the glass-maker, the house painter, and others like them. The distinction which separates these two classes is based upon the fact, that broadly speaking the arts of the first class minister to the enjoyment of man, while those of the latter minister to his needs. They are both alike manifestations of the development of man; but the Fine Arts are concerned mainly with his moral and intellectual growth, and the Lesser Arts with his physical and material well-being. And between these typical arts of the second class and the Fine Arts, there are others, such as engraving on wood or copper, painting on china or glass, carving in wood, the designing of decorations for walls or patterns for fabrics, which may belong to either class according to the degree of merit displayed by the artist.

The origin and purpose of the Lesser Arts are simple and easily understood. These arts, arising from man's natural desire to provide himself conveniently

---

[1] To these we might add the composite art called the Drama, the art of Oratory, and the lost art of Dancing.

with the elementary requirements of food and shelter, clothing and locomotion, grew with the growth of civilization. Their purpose is no less definite; and the principle which lies at their foundation, and which itself furnishes a test of the merit of the works which they severally produce, is utility. So far-reaching is this principle that they are often (and rightly) called the "useful" arts. The characteristic merit, therefore, of a house, of a chair, or of a vessel in metal or clay, is to fulfil the purpose for which it is intended; and beauty of form in them is nothing else than the instant revelation of this capacity. It is mainly[1] by virtue of this revelation that such objects satisfy the eye and mind; and all decoration, or decorative effect, which does not contribute to this revelation, being meaningless, lessens instead of increasing the beauty of the objects it is intended to adorn.

We need say little, therefore, about the Lesser Arts: but we must consider the Fine Arts more at length, for the nature of these latter is more complex, and to this day there is no complete agreement among critical writers concerning either their precise origin, or their exact purpose. We shall have to notice the significance of this disagreement with respect to the art of Poetry, when we come to consider the test of Merit in Literature. Henceforward, therefore, in speaking of "the Arts" and of "Art," I shall refer exclusively to the Fine Arts and to Fine Art.

There are two classifications of the Arts which are helpful. The first divides them into the Arts of the "Eye" and the Arts of the "Ear," according

---

1   I say mainly, because colour and the lustre of polished metal, are elements of beauty in themselves.

as they respectively use one or other of the senses of sight or hearing as their primary channel of approach to the mind. Thus grouped we get the arts of Architecture, Sculpture and Painting placed in broad contrast to the arts of Music and Poetry. By the second they are arranged with reference to the greater or less degree in which they severally depend upon a material basis for the realization of their respective purposes. On this principle Hegel places Architecture *lowest*, and Poetry *highest*, in order of dignity. Architecture is placed lowest because in the manifestations of this art, the material basis is most prominent: and, indeed, it is only the purpose expressed in the arrangement of the materials, which raises the masses of stone or brick reared by the architect to the dignity of works of Art. Next to Architecture is Sculpture. Here, too, the basis is wholly material; but the sculptor gives to the marble or metal, which forms his medium, a significance entirely unlike any which these materials possess in themselves. For out of the dead block he carves the semblance of a living form. From Sculpture we advance to Painting, where the material basis is reduced by the rejection of the third dimension of space to the plane surface of the canvas —that is, to length and breadth. But upon this surface the Painter produces a semblance of material objects which is possessed alike of substance, form, and colour. Then comes Music, where the sole basis of material reality is the volume of sound, but where the sounds are so arranged by the Musician that they represent distinct emotions, and even serve to create the actual emotions which they severally represent in the mind of the hearer. Lastly, there is Poetry, which is so far removed from the material, that its very medium (with the exception of the element of metre) consists solely of symbols—of words, or combinations of words, which recall ideas to the mind.

These two classifications are helpful, as I have said. The facts which they serve to bring into prominence are these. First, the arts require a material basis to work upon, ranging from the stone and brick of Architecture to the word-symbols of Poetry. Second, the main channels by which they approach the mind are the sense of sight, and (in a much less degree) the sense of hearing. Third, and most important, both this material basis and these two channels, are merely the means by which the mind of the artist communicates with the mind of the spectator. Works of Art, therefore, from a cathedral to a sonnet, are symbolic; that is to say they have a quality which is addressed to, and perceived by, the mind, over and above the quality, or qualities, which are perceived by the senses. Now, perhaps, having got so far as this, we can gather up these facts in a general idea and venture upon a definition of Art. *Art, then, is the presentation of the real in its mental aspect.*

In order to realize the significance of this definition we will take each of the Arts separately, and consider (1) its material basis; (2) the means which it employs to bring this material basis under the cognisance of the senses; and (3) the greater or less prominence which it gives to the mental aspect of the reality which it thus presents to the mind.

In Architecture the material basis is of the coarsest kind. It consists of the stone, brick, metal and wood, which, with other materials, are used in the erection of buildings. As this medium is wholly material, the eye is affected in precisely the same manner by the works which the architect produces, as it is by any other external object. All the effects of sunshine, light and shade, colour, atmosphere, site or natural position and surroundings, are at his disposal, and he does not require any artifice, such as we shall see other artists require, in using the channel of sight to approach the mind.[1] And this for two reasons: first, he does not represent life or movement, and, second, his work is possessed of precisely the same attributes of solidity, form, and colour, as any other inanimate external object. Nevertheless, the external masses which he creates, though they are real, are also realities presented in a mental aspect. In other words, they are expressive of ideas. The Gothic Cathedral—to take the most familiar example—is not merely a place where people worship, but it is itself a place of worship—a building so constructed that it expresses the aspirations of man for eternal life in its form and features. This is the thought embodied alike in the profusion of pinnacles, in the sky-piercing spires, and in the upward springing shafts which carry its lofty roof. But, although architecture here presents a place of worship in its mental aspect—that is to say, the Cathedral which the architect builds is representative of his idea of a place of Christian worship—yet the material, or sensuous, element is so prominent, that it is possible for the spectator to be impressed and even delighted by works of architecture, without having any consciousness of the ideas which the architect intended them to severally represent.

In the art of Sculpture the material basis is the stone or metal which

---

1   Unless we make an exception of the "optical corrections" employed by the Greek architects in the construction of certain temples.

is chiselled or moulded by various processes into the forms of animate or inanimate objects. The sculptor has all the attributes of reality, except movement, at his disposal; for his work possesses solidity, form, and, if he chooses, colour, just as much as the real persons or objects which he represents. It is only, therefore, when he represents persons in motion that he needs to employ any artifice to beguile the eye of the spectator. But the absence of this attribute of movement forms a natural limit to the field of external reality which he is free to represent; and as a result of this limit, the special and most appropriate subjects of the art of sculpture are separate figures, or separate busts, or small groups of figures, all alike in repose. These figures he represents with as little accessory detail as possible and in the simplest possible manner; and for this reason—and also because it is difficult to represent drapery in so stubborn a medium as stone or metal—the finest representations of the human figure in sculpture are partially or entirely nude. Nevertheless the mental aspect of the real is far more prominent in the sculptor's work than it is in the architect's; for the sculptor endows the stone or metal figures which he creates with the appearance of life, and presents the idea of the highest perfection of the class of being which is in each case represented. Physical beauty in repose is, therefore, the special subject of the art of sculpture.

In Painting, the material basis is provided by the canvas, board, or other surface, upon which the lines which indicate space, and the artificial colours which represent the natural colours of external objects, are respectively drawn or laid. But in proportion as this basis is less material than that of the sculptor, the painter requires a greater amount of artifice in the means which he employs to bring these lines and colours under the cognisance of the sense of sight: for he has to represent solid objects and real colours by means of lines and colours placed on a flat surface. In order to present solid objects by lines only, he must draw these lines according to rules of perspective—that is, he must draw the several outlines of the external objects which form his picture, in precisely the same positions on his canvas, as they would occupy on the field of vision of a spectator who sees them from a single point of view—and similarly, in order to represent the real colours which external objects of varying distance from the spectator assume, by his artificial colours laid on a uniform surface, he must give the correct values to the colours of each object—that is, he must make these colours more or less bright or strong in proportion as the real objects, whose colours he thus represents, would be more or less distant from the spectator. In this way, by drawing his lines in perspective and by giving the right value to his colours, he makes the flat surface which he thus covers present to the eye the appearance of a landscape or of an interior. Moreover, in painting, the prominence given to the mental aspect of the reality thus represented is greater than in sculpture—and, of course, far greater than in Architecture—for in all cases, whether a historical event or a landscape be the subject of the picture, it is the painter's idea of the event or of the scene, and not the bare external details of the event—so far as they are known—or the exact appearance of nature, that is represented in the picture. In other words the painter idealizes in his representation of the real: he does not merely copy or imitate, but he also interprets and selects. He, like every other artist, presents the real in its mental aspect, and he addresses his work not only to the senses, but also to the mind and understanding of the spectator.

So far we have been concerned with the "arts of the eye." It remains to consider the "arts of the ear"—Music and Poetry. In both of these the material basis is less prominent, and the mental aspect of the realities represented is consequently more significant.

The sole material basis which the musician employs is sound; that is, the sound produced by the human voice, or by one or other of the musical instruments which have been invented, and perfected, in the course of past ages; and this sound is presented alone or in union with words, and is arranged in notes and separated into intervals in accordance with the rules of harmony and musical composition. But in as much as the musician by employing words calls in to his assistance the sister art of poetry, his most characteristic medium is sound alone—inarticulate sound. The obvious characteristic of this medium, considered as a means for the expression of ideas, is its extreme indefiniteness, its vagueness; and corresponding to this vagueness is the characteristic value of music—its power to operate over a wild field of mind, to address itself to the primordial aspects of the universal soul of man. And so the charm of music appeals to the child or the savage, as well as to the learned and highly civilized. Nevertheless, the musician—apart from the rules of musical composition or execution—uses an artifice in approaching the mind through the sense of hearing. He can represent real existences, but only under the conditions of his art. An illustration will serve best to explain how he is limited by these conditions. It is the account which Victor Cousin, the French critic, gives us of the method by which Haydn, while thus recognizing the limits imposed upon him by his art, nevertheless represents a scene so material as the conflict of the elements.

"Give the wisest symphonist a tempest to render. Nothing is easier than to imitate the whistling of the winds and the noise of the thunder. But by what combination of ordered sounds could he present to our sight the lightning flashes which suddenly rend the veil of night, and that which is the most terrific aspect of the tempest, the alternate movement of the waves, now rising mountain high, now sinking and seeming to fall headlong into bottomless abysses? If the hearer has not been told beforehand what the subject is, he will never divine it, and I defy him to distinguish a tempest from a battle. In spite of scientific skill and genius, sounds cannot represent forms. Music, rightly advised, will refuse to enter upon a hopeless contest; it will not undertake to express the rise and fall of the waves and other like phenomena; it will do better; with sounds it will produce in our soul the feelings which successively arise in us during the various scenes of the tempest. It is thus that Haydn will become the rival, even the conqueror of the painter, because it has been given to music to move and sway the soul even more profoundly than painting." [1]

In respect of Poetry I need say only just so much as is necessary to complete this brief review of the arts; for we shall have to consider the various aspects of this special art at length in more than one of the succeeding chapters. Poetry, then, of all the arts, has the least material basis. If we except

---

1 *Du Vrai, du Beau, et du Bien*; leçon ix. pp. 195-6. (ed. 27th).

the element of musical sound contained in metre, rhyme, and alliteration, it uses the senses of sight or hearing, as the case may be, merely to convey its word-symbols to the mind. It employs no artifice to bring these symbols to the mind which it addresses; for the words are perceived naturally by the eye or ear. But the mental aspect of the facts of life and the scenes of external nature, which are thus presented by the ideas, or combinations of ideas, of which these words are the symbols, is all important. Poetry speaks directly to the mind: for ideas, or mental pictures, are the rough material of the poet, and no medium is so powerful to affect the imagination as language. In representing reality the poet is absolutely limited by the very conditions of his art to the mental aspect of the external existences which he portrays.

Chapter II

Literature

We approach the world, that is, all reality external to ourselves, from two sides—the objective and the subjective. At every moment of our lives (except, of course, when animation is temporarily suspended in sleep) we are conscious of the world around us in two separate ways; for the sum of the sensations which make man a sentient being is derived in part from the presence of material existences, animate or inanimate,—that is, from actual contact with so much of the world as at any given moment impinges upon his senses—and in part, from the mental images ever passing and repassing through his mind, which are sometimes connected with these material existences, and sometimes entirely dissociated from them. Thus we have two outlooks upon the world. From both we look out upon realities; but while the former shows us these realities in their objective aspect, the latter shows us them in their subjective aspect.

If we reflect a moment, we must feel that the outlook upon the world which we get through our mind alone, that is, through the images or notions of external existences which we can call up at will by memory and reason, or by both of these acting and reacting upon each other, is by far the wider. As I write, the outlook upon the world which I get through the immediate action of my senses, is confined to the four walls of the room in which I sit, and to such glimpses of buildings, trees, and passers-by, as I chance to see through the open window. But if I turn my mind away from these objects and reflect, my thoughts can range at will over the objects and existences of every country and every age—in fact, over so much of the world as is known to me by my own experience or by that of others. For in this subjective outlook I am no longer confined to my own immediate sensations, but I can draw upon my past sensations, and—what is more important still—upon the sensations of other men—men of every age and every race, whose thoughts and experience have been recorded in buildings, in works of art, in custom, and especially in the written accounts of their opinions, or of their actions, which have been preserved in books or manuscripts. And of all these secondary sources of sensation, the last, which we can gather up in the term literature, is by far the most effective and far-reaching. All art reproduces external reality in its mental aspect; but the arts—except poetry, which is the highest form of literature—employ representations of the objective aspects of reality to assist in the presentation of this mental aspect. But literature, with the sole exception (already noted) of the element of musical sound, does not need this assistance; for literature—as literature—is concerned solely with the subjective outlook upon the world.

In order to make my meaning plain, I will take a simple instance—let us say a battle—and I will try to point out the difference in the manner in which the painter and the historian respectively bring such an event before the mind. I have on my wall a picture in which the painter, representing the objective outlook, shows me the field of battle as I should have seen it, if I had been present at a critical moment, and if I had been placed in a convenient position for seeing what was going on. He shows me the solid masses of men, the flash of steel and the dashes of bright colour, the clouds of smoke, the commander and his staff, with other prominent figures or groups of figures, and the prostrate bodies of the dead and wounded upon the ground. If I look carefully at his picture, he will give me some precise details, such as the colour and form of the various uniforms, and the disposition of the respective armies, as seen from this single point of view and at this particular moment; but all these details are such only as can be perceived by the eye. When I turn away from the picture, I sum up what I have learned by saying, "Now, I know what the battle must have been like, if I had been there." Then I turn to my bookshelves and take down a volume of history which contains an account of the same battle. As I read I find that the historian tells me quite a different class of facts. In the first place he is concerned with the subjective aspect of the event, and, therefore, his outlook is not confined to a single point of view or to a single moment of time. It covers the whole range of facts which together make up the significance of this battle as an event. He tells me the place where it took place, the number and nationality of the respective combatants, the results, immediate and remote, of the conflict, the names of the respective generals, their plans, and the skill which they showed in putting these plans into execution—all these and many other details. Moreover, he shows me how this event is connected with other events which preceded or followed it. Nevertheless, although I have been told all these details, and, perhaps, the historian's own opinions on the conduct of the respective armies, I have not received such a vivid impression of the battle as that which the painter gave me. But while this vivid impression lasted only so long as I was actually looking at the picture, it is far easier for me to recall the description of the historian; and the notion of the battle which has been thus created in my mind, although it requires a longer time to acquire, is, when once acquired, far more complete and permanent. For the facts which he has told me, being all such as I can grasp from my subjective outlook upon the world, can be easily stored in the mind and readily called up by memory to unite in forming a mental picture—that is, an "idea," which is independent of the senses. To contrast the results of the two methods in a single sentence; when I turn from the picture I exclaim, "I have seen the battle": but when I close the book I say, "I know all about the battle; for he has told me everything that took place."

What the writer, therefore, reproduces by his word symbols, is not the external aspect of an event, not the semblance of objects as they are perceived by the senses, but the relationship of man to these events, and the impressions produced upon his mind by these objects. He does not present the building of the town, or the meeting of the council, or the battle; the mountain, or the river, or the valley, but the purposes, the words and the thoughts, which such events and scenes produce either in his own mind or in the minds of others.

Literature, then, in the widest sense, is the record of the impressions made by external realities of every kind upon great men, and of the reflections which these men have made upon them. The subject matter of literature covers the whole range of human life and activity, as well as every known manifestation of physical nature. For not only are actual events and the doings and sayings of actual persons reproduced in it, but the rules deduced from the observation of the conditions of man's life are included in its records. Similarly it presents to us not merely what individual men found to interest them in particular countries in a particular epoch, but also the general laws which have been gradually formulated by long-continued observation of the processes of nature. And so literature plays a very important part in the life of man. It is the greatest of the secondary sources of sensation, and it makes an immense contribution to the sum total of facts—the joint result of the experience of the individual and of the race—which gives to each one of us this subjective outlook upon the world at large.

In order to realize to how large an extent the subjective existence of man is made up of the material of books, we will pause a moment to consider what literature does for us. Through literature we converse with the great dead, with Plato, with Buddha, with Montaigne, with Addison; we walk the streets of Babylon, of Athens, of Rome, of Alexandria; we see great monuments, reared ages ago and long since crumbled to the dust; we recreate the life of distant epochs, and thus by comparison gauge the progress achieved by the men of to-day. Through literature we learn wisdom from Aristotle, geometry from Euclid, law from Justinian, morality from Christ and St Paul. Literature makes the physical features, the inhabitants, the climate, the produce of the antipodes as familiar as those of the neighbouring county. More than this, the masters of creative literature have made regions of their own which they have peopled with the children of their genius. Homer has given us an Aegean of sun-lit islands and purple seas, Dante a dark and mysterious Inferno; Milton a garden of Eden; Shakespeare an Elizabethan England, with landscapes more brightly hued, and men and women more finely real, than the landscapes or the people of the England of Elizabeth; Molière a France more natural and more vivid than the France of the Grand Monarque. And so it is that Odysseus, Antigone, Beatrice, Hamlet, Tartufe and the rest, these spiritual offspring of great souls, live side by side with Moses, Alexander, Cæsar, Joan of Arc, and Henry VIII.: for literature has made the personalities of each almost as familiar to us as those of our dearest or most intimate friends.

There is one point which must be noticed, before we leave this consideration of the subjective outlook upon the world to which literature contributes so largely. It is this: the subjective outlook reacts upon the objective. The knowledge of the world which we gain through our own previous sensations, and through literature, increases our capacity for understanding the objective world, and heightens and intensifies the pleasure which we derive from the contemplation of works of art or the face of nature. It is only by, and through, the subjective aspect of the world that we can rightly appreciate the objective. And that is why I remarked in the preceding chapter, that one of the objects for which we desire critical insight is that we may be able to appreciate not only works of art, but also the external realities of which these works are representations. It is this principle which underlies the truth which Goethe states, when he says that a traveller does not take anything out of Rome which he has not first brought into it.

In conclusion, literature is the brain of humanity. Just as in the individual the brain preserves a record of his previous sensations, of his experience, and of his acquired knowledge, and it is in the light of this record that he interprets every fresh sensation and experience; so the race at large has a record of its past in literature, and it is in the light of this record alone that its present conditions and circumstances can be understood. The message of the senses is indistinct and valueless to the individual without the co-operation of the brain; the life of the race would be degraded to a mere animal existence without the accumulated stores of previous experience which literature places at its disposal.

Chapter III

The Criticism of the Ancient World

We have seen how greatly it is due to literature that our knowledge of men and things, other than those with which we are brought into contact by the direct action of our senses, is so extensive. Indeed, so great is the part that books play in our life, or, at least, in the formation of our several personalities, that to master the contents of certain books of admitted excellence has always been considered a chief element in a liberal education; that is to say, it is a recognized method of introducing the mind to the world at large. But while all literature thus contributes to our subjective outlook upon the world, we can recognize a broad distinction in the manner in which books render us this assistance. In the case of some books the value of the contribution consists mainly, though not exclusively, in the actual facts which they contain; in the case of others, the actual facts are of secondary importance and their chief value consists in the manner in which these facts are brought before our minds. No hard and fast line can be drawn between the two classes, but the difference may be broadly indicated by saying that while the former gives us the facts of life, the latter gives us "pictures" of life.

Let me illustrate the distinction by one or two examples. Such works as Locke's "Essay on the Human Understanding," and Gibbon's "Decline and Fall," must obviously be placed under the head of books in which the facts are of first importance. Equally, the novels of George Eliot, in which she gives us a full and truthful picture of life in the Midland Counties, must be included among those books where the presentation of the facts is of more importance than the facts themselves. And so, too, in the case of "The Story of an African Farm," where we have a picture of rural life in South Africa, or in "Diana of the Cross-ways." Only in this latter work the personality of the central character is so commanding, that the book is not so much a picture as a portrait—a portrait of a beautiful and wayward woman who is exposed to temptation by circumstances and by the very abundance of her own gifts. Here, then, we have two distinct elements, matter and manner; and it is upon the degree in which these elements are respectively present in any given work, that the main division of literature—the division which separates works of creative literature from works of literature, simply so-called, is based.

Now, it will be seen that this distinction is one which has a very important bearing upon criticism, which, as I have already said, is the science of forming and expressing correct judgments upon the value and merit of works of literature. And for this reason, that part of literature which is not creative, employs, not entirely but mainly, the method of science; but creative literature employs—again not entirely but mainly—the method of art. We are confronted, therefore, at the outset with the fact that there are two separate and distinct values to be looked for in books, each of which must be estimated by a separate and distinct test of merit. In literature where the creative element is very slight, or is altogether absent, and where, therefore, the method is the method of science, the man of science, the philosopher, the man who is master of the special subject treated, is the best qualified critic; but with creative literature the case is different. Here, where special knowledge is subordinate, where the facts are the broad facts of life known to all of us, where treatment is all-important and the method of presentation is the method of art, the artist is the ideal critic.

But not only are there these two distinct qualities or values to be found in the works which respectively belong to one or other of these two main divisions of literature, but these two qualities are mingled in varying proportions, and in subtle conjunctions, in the several departments of the works of which both of these main divisions are composed—in Science, Philosophy, History, Biography, the Essay, Prose-Fiction, and Poetry. Moreover, all creative literature, and all literature that is not merely science—that is, all literature in which the writer adds the work of his own mind to the facts which he presents—contains a further quality or value of which I have said nothing at present, but one which is notwithstanding very real and very important. It is the characteristic quality which Poetry shares with its sister Arts, the quality of giving pleasure—aesthetic pleasure; that is pleasure which arises neither from a consciousness of right conduct, nor from an expectation of material profit, but which consists in a sense of enjoyment that is purely self-sufficing and disinterested. Here, then, are three distinct and characteristic elements of excellence, the presence of which can be discerned in varying degrees in works of literature—matter, manner, and the capacity to please. And as each and all are present in varying degrees and in different combinations, both in different classes of books as well as in different works of the same class, it is not surprising that great minds should have approached books from different points of view, should have proposed to measure their merit by different tests, or that the verdict of the critics upon any given work of literature should have been often confused and uncertain.

Nevertheless it is due to these efforts, tentative and inconclusive though many of them were, that we can to-day discern certain principles, the validity of which is definitely established. And in order to understand these principles it is desirable, almost necessary, to know something of the character of the several enquiries which have afforded the most ample contributions to the evolution of criticism.

The first great writer who applied himself to the study of literature, as literature, was Plato. As he was first in the field, and as, too, questions of morality possessed a commanding interest for him, it is not surprising that the first and most obvious quality of literature, namely its matter, should have absorbed his attention, and made him comparatively blind to those other qualities of manner and capacity to please, which we now recognize as being of almost equal importance. Accordingly the sole test by which Plato proposed to estimate the merit of a work of literature,—and indeed that of works of art in general,—was the greater or less degree in which the information which it conveyed corresponded to the external realities of which it treated. Starting with the principle of the interdependence of art and morals, he seems to have regarded the works of both literature and the arts merely as vehicles for the conveyance of the truths of morality. This principle is so important in itself, and holds so important a place in Plato's system of philosophy, that I give a statement of it in his own words.

"Excellence of thought, and of harmony, and of form, and of rhythm, is connected with excellence of character, with good nature, that is, not in the sense of the colourless character which we euphemistically term 'good nature,' but in that of the disposition which is really well and nobly equipped from the point of view of character. . . .

"The qualities which are implied in this excellence of character are conspicuously present in painting and all similiar arts, in weaving and embroidery and architecture, and indeed, in the productions of all the lesser arts, and further in the constitution of bodies and of all organic growths. In all of these, excellence or defectiveness of form can be discerned. And defectiveness of form and rhythm and harmony are associated with deficiencies of thought and of character, while the corresponding artistic excellencies are associated with the corresponding moral excellencies of self-restraint and goodness; indeed, they are directly expressive of them. . . .

"We must look for artists who are able out of the goodness of their own natures to trace the nature of beauty and perfection, that so our young men, like persons who live in a healthy place, may be perpetually influenced for good. Every impression which they receive through eye or ear will come from embodiments of beauty, and this atmosphere, like the health-giving breeze which flows from bracing regions, will imperceptibly lead them from their earliest childhood into association and harmony with the Spirit of Truth, and into love for that Spirit."[1]

Regarding literature and art from this point of view, Plato used criticism as a means of ascertaining to what extent a work of literature conveyed truthful and wholesome information upon the facts of life. In the application of this test of "truth," he found that the Greek literature current in his day—which included in particular the poetry of Homer and Hesiod, the Lyrics of Pindar, and the masterpieces of the Athenian dramatists—was deficient in morality. "Poets and prose-writers," he says, "are mistaken in dealing with human life in the most important respects. They give us to understand that many evil livers are happy and many righteous men unhappy; and that wrong-doing, if it be undetected, is profitable, while honest dealing is beneficial to one's neighbour, but damaging to one's self."[2] In addition to this general charge of immorality based upon the character of the subject matter of Greek creative literature, he finds, by the application of the same test, that its method is also deficient. It is in this latter criticism that the limitations which his age imposed upon him are most apparent. For Plato, not perceiving that literature is by the nature of things concerned exclusively with the subjective outlook upon the world, counts as a defect what is in fact its crowning virtue—that the poet, or writer of creative literature, reproduces in his representations of the real, not realities,

---

[1] *Republic*; p. 400-1 (St.): as translated in the author's "Principles of Criticism."
[2] *Ibid.* p. 392.

but the mental aspects of these realities. Consequently he is led into the absurdity of placing the writer who *describes* a real object—that is reproduces the mental image of that object by his word symbols—as lower in the scale of truthful representation, than the artist who copies the object in line and colour, and still lower than the artificer who makes—to use his own example—the bed which is the material reality upon which both the description and the painting are alike based. In other words the distinction between the truth of the senses and the truth of the idea—or the truth of logic and the truth of art—has not yet been discerned even by so acute a thinker as Plato. And so he condemns the mental pictures which he found in creative literature as being unreal, and therefore useless for purposes of instruction.

To this defect of unreality, due directly to the method of creative literature, Plato adds another defect, also arising, though less directly, out of its method. For the purpose of making effective pictures of life, the poets—and he is thinking especially of the Attic tragedians—are compelled to select and reproduce bad actions and passionate characters, rather than good actions and normal characters. For "the irascible temperament admits of constant and varied reproduction, while the wise and quiet temperament, which scarcely ever varies, is neither easily reproduced nor, when reproduced, readily comprehended."[1] And so an acquaintance with creative literature will tend, he thinks, to foster the emotional element of man's nature to the detriment of the intellectual. "The part of the soul," he writes, "which is forcibly kept down in

---

1 *Ibid.* p. 604.

the case of our own misfortunes, and which craves to weep and bewail itself without stint and take its fill of grief, being so constituted as to find satisfaction in these emotions, is the very part which is filled and pleased by the poets; while that which is naturally the noblest part of us, because it is not adequately disciplined by reason and habit, releases its guard over this emotional part, representing to itself that the sufferings which it contemplates are not part of itself, and that there is no shame in its praising and pitying the unseasonable grief of another who professes to be a good man. On the contrary, the pleasure which it experiences it considers to be so much gain, and it will not allow its contempt for the poem as a whole to rob it of this pleasure. For only a very few can realize that the character of our own emotions must be affected by the manner in which we participate in the emotions of others. Yet it is so, for if we let our own sense of pity grow strong by feeding upon the griefs of others, it is not easy to restrain it in the case of our own sufferings."[1]

Now, in respect of this criticism of Plato, it may be said at once that it combines a marvellous insight into the essential conditions required for the production of great works of art and literature, with a complete misunderstanding of the nature and effects of artistic representation. Both the central principle of the interdependence of art and morals, and the proposal to make "truth" the central test of the merit of the works of both the artist and the poet, are entirely in harmony with the best modern thought. On the other hand the difference between the method of science and the method of

---

[1] *Ibid.* p. 606.

art has become fully known by careful analysis of mental processes, and both the essential truth of the pictures of life presented by poets and novelists, as well as the significance and value of the appeal to the emotions— "pathos" we call it—have alike been recognized. This very criticism of Plato affords a signal example of the importance of the increased psychological knowledge which characterizes the modern era; since the want of such knowledge blinded him to excellences, made him exaggerate faults, and finally condemn in this wholesale way those very masterpieces of Greek literature which the whole civilized world has now learnt to admire.

Aristotle, who was the next great thinker to apply himself to the examination of the processes of artistic and literary production, had the advantage of being able to avail himself of the results of Plato's enquiries. Moreover, he was a master of method; and under the comprehensive scheme which he elaborated for the treatment of all manifestations of human activity and of nature, these artistic processes and the creations which they produced formed a separate and distinct department of enquiry. The work in which he conducted this enquiry is the famous treatise on Fine Art, entitled "concerning Poetry." It is brief, fragmentary, and incomplete, and the results which it embodied appear to have been only partially understood by the ancient world; nevertheless it is the foundation upon which all modern criticism has been based. It follows, therefore, that a knowledge of its chief conclusions is a condition precedent to the comprehension of those principles of criticism which, as I have already remarked, are now definitely accepted, and with which we shall subsequently be concerned.

Aristotle, then, broadly characterized all art and creative literature as processes of imitation or reproduction (μίμησις). He traced their origin, as manifestations of human activity, to the same primitive impulse of imitation as that which makes a child "pick up" the language and the manners of its parents; and found their end, or purpose, to be that of giving pleasure. Taking the tragedy as the most perfectly developed form of poetry (the term in which he includes all creative literature), he analysed the constituents of its subject matter, and in so doing he distinguished those characteristic elements which are to be found in a greater or less degree in every work of creative literature, and upon the nature of which,—both regarded separately and in their respective relationships to each other and to the whole work of which they form part—he was of opinion that the merit or value of the given work depends. These elements are: Plot, or web of incident; Character, or the distinguishing qualities of the persons introduced; Diction, or the literary expression of the thoughts or words of these characters; Sentiment, or the mental basis which governs their actions; Stage-representation, and Musical Accompaniment. Now, in this analysis two points must be noticed. First, that in approaching the study of literature through an examination of this one form—the tragedy—Aristotle has been led to include two elements (the two last, *i.e.* Stage-representation and Musical Accompaniment) which are not properly elements of literary composition at all. And second, that this method of examining a work of literature through its external aspects, suggests to him the characteristic test by which he proposes to measure the merit of any given work, namely by asking, "Is this work constructed in the best possible manner, having in view both the form of literature to which it properly belongs, and the general purpose of art, which is to give pleasure ? "Aristotle also, continuing his analysis, discusses certain lesser elements in literary composition, such as the construction of the plot, its "development" and "solution," the arrangement of the "episodes," using terms which are still used in the sense in which he used them; and he distinguishes and contrasts the respective characteristics of tragedy, comedy, and epic, as forms of poetry.

In this formal criticism Aristotle does little more than to tell us not to write an epic as we should a tragedy, nor a lyric as an epic. The infinitely wider acquaintance with the external characteristics of the various forms of literature which has followed the discovery of printing, has made such information, and the rules by which it is conveyed, seem superfluous and unmeaning. Nevertheless, we shall find that a knowledge of these formal characteristics is still useful in enabling us to detect the more essential elements of literary excellence. And, as a matter of fact, modern criticism commenced with an application of these formal rules to contemporary literature, and it was the perception of their inadequateness, as thus applied by the seventeenth century critics, which led to the great advances subsequently achieved, which we shall have to trace in outline in the succeeding chapter.

But Aristotle did much more than this. Incidentally he corrected the misconception of the nature of the method of creative literature which led Plato into such astonishing errors. In so doing he has enunciated certain artistic principles which are as permanently valid as Plato's principle of the interdependence of art and morals. To Plato's charge of unreality, he replies that the pictures of life given by creative literature are not unreal in the sense of being inconsistent with the facts of life; but that their truth is of a different order from the truth of science. Plato being absorbed with that first aspect of literature in which it appears as a source of information, made no distinction between works of creative literature and literature in general. Aristotle shows that the reality or truthfulness of these two kinds of literature cannot be measured by the same test. Taking history as typical of those works of literature in which the actual facts are of first importance, and poetry as typical of those works of literature in which the treatment of the facts is more important than the facts themselves, he writes:—

"The business of the poet is to tell, not what has happened, but what could happen, and what is possible, either from its probability, or from its necessary connection with what has gone before. The historian and the poet do not differ in using or not using metre—for the writings of Herodotus could be put into metre without being any the less a history, whether in metre or not—but the difference lies in this fact, that the one tells what has happened and the other what could happen. And therefore poetry has a wider truth and a higher aim than history; for poetry deals rather with the universal, history with the particular." [1]

In these masterly sentences Aristotle has once for all characterized the method of creative literature, and distinguished such literature from all other branches of letters.

---

1 *Poetics* : p. 1451^b. Translation as before.

With equal success he replies to Plato's second charge—the charge that such creative literature, being compelled to be sensational by the conditions of successful production, fostered the emotional part of man's nature to the detriment of the higher and intellectual. Taking the appeal of Tragedy to the typical passions of "fear" and "pity" as his text, he replies to this objection of Plato by an argument based upon a medical illustration. The appeal of poetry to the passions instead of permanently fostering the emotional element, purges man's nature by carrying off any excess of this element. When emotion is artificially excited by witnessing a tragedy performed on the stage, the moral system of the spectator is relieved, just as a man's physical system is relieved by a purging medicine. He writes:—

"Tragedy . . . is an imitation of a serious and complete action which has magnitude. The imitation is effected by embellished language, each kind of embellishment varying in the constituent parts. It is acted, not narrated; and it uses the agency of pity and fear to effect a purging of these and the like emotions. [1]

Thus Aristotle justifies and explains the value and meaning of pathos. And indeed, if we reflect a moment we shall probably be able to find something in our own every-day experience which is in accordance with the words of the great Greek thinker. If we recall the feelings with which we have left the theatre after witnessing a performance of a tragedy, or even the less definite sensation with which we have closed a powerful and well-written novel, we

---

1   *Ibid.* p.1449^b.

Chapter III   The Criticism of the Ancient World   179 shall probably remember that there was a distinct sense of relief present in our minds. For a few hours we had forgotten our own difficulties and troubles in the sympathy which was aroused in us for the imagined characters of the dramatist or the novelist. If we had given expression in words to this feeling we should have said to ourselves, "Well, after all, my troubles are not so bad as these." And this feeling—based upon a comparison of the circumstances of our own life with those of others—made us more reconciled to our own lot in life, and perhaps, taught us to understand better the meaning of human life as a whole.

The opinions of these two great thinkers embody what was truest and most far reaching in the thought of the ancient world on the subject of literature. There were subsequent writers, both Greek and Roman, who dealt with the same subject; but their work has added nothing to the broad principles thus laid down by Plato and Aristotle. Criticism in the restricted sense of the study of the external characteristics of great authors—such as style of composition, the use of simple or florid language, dialect, and so on, with the authorship and integrity of the actual texts of the several works respectively attributed to them—was practised especially by the Greek scholars of the great literary centre of Alexandria. And as we have already noticed,[1] literary criticism in this restricted sense—in fact the only sense in which it was understood by the ancient world—found its origin in the work done by these scholars between the years 300 and 150 B.C. But even the author of the

---

1 Ch. I. p. 1.

famous treatise on "the Sublime"—generally said to be Longinus, who lived in the third century A.D.—although he enlarges upon many of the lesser aspects of successful literary composition, never gives us any ground to believe that he had understood the deep significance of those broad and far-reaching principles which constitute the real merit of this criticism of Plato and Aristotle, and make it, as I have said, embody and express all that is best in the critical thought of the ancient world. The statement of these principles is necessarily incomplete and indistinct; nevertheless it is just here that the thought of the best era of the ancient world unites with modern thought: and it was by taking these incomplete and indistinct expressions as a basis that criticism was able to advance again after so many centuries.

Among the authors who themselves contributed to form the great literature of ancient Rome, there were, of course, some who turned their thoughts to an examination of the forms and methods of literature. But Cicero and Quintilian—to mention the most important—do not advance beyond a re-statement of the comments of Plato and Aristotle upon the more obvious aspects of literary and artistic representation; while the criticism of Horace's "Art of Poetry" consists either of direct transcripts from Aristotle, or of sensible common-places. These latter are expressed with the neatness and facility which we should naturally expect from so great a master of composition in verse; but they neither possess—nor pretend to possess—any value as original contributions to the subject of which they treat.

Chapter IV

Modern Criticism

Before we begin to examine the advances respectively made by certain modern critics, it will be useful to sum up the results which the researches of Plato and Aristotle have so far revealed.

From Plato we have got the principle of the interdependence of art and morality. Not only must the great artist or poet be a good man, but good art and bad art tend respectively to make society moral or immoral. Also, the equally important principle that "truth," in the sense of the essential correspondence of the representation with the reality on which it is based, is the highest merit of a work of art or of a work of creative literature.

Our debt to Aristotle is still greater. To him we owe:—

The identification of poetry, or creative literature, with Fine Art, and the tracing of the characteristic process of both alike to the primitive instinct of imitation.

The detection of the essential characteristic of creative literature, and the definition of it as the presentation of universal, or typical, instead of particular or actual facts—the same truth as that which we now express subjectively, when we say that idealization is the characteristic process of the artist mind.

The distinction between creative literature and literature in general, and the consequent necessity for measuring the truth of the former by reference to the method of art, and the truth of the latter by reference to the method of science.

The justification of the use of pathos, or the exhibition of imagined suffering; and the explanation of its special purpose and method.

In addition to this we have got an analysis of the constituent elements of a typical form of creative literature, and the use of these various elements of plot, character, etc., expressed in a system of formal rules. In harmony with this method we have symmetry, or structural perfection, proposed as the measure of artistic excellence,—a test of the merit of creative literature which is the counterpart of that proposed by Plato.

Modern criticism began with an application of this last formal, and, as we now call it, least valuable part of Aristotle's theory of art and literature. The ample growth of creative literature in Europe which followed the Renaissance, had been itself succeeded by an epoch of mingled reflection and creation. In this epoch—the xvii and xviii centuries—the study both of nature and of literature was recommenced with fresh ardour and more successful equipments. It was then, when this new literature came to be passed under review, that attention was again turned to the subject of criticism. It was only natural that those writers who began to measure the merit of the modern works should have had recourse to Aristotle's rules; for the "Poetics"—for all that it was written 2000 years ago—was the only work which contained any approach to a definite system of criticism. But it was also to be expected—as in fact proved to be the case—that these canons, based upon a study of the epics of Homer and the works of the Athenian dramatists, would prove inadequate when applied to works which reflected in their changed forms the changed conditions of the modern era. It was strange that this should have been overlooked; nevertheless it was the case, and during the seventeenth and part of the eighteenth century criticism consisted mainly in a knowledge of the formal rules contained in the Poetics, and the work of the critics consisted in the application of these rules more or less rigorously to contemporary literature. In France, especially, which was at this time the centre of European thought and manners, a splendid dramatic literature was produced which was absolutely moulded upon classical models. "Following, or thinking they followed the ancients," Mr Saintsbury writes, "French dramatists and dramatic critics adopted certain fixed rules according to which a poet had to write just as a whist-player has to play the game." [1] The general effect of this artificial system may be seen from the result which is produced upon the great poets of the French "Classical" drama—Corneille and Racine. "This was the source," says Demogeot, "of that severe unity to which Corneille submits and of which Racine bears the yoke so lightly. This was the source of that small number of characters, ever restrained to the indispensable requirements of the plot; of that rapid and uninterrupted progress of a sole and complete action; of those wide

---

1 In his "History of French Literature."

deserted porticoes where the persons of the dialogue meet, vague regions, characterless and nameless, the scene of an ideal action carefully purged of every vulgar episode, in such wise that we might say that there is not so much a *unity* as a *nullity*, of time and place. This immaterial and spiritual action, seems to exist by itself, like thought, and to occupy neither time nor space."

Now this application of Aristotle's rules was both ignorant and mistaken. It was ignorant, because these critics, taking their knowledge of the Poetics for the most part second-hand, frequently misinterpreted his meaning; while the models which they adopted were often not the Greek models at all, but those pseudo-classical models of which the dramas of Seneca were the recognized examples. It was mistaken, because the conditions under which the Greek works were composed were altogether different from the conditions of the modern world. Yet it was possible in France, since the French masters wrote deliberately with an eye upon those very classical and pseudo-classical models upon which this formal criticism was based. But in England the case was different. The greatest of the English masters, the poets of the Elizabethan and Stuart period, rebelled against the servitude to pseudo-classical models: they drew their inspiration from the same sources as those which quickened the national life. The opulence of ideas which followed the recovery of the lost literatures of Greece and Rome, the extension of scientific knowledge, and the discovery of the new world of America and of the ocean highway to the East—this, combined with the energy begotten of a period of national expansion, was sufficient to provide them with a creative impulse which refused to be confined within the limits of any previously developed poetic forms.

Nevertheless, so strong was the influence of the accepted critical creed during the period of French predominance, that Addison, when he set himself to vindicate the greatness of Milton's genius, was compelled to show that "Paradise Lost" conformed to the Aristotelian tests. It was this application—this attempt to put the contents of a gallon into a pint-measure—which showed him the insufficiency of any system of critical rules based upon a study of the literature of a single epoch, however splendid, and led him to discover a new principle of poetical appeal, and consequently a new test of merit by which the new forms—indeed, all forms—of creative literature could be measured. In his criticism of "Paradise Lost," Addison confines himself, mainly but not entirely, to an application, and an explanation, of Aristotle's canons. But in the "Essay on the Pleasures of the Imagination" he avails himself of the new knowledge of the processes of thought embodied in the writings of Descartes, Hobbes and Locke; and it is with the assistance of this new psychological knowledge, that he discusses and applies the principle of the appeal of art to the imagination, which marks the cardinal difference between ancient and modern criticism.

First, then, we will look for a moment at Addison's criticism of "Paradise Lost," as being a typical example of the method of this formal criticism, and afterwards we will notice the character and significance of the new principle of poetic appeal.

Addison gives us the plan of his criticism of "Paradise Lost" in the last of the eighteen papers in the *Spectator* which he devotes to the subject. Four papers are assigned to the examination of the poem under the respective heads of Fable (or Plot), Characters, Sentiments, and Language; that is to the four constituent elements of Aristotle's analysis of the Tragedy which are present in an Epic poem. Two papers are given to the "Censures which the author may incur under each of these heads;" and the remaining twelve are devoted to a consideration of each of the twelve books of the poem in turn; and in this consideration he points out the "particular beauties" which belong to each book, and tells "wherein these beauties consist." As the result of this examination, he pronounces a general verdict of approval; but at the same time he indicates certain deficiencies. Milton, he says, "excels in general under each of these heads." On the other hand, he finds the "plot" of "Paradise Lost" to be deficient in two respects. First because "the Event is unhappy;" for Aristotle, while he says that the plot of a tragedy should terminate in a disaster, lays down the general rule that an epic should end happily. And secondly, because it contains too many "digressions." Similarly, he finds a defect in Milton's "characters." This defect consists in the introduction of "two actors of a shadowy and fictitious nature, in the persons of Sin and Death." These allegorical characters he holds are not suitable for an epic poem, because "there is not that measure of probability annexed to them, which is requisite in writings of this kind." In advancing this criticism he makes a distinction between them and the character of Satan; for this latter was to all intents and purposes a human character. Once more he complains that Milton's "Sentiments" are marred by the "unnecessary ostentation of learning" shown in his discussions on "Free-will and Predestination, and his many glances upon History, Astronomy, Geography and the like."

But these examples are sufficient to indicate the kind of results obtained from the attempt to estimate the merit of a work of creative literature by the application of these formal rules. They have been cited as illustrations of the barrenness of this method, and not as specimens of Addison's criticism. It is necessary, therefore, to add at once that Addison himself compares the defects thus revealed to "spots on the sun," and that he occupies twice as much space in the more congenial task of indicating those beauties in "Paradise Lost, which appear more exquisite than the rest." In this appreciation he detects and emphasizes most of the characteristic excellences of the great English Epic. In particular he decides—and all subsequent critics have agreed with him—that Milton's dominant quality is sublimity.

"Milton's chief Talent, and indeed his distinguishing Excellence, lies in the Sublimity of his Thoughts. There are others of the Moderns who rival him in every other Part of Poetry; but in the Greatness of his Sentiments he triumphs over all the Poets, both modern and ancient, Homer only excepted. It is impossible for the Imagination of man to distend itself with greater Ideas, than those which he has laid together in his First, Second, and Sixth Books." [1]

But it is in the "Essay on the Pleasures of the Imagination" that Addison's great contribution to the science of criticism is to be found. Let me try to state in a few words what was the precise nature of the advance, which is embodied in the proposal to measure the merit of works of creative literature by the degree in which they severally appeal to the imagination.

To do this, it is necessary to look back a little. Aristotle, in showing that

---

[1] *Spectator*, No. 279.

the test of truth could not be applied to measure the value of poetry in the way in which Plato had applied it, established the fact that works of creative literature, as being works of art, represented external realities in a different manner from that in which non-creative or scientific literature would represent them. Rightly considered he said such representations were not less but *more* truthful; because under the method of art it was the most essential aspects of realities that were reproduced. Addison, by applying the new psychological knowledge of his age—in particular the doctrine of association of ideas—to the study of literature, notices that works of art, whether statue, painting, or creative literature, by virtue of the reproduction of these essential aspects of reality, work upon the mind of the spectator in a different way than the corresponding raw material (so to speak) of reality: that, in other words, by virtue of the imagination of the artist thus embodied in their sensible atributes they call up images more rapidly and more vividly in the mind with which they are so brought into contact. And from this observation he passes to the conclusion that the characteristic merit of such works can be best measured by the possession of this quality—the quality of appealing to the imagination.

It is interesting to trace the steps by which Addison arrived at this conclusion. But it is necessary to notice first of all that he is well aware that "the faculty of the imagination" is nothing more than a convenient term for describing one aspect of the action of the mind as a whole. "We divide the soul," he says, "into several powers and faculties," but, "there is no such division in the soul itself, since it is the whole soul that remembers, understands, wills, or imagines."

In commencing his examination of the effects of this faculty of the imagination, or fancy, he points out that it is the sense of sight which provides the mind in the first instance with the "images" subsequently reproduced in thought: and he describes briefly the mental process to which these sense-impressions are submitted.

"It is this sense," he writes, "which furnishes the Imagination with its Ideas, so that by the Pleasures of the Imagination or Fancy (which I shall use promiscuously) I here mean such as arise from visible Objects, either when we have them actually in our View, or when we call up these Ideas in our Minds by Paintings, Statues, Descriptions, or any the like Occasion. We cannot indeed have a single Image in the Fancy that did not make its first Entrance through the Sight; but we have the power of retaining, altering, and compounding those Images which we have once received into all the Varieties of Picture and Vision that are most agreeable to the Imagination; for by this Faculty a man in a Dungeon is capable of entertaining himself with Scenes and Landscapes more beautiful than any that can be found in the whole Compass of Nature."[1]

He then divides these pleasures into two kinds—primary and secondary. Of these the primary pleasures arise from "objects before our eyes"; the secondary, from "the ideas of visible objects, where the objects are not actually before the eye, but are called up into our memories, or formed into agreeable visions of things that are either absent or fictitious." Moreover he finds that while the works of nature are more effective in producing the first class, the

---

1 *Ibid.* 411.

works of art are more effective in producing the second. It is the secondary pleasures, therefore, with which art and literature are concerned; and these are caused not by real objects but by the representations of these objects. But here again he distinguishes between the two kinds of representations produced respectively by the "arts of the eye" and the "arts of the ear." In the case of those of Architecture, Sculpture, and Painting, there is a physical form perceptible by the sight: but in the case of the representations of music and creative literature the sole physical basis is the sound of the notes or words, or the sight of the word-symbols which indicate articulate sounds.

In all cases alike he traces the secondary pleasures of the imagination to "that action of the mind, which compares the ideas arising from the original objects with the ideas we receive from the statue, picture, description, or sound that represents them."

In creative literature, where the ideas are "raised by words," the part played by the imagination is twofold.

In the first place there is the working of the imagination in the mind of the poet:—

"Because the Mind of Man requires something more perfect in Matter than what it finds there, and can never meet with any Sight in Nature which sufficiently answers its highest ideas of Pleasantness; or, in other words, because the Imagination can fancy to itself Things more "Great, Strange, or Beautiful, than the Eye ever saw, and is still sensible of some defect in what it has seen; on this account it is the part of a Poet to humour the Imagination in its own Notions, by mending and perfecting Nature where he describes a Reality; and by adding greater Beauties than are put together in Nature, where he describes a Fiction.

He is not obliged to attend her in the slow Advances which she makes from one Season to another, or to observe her Conduct in the Successive Production of Plants and Flowers. He may draw into his Description all the Beauties of the Spring and Autumn, and make the whole year contribute to render it the more agreeable. His Rose-trees, Woodbines, and Jessamines may flower together, and his Beds be cover'd at the same time with Lilies, Violets, and Amaranths. His Soil is not restrained to any particular Sett of plants, but is proper either for Oaks or Mirtles, and adapts itself to the products of every Climate. Oranges may grow wild in it; Myrr may be met with in every Hedge, and if he thinks it proper to have a Grove of Spices, he can quickly command Sun enough to raise it. If all this will not furnish out an agreeable Scene, he can make several new Species of Flowers, with richer Scents and higher Colours than any that grow in the Gardens of Nature. His Consorts of Birds may be as full and Harmonious, and his Woods as thick and gloomy as he pleases. He is at no more Expense in a long Vista, than a short one, and can as easily throw his Cascades from a precipice half a mile high, as from one of twenty yards. He has his choice of the Winds, and can turn the Course of his Rivers in all the Variety of Meanders, that are most delightful to the Reader's Imagination. In a word, he has the modelling of Nature in his own hands, and may give her what Charms he pleases, provided he does not reform her too much, and run into Absurdities, by endeavouring to excel." [1]

---

1 *Ibid.* 418.

In the second, there is the characteristic power, possessed by creative literature thus composed, to appeal to the imagination of the hearer or reader. "Words, when well chosen, have so great a Force in them, that a Description often gives us more lively Ideas than the Sight of Things themselves. The Reader finds a scene drawn in stronger Colours, and painted more to the life in his Imagination, by the help of Words, than by an actual Survey of the Scene which they describe. In this case the Poet seems to get the better of Nature; he takes, indeed, the Landskip after her, but gives it more vigorous Touches, heightens its Beauty, and so enlivens the whole Piece that the Images which flow from the Objects themselves appear weak and faint in Comparison of those that come from the Expressions. The Reason, probably, may be because in the survey of any Object we have only so much of it painted on the Imagination, as comes in at the Eye; but in its Description the Poet gives us as free a View of it as he pleases, and discovers to us several parts, that either we did not attend to, or that lay out of our Sight when we first beheld it. As we look on any Object, our Idea of it is, perhaps, made up of two or three simple Ideas; but when the Poet represents it, he may either give us a more complex Idea of it, or only raise in us such Ideas as are most apt to affect the Imagination."[1]

This element being of such importance, the merit of creative literature can be estimated by reference to it. And so Addison writes that "the talent of affecting the Imagination" is the "very life and highest perfection" of

---

1 *Ibid.* 416.

poetry. Here, then, we have a test of merit elastic enough to be applied to all forms, and all developments, of creative literature, but one which takes into account the element of "pleasure,"—the last of the three characteristic qualities which belong to it—as well as those of "matter" and "manner." It is this application of psychology to the study of literature which characterizes modern criticism, and all subsequent critics have consciously or unconsciously availed themselves of the principle of appeal thus formulated and interpreted by Addison.

Chapter V

How Creative Literature Appeals to the Imagination

We have now, thanks to Addison's application of the seventeenth century psychology to the study of literature and art—the three essential tests of truth, symmetry, and the appeal to the imagination, corresponding respectively to the three dominant aspects of creative literature, matter, manner, and capacity to produce pleasure. But before we proceed to discuss the applications of these tests by contemporary writers, and the questions of criticism which arise out of the varying degrees of prominence which are severally assigned by individual minds to them, we must glance at the work of two modern critics—the *Laocoon* of Lessing, published in 1766, and the Lectures of Victor Cousin, *Du Vrai, du Beau et du Bien* delivered in 1818 and published in 1853.

Both of these writers recognize that the appeal of art is chiefly addressed to the imagination, and only in a lesser degree to the understanding, and the senses; but their respective examinations of the nature of this appeal proceed from two opposite points of view. Lessing, concerning himself with the objective point of view, tells us what elements and aspects of reality the poet and the painter must respectively strive to reproduce, if their several representations are to possess this power; Cousin, on the other hand, writing from a subjective point of view, traces the process by which the raw material provided by the senses is converted by the artist's (or poet's) mind into an idea or form, which, when expressed in the medium appropriate to his art, will appeal most powerfully to the imagination of the spectator. More briefly, Lessing shows us how the artist in representing a reality must modify the material attributes of the original to suit the limitations of his art; and Cousin, how the "idea" or mental aspect of reality, the reproduction of which is the special object of art, is formed in the artist's mind.

The manner in which Lessing pursues his enquiry is interesting both in itself, and because it is a further development of the formal, or external, criticism of Aristotle in the "Poetics." Commencing with a discussion of the date of the famous piece of sculpture, the Laocoon[1] group (from which his treatise takes its title), he notices that there is a remarkable similarity between it and Virgil's description of the death of Laocoon and his two sons in the Second Aeneid. He then argues that, apart from any historical evidence, the date of the sculpture can be fixed by artistic considerations: for if the poet copied the artist he would naturally omit certain details unsuitable for his representation of the scene in *words*; while, similarly, if the artist copied the poet he would omit certain details in the poet's description which are unsuitable for the sculptor's representation in *stone*. Accordingly he considers

---

1 See *Frontispiece*.

and compares the details of the two representations, and finally decides that the artist copied the poet, because the differences in treatment which the sculpture shows as compared with Virgil's description are only those which the sculptor would be compelled to make by the character of his medium. In particular he points out that while Virgil tells us that Laocoon utters terrible cries, the sculptor has invested his face with an expression of noble calm. That, he says, is just what we should expect, since it is impossible to express in marble the agonized suffering which Virgil expresses by his words: —

> Clamores simul horrendos ad sidera tollit:
> Quales mugitus, fugit cum saucius aram
> Taurus, et incertum excussit cervice securim.[1]

The attempt to do this would have resulted in a grimace that must have been either ridiculous or horrible—for sculpture should express physical beauty in repose. On the other hand, if Virgil had seen the sculptured group, and founded his description upon the representation of the death of Laocoon which it gives, he could never have omitted to reproduce in his description the expression of sublime endurance which Laocoon wears—for it is just as easy to describe in words this sublime endurance as it was to express the agonized outcry.

From this comparison Lessing enlarges upon a discussion of the

---

[1] At the same time he raises terrible cries to heaven: cries like the bellowings of a wounded bull that has shaken the ill-directed axe from his neck, and fled from the altar of sacrifice.

respective methods of painting, as representative of the "arts of the eye," and poetry, as representative of the "arts of the ear." And in the course of this discussion he analyses very carefully the means for representing reality which are respectively at the disposal of these two typical arts.

Poetry, he says, "employs articulate sounds *in time*"; that is, sounds which are uttered successively. Painting, "forms and colours *in space*"; that is, which co-exist side by side. The aspect of reality which is most suitable for the painter is "a visible and stationary action [or a group of objects], the different parts of which are developed in juxtaposition in space": that which is most suitable for the poet is "a visible and progressive action, the different parts of which happen one after another in sequence of time." The painter, therefore, can only imitate actions *indirectly*; that is, by painting bodies so disposed as to suggest action. Similarly, the poet can only imitate bodies *indirectly*; that is, by telling us of the actions or effects of such bodies, animate or inanimate. And so the painter, when he represents an action, must choose that single moment of the action, which best suggests what has gone before and what is to come after: and the poet, when he represents a body, must select that single property of the body, which awakens the most vivid picture of it in the mind. A simple instance will help to explain this closely reasoned argument. Let us take a common object; say a ship. The painter represents this object by presenting on his canvas so much of its form and colour as meets the eye of a spectator from a single point of view. The poet, on the other hand, adds to the word-symbol which recalls the idea of a ship to the mind, a single characteristic epithet—the "swift ship." That is only a very simple example, but if I add a remark of Mr

Meredith (made in "Diana of the Crossways") I think it will serve to explain Lessing's meaning.

"The art of the pen," Mr Meredith writes, "is to rouse the inward vision, instead of labouring with a drop-scene brush, as if it were to the eye; because our flying minds cannot contain a protracted description. That is why the poets, who spring imagination with a word or a phrase, paint lasting pictures. The Shakespearian, the Dantesque [pictures], are in a line, two at most." But the great example is the device which Homer uses to give us a sense of the beauty of Helen. Instead of telling us the colour of her cheeks, or the shape of her mouth, nose and eyes,—instead of enumerating in succession the several elements which together make up her beauty of face and form—he tells us of the *effect* which the sight of her produced upon the oldest and wisest of the men of Troy. These elders—the men who would be least likely to be affected by a woman's beauty— when they saw her graceful presence, forgot the wrong which she had done, and the suffering which she had brought upon her country:—

Οὐ νέμεσις Τρῶας καὶ ἐϋκνήμιδας Ἀχαιοὺς
Τοιῇδ' ἀμφὶ γυναικὶ πολὺν χρόνον ἄλγεα πάσχειν·
Αἰνῶς ἀθανάτῃσι θεῇς εἰς ὦπα ἔοικεν.[1]

And what applies to human beauty, applies equally to the beauty of nature; and, therefore, descriptions of scenery are, as such, unsuitable subjects for the poet. It is not that the poet cannot describe such scenes. He can do this because he uses a medium, words or language, which is capable of recalling to

---

1   *Iliad* III. 156-8. No wonder that the Trojans and well-greaved Achaeans endure evils so long a time for such a woman—she is terribly like the deathless goddesses to look upon.

the mind any and every conceivable idea. But the writer of creative literature has a different aim from that of the historian or the philosopher. He is an artist, and must employ the method of art; that is, he must compose descriptions which appeal to the imagination and not merely to the understanding. Lessing, although he does not deliberately use the psychological principle of the appeal to the imagination—because, as I have already remarked, he approaches the productions of the respective arts from an external, or formal, point of view—gives us an admirable statement of the application of the principle to the representations of creative literature.

"Since the symbols of speech," he writes, "are symbols adopted by ourselves, it is perfectly possible for us by means of them to indicate the consecutive appearance of the parts of a body as completely as we can perceive those same parts of a body in juxtaposition in nature. But this is an attribute of speech and of its symbols in general, an attribute, too, which does not minister specially to the purposes of poetry. The poet's object is not merely to be intelligible, his representations must be something more than clear and distinct (*this* is sufficient for the prose writer). He desires to make the ideas which he arouses in us so vivid that, as they flash through our mind, we believe that we are experiencing the true, objective impressions produced by the physical originals of these ideas, and in this moment of our illusion we cease to be conscious of the medium which he employs for this purpose, that is, his words. It is this principle which forms the basis of the explanation of the poetical picture."[1]

---

1 *Laocoon*, XVII., as translated in the author's *Principles of Criticism*.

Cousin's researches form a direct contrast and an admirable supplement to those of Lessing. While Lessing's analyses were conducted upon Aristotelian lines, the broad conclusions of the French critic are admittedly based upon the philosophy of Plato. His object, he tells us, is "to offer at least an outline-sketch of a regular and complete theory of beauty and art." For this purpose he considers in turn; (1) subjective beauty, or the faculties to which man owes his consciousness of beauty; (2) objective beauty, or the qualities which respectively make an action, a thought, a person or a material object, beautiful; (3) the nature of art, or the processes by which the beautiful in real existences is reproduced; and (4) the means and therefore the aims, which respectively belong to the several arts, or how the arts are separated. On all of these aspects of beauty he writes with precision and philosophic insight, but his most important contribution to the science of criticism consists in his masterly exposition of the process of idealization—the process which, as we have already seen, is identical with Addison's operation of the imagination in the mind of the poet, and is now recognized as the characteristic process of the artist mind.

"We desire," he says, "to see and feel again the natural beauty, physical and moral, which delights us in the world of reality; and we, therefore, endeavour to reproduce it *not such as it was, but such as our imagination represents it to us. Thence arises a work original and proper to man, a work of art.*"[1] The artist neither creates in the sense in which we speak of God as the creator, nor does he merely imitate. He finds his materials in the world

---

1 *Du Vrai, etc.* VIII.

of reality, but he reproduces these materials in a changed form. This change of form is the result of the process of idealization. "The true artist," Cousin writes, "has a profound feeling and admiration for nature; but everything in nature is not equally admirable." What the artist reproduces is an "idea" of the reality which is the subject of his representation; an idea formed in his mind by a double process of selection and omission. If he represents an action, or a person, or an object, it matters not; in all cases in forming this idea he omits defects which were present in the original, and adds excellences which that original did not possess. In a word he idealizes his subject. Idealization, then, is "the unconscious criticism of nature by the human mind," [1] and it is an idealized reality, and not reality itself, which the artist reproduces in the appropriate medium of his art. In the words of Cousin, the end of art is the expression of moral beauty by the assistance of physical beauty. "The latter is for art only a symbol of the former. In nature this symbol is often obscure; art in rendering it clear attains effects which nature does not always produce. Nature has another means of pleasing us, for once again I say she possesses in an incomparable degree that which causes the greatest charm of the imagination and the eyes, life; art touches us in a higher degree, because, in making the expression of moral beauty its first aim, it appeals more directly to the source of the deepest emotions. Art can be more pathetic than nature, and pathos is the sign and the measure of beauty of the highest class." [2]

---

1 *Principles of Criticism.*

2 *Du Vrai, etc.* VIII.

And of all the arts, poetry, or creative literature, is that in which the idealizing process can work most freely. In the first place, its medium, language, is the most flexible of all the mediums which the respective arts employ, and in the second it is the actual medium of thought, and as such enables the artist to communicate most directly with the mind of the spectator.

"Speech," he writes, "is the instrument of poetry; poetry moulds it to its uses and idealizes it that so it may express ideal beauty. It gives it the charm and majesty of metre, it turns it into something that is neither voice nor music, but which partakes of the nature of both, something at once material and spiritual, something finished, clear, and precise, like the sharpest contours and forms, something living and animated like colour, something pathetic and infinite like sound. A word in itself, above all a word chosen and transfigured by poetry, is the most energetic and the most universal of symbols. Equipped with this talisman of its own creation, poetry reflects all the images of the world of the senses, like sculpture and painting; reflects feeling like painting and music, rendering it in all its variations—variations which music cannot reach, and that come in a rapid succession which painting cannot follow, while it remains as sharply turned and as full of repose as sculpture; nor is that all, it expresses what is inaccessible to all other arts, I mean thought, thought which has no colour, thought which allows no sound to escape, which is revealed in no play of feature, thought in its loftiest flight, in its most refined abstraction." [1]

---

1   *Ibid.* ix. Translation from *Principles of Criticism*.

Chapter VI

Contemporary Criticism

In spite of the fact that great thinkers have from time to time applied themselves to the consideration of the processes of literary composition, and of the relation of these processes to the processes of artistic representation in general, it is only to-day that any definite principles of judgment in literature seem to have at length emerged from the nebulous mass of thought which has thus gathered in the course of centuries round the subject. I say "to-day," for nothing is more astonishing to the student of literature than the blindness which great—sometimes the greatest—men have shown in contemplating the work of their fellows, and especially that of contemporary authors. Putting on one side for a moment the verdicts of what we may call the "professional" critics of the eighteenth and nineteenth centuries—critics whose purpose was often frankly "destructive"—we are confronted by the record of a Voltaire declaring that Hamlet was "a rude and barbarous piece—such a work as one might suppose to be the fruit of the imagination of a drunken savage"; of a Goethe expressing the opinion that the *Inferno* of Dante was "abominable, the *Purgatorio* dubious, and the *Paradiso* tiresome"; of a Byron insensible to the charm of an entire choir of English lyric singers, of a Matthew Arnold, acutely sensitive to the beauty and power of the ancient and mediæval masters, yet blind to the genius of the greatest of his great contemporaries—Tennyson, Browning, Swinburne, Rossetti, and William Morris. While as for this professional criticism—the criticism of which the great reviews which flourished in the early part of the present century have been the chief depositories—there is no more humiliating record of the littleness of human nature than is afforded by the egregious blunders and the envenomed sentences of its exponents. The story is writ large in the pages of the literary journals, and both Wordsworth in his "Essay Supplementary,"[1] and quite recently Mr Dowden in his essay on the Interpretation of Literature,[2] have collected and exhibited the most extraordinary examples of the mingled perversity and obtuseness which even great writers have displayed in the endeavour to perform an impossible task.

But to-day the practice of attempting to estimate the merit of works of literature—whether contemporary or belonging to past ages—by the application of formal or technical tests has become entirely discredited, if, indeed, it is not practically extinct. Such tests, even if they were perfectly understood by the critic who applies them, would measure excellences or defects which are appreciable by only a limited class, while they leave untouched those broad and dominant qualities, which, appealing to all persons

---

[1] To the Preface of his edition of 1815.
[2] *Contemporary Review*, 1886.

of ordinary intelligence, can alone form the basis of that universal recognition which is the sign and seal of the highest merit. The practice of attempting verdicts upon new works of literature is still maintained in the ordinary criticism of the journals; but while there is much that is often both unbiassed and enlightened in this criticism, it is well understood that the writers of these reviews or notices do not claim to give a binding verdict: that, indeed, the conditions under which such criticisms are for the most part written preclude their writers, however well qualified they may otherwise be, from forming any but a superficial estimate. The criticism embodied in the ordinary "reviews" of the journals we may therefore put on one side as ineffective. Nevertheless the study of literature has never been pursued so widely in England, nor pursued with such happy results, as it is to-day. But before we consider the motives and principles of contemporary English criticism as thus understood, it will be desirable to refer very briefly to some of the more striking of the results embodied in the work of its most distinguished exponents.

Wordsworth, in his protest against the assumptions of the professional critics, has put his finger upon the inherent weakness of any system of criticism which attempts to measure new works of creative literature by rules based solely, or mainly, upon a knowledge of previously existing models. The external qualities which this formal and technical criticism measures exist in complete independence of the element of originality; and it is to the fact that no allowance has been made for this unknown quantity that the failure of this criticism is chiefly due. Smarting under the mingled injustice and indifference with which his own work had been received, he writes:—

"If there be one conclusion more forcibly pressed upon us than another by the review which has been given of the fortunes and fate of poetical works, it is this: that every author, as far as he is great and at the same time *original*, has had the task of creating the taste by which he is to be enjoyed; so has it been, so will it continue to be. . . . The predecessors of an original genius of a high order will have smoothed the way for all that he has in common with them; and much he will have in common; but, for what is peculiarly his own, he will be called upon to clear and often to shape his own road; he will be in the condition of Hannibal among the Alps."[1]

He has also stated with perfect clearness the reason why such formal tests as structure of plot, perfection of metre, purity or elegance of diction, and others on which the professional critic bases his verdict of approval or condemnation, cannot in themselves afford the material for a binding verdict. Mere technical or formal perfection can be attained in works which are destitute of that quality which is essential to secure the permanent appreciation of mankind—the quality of giving pleasure. On the other hand, works which are deficient in such technical excellences may possess this quality in a high degree. The foundation of this quality of giving pleasure is, as we have seen, the power of appealing to the imagination, and it is precisely the greater freedom with which the poet can avail himself of this appeal that constitutes the higher value of the poetic presentation of the facts of life. But the imagination to which the poet appeals is not that of the critic, but that of the

---

1 *Essay Supplementary.*

general reader—of the person possessed, not of technical knowledge, but of ordinary everyday intelligence. Indeed, so far from technical qualities affording an absolute basis for the measuring of poetic excellence, these qualities may be developed to a degree that makes them actually hinder the general appreciation or acceptance of the work. "The poet writes," he says[1], "under one restriction only, namely, that of the necessity of giving immediate pleasure to a human being possessed of that information which may be expected from him, not as a lawyer, a physician, a mariner, an astronomer, or a natural philosopher, but as a man. Except this one restriction, there is no object standing between the poet and the image of things; between this and the biographer and historian there are a thousand."

In other words, the power of giving pleasure by an appeal to the imagination of the reader, is the essential quality which a work of creative literature ought to possess (for it is only by virtue of this quality that the general sense of mankind can be satisfied), and this quality is one which lies outside the reach of any technical test.

But it is in the critical writings of Matthew Arnold that we find the highest example of contemporary English criticism. In his two volumes of "Essays in Criticism" we have studies of foreign and English authors, which exhibit more fully than any similar writings the changed spirit of which I have spoken. It is, of course, impossible within the limits at my disposal to give any conception of the luminous treatment, the lucid expression, or the wealth of illustration

---

1 Observations, prefixed to the second edition of *Lyrical Ballads*.

which characterize these studies of individual authors; all that can be said here is that the great object which Matthew Arnold the critic has seemed to have placed before him, is to interpret—to gather up all the facts which are of use as indicating the special conditions of the author's personality, and the special motives of his work, and then of tracing the connection between these conditions and the excellences or defects which characterize his work. In short, of providing the reader with that preliminary basis of information which will enable him to read the work of the author with both discrimination and appreciation.

Indirectly, however, in the course of these studies of particular authors he has enunciated certain principles of general application.

(1) He has emphasized and defined the close connexion between the author and the age in which he lives, by pointing out that in every work of creative literature two distinct factors can be discerned—the personality of the writer and the mental atmosphere of the age. Gray is a case in point, and in his essay on his poetry he takes him as an example of a genius planted in an unfruitful soil, and therefore doomed to comparative sterility.

"Gray," he writes, "with the qualities of mind and soul of a genuine poet, was isolated in his century. Maintaining and fortifying them by lofty studies, he yet could not fully educe and enjoy them; the want of a genial atmosphere, the failure of sympathy in his contemporaries, were too great. Born in the same year with Milton, Gray would have been another man; born in the same year with Burns, he would have been another man. A man born in 1608 could profit by the larger and more poetic scope of the English spirit in the Elizabethan age; a man born in 1759 could profit by that European renewing of men's minds of which the great historical manifestation is the French Revolution."[1]

(2) He has broadly characterized the philosophic aspect of all poetic representations of reality by the luminous expression that Poetry is a "criticism of life." That is to say, that the poet or novelist by creating ideal pictures of life, provides an ideal standard with which the facts of real life can be contrasted. And since such a comparison of the real with the ideal helps us to understand the general purpose and conditions of human existence, he defines the special quality of poetic thought as its "interpretative power." In particular, he has distinguished with precision the truth of poetry from the truth of science, and he has told us why it is that poetry by virtue of this power of interpretation becomes, as Wordsworth has said, "the breath and finer spirit of all knowledge." It is because it appeals to the *whole man*, to the emotions and feelings as well as to the reason. If we understand this interpretative power, as thus defined, to be the subjective aspect of the appeal to the imagination—or the effect in the mind of the hearer or reader which the appeal of poetry produces—we shall find in the following passage a precise analysis of the effects of this appeal in the case of that art—poetry—which possesses it in the highest degree.

"The grand power of poetry is its interpretative power; by which I mean, not a power of drawing out in black and white an explanation of the mystery of the universe, but the power of so dealing with things as to awaken in us a

---

[1] *Essays in Criticism*, II.

wonderfully full and intimate sense of them, and of our relations with them. When this sense is awakened in us as to objects without us, we feel ourselves to be in contact with the essential nature of these objects, to be no longer bewildered and oppressed by them, but to have their secret, and to be in harmony with them; and this feeling calms and satisfies us as no other can. Poetry, indeed, interprets in another way besides this; but one of its two ways of interpreting, of exercising its highest power, is by awakening this sense in us. I will not now enquire if this sense is illusive, whether it can be proved not to be illusive, whether it does absolutely make us possess the real nature of things; all I say is, that poetry can awaken it in us, and that to awaken it is one of the highest powers of poetry. The interpretations of science do not give us this intimate sense of objects as the interpretations of poetry give it, they appeal to a limited faculty and not to the whole man. It is not Linnaeus or Cavendish or Cuvier who gives us the true sense of animals, or water, or plants, who seizes their secret for us, who makes us participate in their life, it is Shakespeare, with his

'daffodils

That come before the swallow dares, and take

The winds of March with beauty;'

it is Wordsworth, with his

'Voice ... heard

> In the spring-time from the cuckoo-bird,
> Breaking the silence of the seas
> Among the farthest Hebrides;'

it is Keats with his

> 'Moving waters at their priest-like task
> Of cold ablution round Earth's human shores;'

it is Chateaubriand, with his '*cîme indéterminée des forêts;*' it is Senancour, with his mountain birch-tree; '*Cette écorce blanche, lisse et crevassée; cette tige agreste; ces branches qui s'inclinent vers la terre; la mobilité des feuilles, et tout cet abandon, simplicité de la nature, attitude des déserts.*' " [1]

(3) Poetry of the highest class must exercise this power of interpretation, this appeal to the imagination (or, as Arnold himself calls it, to the "imaginative reason"), within a given sphere; and the accent of the masters of such poetry is the "high seriousness of absolute sincerity."

"For supreme poetical success more is required than the powerful application of ideas to life; it must be an application under the conditions fixed by the laws of poetic truth and poetic beauty. These laws fix as an essential condition, in the poet's treatment of such matters as are here in question, high

---

[1] *Ibid*, I.

seriousness—the high seriousness which comes from absolute sincerity."[1] And such poetry must be essentially moral; that is to say, it must be such as to satisfy the general sense of mankind as embodied in the principles of morality.

"It is important, therefore, to hold fast to this: that poetry is at bottom a criticism of life; that the greatness of a poet lies in his powerful and beautiful application of ideas to life—to the question: How to live. Morals are often treated in a narrow and false fashion; they are bound up with systems of thought and belief which have had their day; they are fallen into the hands of pedants and professional dealers; they grow tiresome to some of us. We find attraction, at times, even in a poetry of revolt against them; in a poetry which might take for its motto Omar Kheyam's words: 'Let us make up in the tavern for the time which we have wasted in the mosque.' Or we find attractions in a poetry indifferent to them; in a poetry where the contents may be what they will, but where the form is studied and exquisite. We delude ourselves in either case; and the best cure for our delusion is to let our minds rest upon that great and inexhaustible word *life*, until we learn to enter into its meaning. A poetry of revolt against modern ideas is a poetry of revolt against *life*; a poetry of indifference towards moral ideas is a poetry of indifference towards *life*."[2]

To Mr Ruskin in the field of the Fine Arts, and to William Morris in the field of the Lesser Arts, we owe an unhesitating application of the principle of the interdependence of art and morality. The general character of Mr Ruskin's

---

1 *Ibid*, II.

2 *Ibid*, II.

criticism of works of architecture and painting is sufficiently expressed in his own words. "In these books of mine," he writes, "their distinctive character as Essays on Art is their bringing everything to a root in human passion or human hope." And nowhere else do we find a stronger assertion of the inseparable connection of morality and poetic excellence than in the following passage.

"All right human song is, similarly, the finished expression, by art, of the joy or grief of noble persons for right causes. And accurately in proportion to the rightness of the cause, and purity of the emotion, is the possibility of the fine art. . . . And with absolute precision, from highest to lowest, the fineness of the possible art is an index of the moral purity and majesty of the emotion it expresses. . . . And that is so in all the arts; so that with mathematical precision, subject to no error or exception, the art of a nation, so far as it exists, is an exponent of its ethical state."[1]

Moreover Mr Ruskin (like Matthew Arnold) has added increased precision to the principle of the appeal to the imagination. The ideas which poetry and the arts can powerfully stir in the mind by virtue of this appeal, must be ideas which are in harmony with the best traditions of the race.

"I do not say, therefore, that the art is greatest which gives most pleasure, because perhaps there is some art whose end is to teach and not to please. I do not say that the art is greatest which teaches us most, because perhaps there is some art whose end is to please and not to teach. I do not say that the art is greatest which imitates best, because perhaps there is some art whose end is to

---

[1] *Lectures on Art*, III., §67.

create and not to imitate. But I say that the art is greatest which conveys to the spectator, by any means whatsoever, the greatest number of the greatest ideas; and I call an idea great in proportion as it is received by a higher faculty of the mind, and as it more fully occupies, and in occupying, exercises and exalts, the faculty by which it is received. If this, then, be the definition of great art, that of a great artist naturally follows. He is the greatest artist who has embodied, in the sum of his works, the greatest number of the greatest ideas."[1]

On the other hand there are contemporary writers who emphasize the important principle of the "freedom" of art.

Their point of view is expressed in the phrase "Art for art's sake" and the principle which they apply is excellently stated by Mr Swinburne—himself distinguished beyond all living masters of song for the perfection of his verse.

"No work of art has any worth or life in it that is not done on the absolute terms of art, that is not, before all things and above all things, a work of positive excellence, as judged by the laws of the special art to whose laws it is amenable." And of poetry he writes:—

"The worth of a poem has properly nothing to do with its moral meaning or design; the praise of Caesar as sung by a Virgil, of a Stuart as sung by a Dryden, is preferable to the most magnanimous invective against tyranny, which love of country and of liberty could bring from a Bavius or a Settle."[2]

And again:—

---

1 *Modern Painters*, I. Pt.1., Sect.1., ch.ii., §9.
2 *Essays and Studies.*

"In all great poets, there must be an ardent harmony, a heat of spiritual life, guiding without restraining the bodily grace of motion, which shall give charm and power to their least work; sweetness that cannot be weak, and force that will not be rough. There must be an instinct and resolution of excellence which will allow no shortcoming or malformation of thought or word, there must be also so natural a sense of right as to make such a deformity or defect impossible, and leave upon the work done no trace of any effort to avoid or to achieve."[1]

This doctrine, although it can scarcely be maintained in the extreme form in which it is here stated by Mr Swinburne, is valuable as emphasizing the independence of Art. Although creative literature, and the arts in general, often draw their inspiration from religion and patriotism, they must not be identified with either the one or the other. And again, although the test of truth requires that what the poet writes should be in harmony with the general sense of mankind, a poem or other work of creative literature must not be condemned as inartistic, because the views which it contains are repugnant to the individual critic, or contrary to the received opinions of the majority of his fellow countrymen. It is very difficult, of course, to fix the line, so as to distinguish between what is merely a divergence from a temporary or local standard of sentiment or conduct, and what is really inconsistent with the principles of morality, and can never, therefore, be in agreement with the general sense of mankind. Owing to this natural difficulty, and a failure to pay

---

[1] *Essays and Studies.*

due respect to the independence of Art, charges of "obscurity" and "immorality" have been made almost invariably against the works of great writers by their contemporaries. One or two examples will serve to illustrate both the reality of the difficulty, and the nature of the distinction between a divergence from conventional or national sentiments, and a disagreement from the general sense of mankind. Coleridge's "Cristabel" appeared to the Edinburgh reviewer of that day to be "a mixture of raving and drivelling." Wordsworth's Ode on "Intimations of Immortality" ". . . the most illegible and unintelligible part" of the volume to which it belonged. Shelley was advised to publish "a glossary of words" with his poems. The writings of Southey and Wordsworth, now regarded as our most spiritual poets, were originally regarded as dangerous in their moral teaching, since the Lake School found its inspiration in the writings of Rousseau, and was tainted by his discontent at the organization of society. Charles Kingsley's *Yeast* was condemned by the *Guardian*. "It is the countenance the writer gives to the worst tendencies of the day, and the manner in which he conceals loose morality in a dress of high sounding and philosophic phraseology which calls for plain and decided condemnation." But these examples, which might be almost indefinitely multiplied, will suffice to show that the student of creative literature should hesitate before he pronounces an adverse verdict on a new author on either of these grounds; for not only does the artistic merit of creative literature depend upon the recognition of this freedom of art, but its moral value, as one of the forces which make for progress, is also involved. The idea is well expressed by Mrs Browning in *Aurora Leigh*—a book which contains, as she tells us, her "highest convictions upon Life and Art." Of the poets, she says that they are "the only truth-tellers now left to God":—

> "The only speakers of essential truth,
>
> Opposed to relative, comparative.
>
> And temporal truths: the only holders by
>
> His sun-skirts, through conventional gray glooms,
>
> The only teachers who instruct mankind
>
> From just a shadow on a charnel-wall
>
> To find man's veritable stature out
>
> Erect, sublime, —the measure of a man."

To this appeal against the tyranny of convention, she adds an equally impassioned appeal against the tyranny of the professional critic.

> "And whosoever writes good poetry,
>
> Looks just to art. He does not write for you
>
> Or me,—for London or for Edinburgh;
>
> He will not suffer the best critic known
>
> To step into his sunshine of free thought
>
> And self-absorbed conception and exact
>
> An inch-long swerving of the holy lines.
>
> If virtue done for popularity
>
> Defiles like vice, can art, for praise or hire,

> Still keep its splendor and remain pure art?
> Eschew such serfdom. What the poet writes,
> He writes; mankind accepts it if it suits,
> And that's success: if not, the poem's passed
> From hand to hand, and yet from hand to hand,
> Until the unborn snatch it, crying out
> In pity on their fathers' being so dull,
> And that's success too."

Nevertheless, important as this doctrine undoubtedly is, it cannot be maintained in the extreme form in which Mr Swinburne advances it, when he says, "No work of art has any worth or life . . . . that is not . . . . a work of positive excellence, as judged by the laws of the special art to whose laws it is amenable." In the first place, obedience to the laws of art is not alone sufficient to produce that sense of delight in the ideal representation of nature and human life which a work of art must produce, if it is to be accepted by humanity. If we examine the actual conditions under which this sense of delight is produced, we can find a psychological basis for the opposite contention, that the supreme test of merit is agreement with the general sense of mankind. The feeling of pleasure which arises from contact with a work of art is not produced solely by the external stimulus *i.e.*, the picture or the poem, which appeals to the senses and through them to the imagination, but it depends also upon the effect caused by the re-action of the mind of the person so affected. Now in this second factor—the mind of the person as a whole—the social medium, or general body of contemporary ideas, plays its part. Consequently, if the artist wishes to please, he must present the materials which form the subject of his work in a manner which will agree, and not disagree, with the sentiments embodied in these contemporary ideas. Indeed, the argument may be carried farther; and it may be maintained that it is the adjustment of the rules of the particular art to suit the requirements of the human mind which constitutes the prime merit of the artist.

Or, to approach the question from another side, in a poem, or a picture, or a musical composition, there is one aspect which appeals solely or mainly to persons who are trained in the particular art, while there is another which appeals to all and every one of ordinary intelligence. These latter must by the nature of things be more numerous than the former: and although it would be absurd to consult their opinion in matters of purely technical importance, yet in the question of the general effect of the particular work of art they must be consulted; since the poem or picture, as the case may be, is not produced for poets and artists solely, but for all the world. That the public in general do claim and exercise the right of deciding on the worth of a work of art, and do in fact pronounce the verdict of success or failure, is a matter of common knowledge. Should not, therefore, the faculty of taste or correct judgment which is the property not of a particular class or profession, but generally of all intelligent persons, be the true test, and not the rules of the specific art which are known only to the few? It is quite true that this "taste" will vary from one age to another, and will differ in different societies, just as the standard of morality varies; but even allowing for these variations there still remains a sufficient basis of agreement to constitute a faculty of taste of permanent validity. If we accept the existence of this faculty of taste, and maintain that "agreement with the general sense of mankind," is the true test, then the effect of a work of art on the world in general must be considered, and its influence for good or bad becomes a factor which cannot be overlooked.

Here we come upon the main drift of Mr Ruskin's teaching; "every principle of painting which I have stated," he says in *Modern Painters*, "is traced to some vital or spiritual fact; and in my works on architecture the preference accorded finally to one school over another, is founded on a comparison of their influences on the life of the workmen—a question by all other writers on the subject of architecture wholly forgotten or despised." According to Mr Ruskin, then, the effect of a work of art for good or bad is not only a factor in its excellence, but a factor of supreme importance; and this conviction is the foundation upon which he, like Plato, has based his whole theory of art. And so he decides with reference to each branch of the arts. In painting, "no vain or selfish person can possibly paint, in the noble sense of the word. . . . Mere cleverness or special gift never made an artist." In architecture, the Gothic style is adjudged to be the best on the same grounds. "In one point of view, Gothic is not only the best but the only rational architecture, as being that which can fit itself most easily to all services, vulgar or noble. Undefined in its slope of roof, height of shaft, breadth of arch, or disposition of ground plan, it can shrink into a turret, expand into a hall, coil into a staircase, or spring into a spire, with undegraded grace, and unexhausted energy. . . ." And as we have seen, in his opinion the greatest artist is the artist "who has embodied in the sum of his works, the greatest number of the greatest ideas." Moreover, he applies this principle no less rigorously to individuals. In his lecture on the realistic school of painting, although he acknowledges Rossetti as "the chief intellectual force in the establishment of the modern Romantic School in England," yet he decides that Holman Hunt is, "beyond calculation greater, beyond comparison happier, than Rossetti," because of his faith in the truths of the Christian religion. "To Rossetti, the old and new Testaments were only the greatest poems he knew; and he painted scenes in them, with no more actual belief in their relation to the present life and business of men, than he gave also to the 'Morte d'Arthur' and the 'Vita Nuova.' But to Holman Hunt the story of the New Testament, when once his mind entirely fastened on it, became what it was to an old puritan or an old catholic of true blood,— not merely a reality, not merely the greatest of realities, but the only reality. So absolutely . . . that in all subjects which fall short in the religious element his power also is shortened, and he does those things worst which are easiest to other men."[1]

And so we have a statement from Mr Ruskin of the relations of morals and art which is precisely opposite to that of Mr Swinburne ". . . the praise of a Cæsar as sung by a Virgil, of a Stuart as sung by a Dryden, is preferable to the most magnanimous invective against tyranny which love of country and of liberty" could inspire. Nevertheless it is significant of the difficulty of the subject that neither of these masters of criticism are perfectly consistent.

---

1 *Lectures on Art* II. p. 9.

When Mr Ruskin writes of the faculty of the imagination, he declares, in terms scarcely less definite than those of Mr Swinburne, that this, the distinctive faculty of the artist being, is supreme, and the subject matter of secondary importance. "There is no reasoning in it; it works not by Algebra nor by integral Calculus; it is a piercing, pholas-like, mind's tongue, that works and tastes into the very rock-heart; no matter what be the subject submitted to it, substance or spirit. . . . Every great conception of poet or painter is held and treated by this faculty."[1] While Mr Swinburne, when he comes to criticise a special poem, finds the blemish to consist in certain social and moral views which offend him; so he writes of the "passing perversities of Christianized Socialism or bastard Cassarism, which disfigure and diminish the pure proportions and noble charm of *Aurora Leigh*."[2]

Both views embody a truth, but not *the* truth. Mr Ruskin's test of conveying "the greatest number of the greatest ideas" is appropriate, when applied to a work of art in its external or objective aspect—the aspect in which art as a whole is regarded as being "the interpretation or expression of moral beauty by the assistance of physical beauty": [3] but it fails if it is applied to a work of art in its internal or subjective aspect—the aspect in which a work of art appears as the expression of the artist's mind, as a "conception converted into a creation."[4] Mr Swinburne's test of "obedience to the rules of the specific

---

1 *Modern Painters.*
2 *Study of Victor Hugo.*
3 *Cousin.*
4 *Idem.*

art" is appropriate only when applied to a work of art in its external aspect. In forming his conception the artist should be guided by the test of "great ideas"; in executing his conception he must be guided by the "rules of art." He, on the one hand, can never be, by the nature of things, so independent of the mass of mankind, as to make artistic excellence his sole object; on the other, moral worth, however distinctive, can never of itself suffice to endow his work with the characteristic charm of art.

Chapter VII

The Exercise of Judgment in Literature

The preceding chapters have contained examples of the points of view from which certain great thinkers, ancient and modern, have looked at literature. These examples show us, to some extent at least, what are the main qualities which criticism teaches us to admire in works already accepted as part of the literary heritage of mankind, and to look for in new works which have not yet won this acceptance.

Broadly speaking, the development of criticism, as shown by a comparison of the writings of critics in different ages, does not consist so much in the recognition of new qualities as in the more complete comprehension, and the more exact definition, of qualities recognized from the very first: and consequently in the application of new and more appropriate tests by which these essential qualities can be detected. As we have already noticed, the three characteristic qualities of literature as a whole are matter, manner, and the quality of giving pleasure. By *matter* is meant the quality of containing "thought," or contributing to the subjective outlook upon the world; by *manner*, the quality of presenting this "thought" by the method appropriate to the special form of literature to which the given work belongs; while, if a work of literature is to give pleasure, we know that it must be possessed of the characteristic power of a work of art, that is to say, it must "appeal to our imagination," or produce in us that "intimate sense of things" which makes poetic truth more convincing—more easily assimilated by the mind—than scientific truth.

Now all of these qualities were discerned from the first moment when men began to regard literature (and the arts) as a separate and distinct field for the exercise of the higher faculties. Plato, for example, was conscious of the existence of all of these qualities, and he selected the conveying of thought, and thought of the best kind, as the most essential and commanding quality of literature as a whole. But the test by which he proposed to measure the existence of this quality was the degree in which the representations of creative literature approached that naked description of reality which is to be found in those forms of literature in which an element of creation does not enter. In other words he proposed to test the truth of a *representation* by a test which is applicable only to an *imitation*. Or, as Aristotle showed, he did not distinguish between the aspects of reality which the poet sought to represent and those which the historian sought to represent—between the truth of feeling and the truth of reason. Aristotle again, perceiving that works of creative literature conveyed information to the mind in a different way from that in which works of history or philosophy did, thought that the best way of measuring this characteristic quality was to observe the different forms in which the poetic compositions of recognized merit were composed. But we now take it for granted that a writer of fiction, either in verse or prose, will adopt the appropriate and necessary form of composition, and we look mainly, though not entirely, at the effect which he has produced by his composition as a whole; and, if we find that his creation possesses the essential quality of appealing to the imagination, we do not trouble ourselves to consider whether in attaining this supreme purpose he has moulded his materials into the precise form of any previously existing model.

If we call the canons which concern such lesser elements as construction of plot, metre, language or diction, and the rest "rules," and those which concern these essential qualities "principles," and thus make a distinction between "rules" and "principles," we can express the change which has taken place in the spirit of criticism by saying that criticism tends in an increasing degree to disregard rules, and to concentrate its attention upon principles. For whereas the application of these rules reveals excellences or defects which vary in importance from one epoch to another, the principles are concerned with qualities of universal importance—that is to say with qualities which are connected with some elementary characteristic of the mind of man. For the appreciation of such qualities is not subject to change under the shifting conditions of human life. The validity of criticism, therefore, depends upon the capacity to distinguish between the permanent elements which are covered by these principles, and the varying elements which are covered by these rules.

The effect of this change is shown in the manner in which the contemporary critic approaches the examination both of works of established reputation and of those new works, the value of which is as yet undetermined. If he concerns himself with the former he does not seek to *estimate* so much as to *interpret*. He does not search for defects or failures—or if he does, it is with a view of bringing the contrasting merits into stronger relief—but he is rather busied with the discovery and explanation of the qualities revealed by the application of tests based upon a recognition of these principles. He is concerned more with the reader than the author; for his chief aim is to make us understand the special conditions of the author's social and material environment, and of his personal endowment, and to show how these determining conditions are reflected in the character of his work. In this way, by putting us in possession of information which enables us to understand the author's motives and points of view, the critic enables us to estimate for ourselves. In a word, criticism as applied to works of this class, has become the interpretation of literature. In approaching the examination of contemporary works, the critic has a more difficult task. He can at best only give a provisionary verdict; but for the formation of this verdict he relies upon tests which are intended to measure the characteristic merits of matter, manner, and the appeal to the imagination,—and puts on one side the rules which deal with technical and less permanent qualities. Of course, there is no question here of the necessity of observing the recognized rules of grammar and prosody. In general, the compositions in which such rules are violated would not come under the category of literature, and would not, therefore, demand the attention of the critic. I say "in general," because it must be remembered that these rules are themselves based upon the observed practice of great writers; and that the source from which they derive their validity is literary usage. A certain latitude, therefore, must be observed in applying them, for the literary usage which made them, can also extend them: and moreover the spirit of the rule may be obeyed when its letter is broken. With this exception, contemporary criticism tends more and more to base its tentative judgments of new works upon such principles, as are intended to reveal the presence or absence of those qualities which past experience has taught us to recognize and admire in previous efforts of human genius. And as we have to read contemporary literature as well as the masterpieces, a knowledge of these principles is necessary to enable us to exercise for ourselves a certain judgment in the selection and appreciation of the books which are every day being offered for our consideration. Such contemporary books have a value and attractiveness of their own, which is independent of their literary merit, strictly so-called. They are instinct with the movement of the life around us; they reflect and even discuss questions, the solution of which has an immediate interest for each and all of us; they are vitalized, at any rate for the moment, by the mere fact that they have come straight from the brain of a neighbour. Moreover, unless it be supposed that the fountain of English literature is being suddenly dried up, it is among these contemporary works of literature that we must look for the masterpieces of the future.

Let us see if we can gather up what we have already learnt about these principles into a statement sufficiently clear to be of practical value in guiding us to form a judgment upon books.

The first principle—first in order of historic evolution and first in importance—is the principle of truth. The characteristic quality, which this principle leads us to expect and require in a work of literature, is the essential correspondence between the body of information which the work conveys to our minds and the external realities, or facts of life, of which it treats. This is the principle of the highest validity, for it serves to test the most important of all the qualities by virtue of which a work of art or literature is felt to be in agreement with the general sense of mankind, and, therefore, accepted as a permanent contribution to the intellectual heritage of man. To contribute a new thought to the world is the highest merit of a work of literature in general, and to contribute this thought in the delightful manner which arises from the appeal to the imagination, is the highest merit of a work of creative literature. Truth, then, is the final test of merit in literature: for if we had to choose between the sacrifice of matter or of manner, we should prefer to lose the latter. For a work which has no correspondence with the facts of life—or which violates any of the universal and fundamental beliefs of mankind—is worthless, however great its purely artistic qualities may be.

But the truth which is required in literature is "essential" truth. That is to say, the nature of the correspondence between the matter of the book and the reality to which it refers will vary in the different forms of literature. And in order to ascertain the presence of this correspondence the test of truth must be applied in the varying degrees appropriate to the several forms. The truth which we expect from the philosopher, the historian, or the biographer, is the actual fact, the "whole truth and nothing but the truth" of a witness giving evidence in a court of law, an entire statement of the necessary facts which is obscured neither by a *suppressio veri* nor a *suggestio falsi*. Perfect candour in the presentation of the sources of information, perfect accuracy in dates, figures, and in the sequence of events or the marshalling of facts, absolute impartiality of opinion where there is a conflict of evidence. From the essayist, the descriptive writer, and the traveller, we require a less rigorous reproduction of the facts which form the foundation of his opinions, or of his pictures of men and places. For here the personal element is more pronounced, and the process of idealization converts his rendering of the facts into representations rather than mere descriptions. That is to say, he tells us not so much what he saw or learnt, but the thoughts and feelings which the scenes of natural objects, or his contact with other men, produced in his mind. And it may well be that he can give us a more real, and therefore more truthful picture of men and manners, and even of natural scenery, by a free use of the idealistic method of art; by selecting certain features for prominent treatment, by subordinating, or even omitting, details which he considers likely to weaken the total effect which he desires to produce in our minds.

Again, there is the truth which we require in creative literature, whether fiction or poetry. This is the truth of art, for the character and events of the poet and novelist are typical, not actual. The scenes which the poet (or novelist) describes, and the characters which he draws, have no existing originals. The originals are the creations of his mind, as well as the representations, and the proper truth which belongs to fiction is the truth of idea; that is to say, the generalized experience of the individual author must correspond to the generalized experience of the community or of the race. To take examples,

"Middlemarch" is not Nuneaton, nor is "Maggie Tulliver" Mary Ann Evans in her girlhood; but if we wanted to get an idea of what life in a Midland town was like, or an idea of the sort of girl that "George Eliot" must have been, where could we get them better than by reading the novels in which the accounts of Middlemarch and of Maggie Tulliver respectively occur? Here are examples of the generalized experience of an individual producing the truth of idea. For no one could fail to recognize the essential correspondence between the descriptions and characters of "George Eliot," and the generalized realities and facts, upon which they are based. Even higher and more permanent is the essential truth of those creations which are based upon a mingling of personal experience and of that universal experience which is embodied in the spiritual traditions of the race. If we wish to "get an idea" of the supreme devotion which is produced by the passion of love, we do not think of the engagement and marriage of one of our acquaintances, but of the story of "Romeo and Juliet"; our idea of devotion to a woman's ideal of duty is based upon the conduct of the Antigone of Sophocles; our idea of knightly duty upon the Arthur of the "Idylls of the King." The truth of idea which is thus attained in the works of the great poetic masters is in a certain sense superior to the truth of history or biography, or of any mere transcript from reality. Its superiority is due to the fact that the conceptions which it embodies are based upon the generalized experience of more than one age, and of more than one country; that, in fact, it epitomizes the experience of the race. And so, as Aristotle says, "poetry has a wider truth and a higher aim than history; for poetry deals rather with the universal, history with the particular." Or it becomes, as Wordsworth says, "the breath and finer spirit of knowledge."

This truth of idea which we require in a work of creative literature, whether in prose or verse, is in its essence an agreement between the opinions and feelings of the poet or novelist and the general sense of mankind. And since the general sense of mankind on matters of the highest importance is embodied in the code of social laws, the observance of which is called "morality," it follows that the connection between the highest and best creative work and morality is by no means an artificial connection. The morality of one country or of one society differs in certain respects from that of another; the morality of the West is markedly different from the morality of the East: but notwithstanding these differences there are certain principles which—as principles—are universally accepted by all civilized societies. A novel or poem which represents that an immoral man (in this sense) is happier than a moral man, does not possess the truth of idea which is the proper truth of creative literature; for the experience which the author has embodied in his creation does not correspond with the generalized experience of the race as expressed in the laws of morality. Such works, therefore, are condemned by an application of this principle of truth. As morality is the aggregate experience of a given society, or of society in general, the matter of books which are in conflict with morality is *ex hypothesi* condemned by this supreme test of truth.

Secondly, there is the principle of symmetry. It is the adaptation of the external qualities of the given work to the special purpose which it is intended to achieve. As applied to the arts in general it enjoins and requires that the artist should in each case both select such attributes of reality as can be best reproduced by the means at the disposal of his special art, and also confine himself to the employment of these appropriate means in reproducing these aspects. From this external point of view, symmetry is resolved into "composition," or the right selection and the right disposition of materials. As applied to literature, the principle has a twofold significance. In the first place, it applies to literature as a whole; in the second, in addition to this general application, it applies in a special sense to creative literature where the method of artistic representation is employed. In the first case, it requires that the external qualities of literary compositions, *i.e.*, *length* of composition and *form* of composition (prose or verse, narrative, dialogue, or union of narrative and dialogue), should be suitable to the subject matter of which these compositions severally treat. That is a comparatively simple and obvious requirement: for,— to take two extreme instances—a historian, having a great mass of facts to set out, would naturally choose the narrative form, and write in easy prose unfettered by metre, or by any structural limitation of length; while the poet, when he wishes to give expression to a single thought, just as naturally selects a rigidly limited poetic form, such as the sonnet, where he can endow a dozen lines with so much beauty of literary workmanship that his single thought shines like a jewel in an exquisite setting. In this sense, the principle of symmetry applies to all literature, however humble its purpose or form may be. Even a manual of history or science requires to be written with a certain regard for arrangement; that is to say, the subject should be presented as a whole, the facts must be marshalled in their due order, what is essential must be brought into prominence, what is merely accessory must be kept in due subordination.

In the second sense the principle of symmetry applies to creative literature only, since such literature alone employs the method of art in its representations of reality. Here the principle enjoins not merely that the given work should be composed in a manner consistent with the external requirements of the form of poetic literature to which it belongs, but that the limitations imposed upon the artist by the medium in which his creations are expressed should be respected. This medium is, briefly, word-symbols, written or spoken, and capable of expressing the attribute of time by the sequence in which they are presented to eye or ear. Thus understood, the principle of symmetry requires that the artist in words should select for representation certain definite aspects of reality, and not all reality. If therefore a poetic composition is to possess the quality of symmetry, it must, first, be limited as a whole to the presentation of these appropriate aspects of the general mass of the reality—objective or subjective—on which it is based, and, second, in the several elements of dialogue, narrative, description, and soliloquy, the medium of words must be used only to represent such aspects in the respective objects, actions, states of mind, or scenes of material reality to which these elements severally refer, as can be appropriately reproduced by words regarded not as a means of conveying thought, but as a means of presenting mental pictures—that is of appealing to the imagination. The rules which limit and control the artist in words in the use of his medium have been sketched in outline by Aristotle in the *Poetics*, and this outline has been filled in with detail by the fuller researches of Lessing in his study of the respective methods of the contrasting arts of the "eye" and "ear". As I have already pointed out this principle is made by Aristotle the chief measure of the merit of creative literature: and in taking the tragedy as the most highly developed form of such literature, he naturally insists upon the doctrine of the supremacy of the plot. For in the stage play, and to a scarcely less degree in the novel, it is in the construction of the plot that the widest scope is given to the artist in words for the manifestation of both excellence and deficiency of composition. And so he writes from this standpoint of symmetry, that the plot is "the central principle and soul, so to speak, of tragedy; character is second in importance." And with Aristotle the construction of the plot includes both the selection of suitable materials, and the effective arrangement of these materials by investing the central action with a distinctive prominence, and by keeping the "episodes" in due subordination to this central action, while at the same time they are directly ancillary to it. But whereas Aristotle deals with the symmetry, or correct disposition, of the work as a whole, Lessing tells us how to apply the principle to its separate elements: not how to compose a plot, but how to compose a description of a person, an object, an action, or a scene. Some of the most striking results of Lessing's inquiry have been already set out in Chapter V, and they need not, therefore, be repeated here. They are summed up in Mr Meredith's notable sentence, "The art of the pen is to rouse the inward vision . . . because our flying minds cannot contain a protracted description. The Shakespearian, the Dantesque [pictures], are in a line, two at most." But it will be useful to add the account of character drawing which Sir Walter Besant gives in his "Art of Fiction." It is written in a practical spirit and relates primarily to prose fiction.

"As for the methods of conveying a clear understanding of a character, they are many. The first and the easiest is to make it clear by reason of some mannerism or personal peculiarity, some trick of speech or of carriage. This is the worst, as may generally be said of the easiest way. Another easy method is to describe your character at length. This also is a bad, because a tedious, method. If, however, you read a page or two of any good writer, you will discover that he first makes a character intelligible by a few words, and then allows him to reveal himself in action and dialogue. On the other hand, nothing is more inartistic than to be constantly calling attention in a dialogue to a gesture or a look, to laughter or to tears. The situation generally requires no such explanation: in some well-known scenes which I could quote, there is not a single word to emphasize or explain the attitude, manner, and look of the speakers, yet they are as intelligible as if they were written down and described. That is the highest art which carries the reader along, and makes him see without being told, the changing expressions, the gestures of the speakers, and hear the varying tones of their voices. It is as if one should close one's eyes at the theatre, and yet continue to see the actors on the stage as well as hear their voices. The only writer who can do this is he who makes his characters intelligible from the very outset, causes them first to stand before the reader in clear outline, and then with every additional line brings out the figure, fills up the face, and makes his creatures grow from the simple outline more and more to the perfect and rounded figure."

Only such works, therefore, as are possessed of this quality of symmetry—that is to say, in which the materials are so disposed and arranged both in the mass and in detail as to catch the "flying mind"—can appeal to the imagination. And so the test of symmetry is indirectly a means by which the presence of this dominant artistic quality can be discovered and measured in a work of literature.

Thirdly there is the principle of idealization. This is a principle which applies only to creative literature, that is to say to such works of literature as are also works of art; which, therefore, must possess that characteristic quality of a work of art which we call from a subjective point of view, "to give pleasure," and from an objective point of view, "beauty." As applied to creative literature this principle enjoins and requires not merely that the mental aspect of reality should be presented by the author, but that a selection from this mental aspect of reality should first be made, and that the selection so made should exclude such matter as affects unpleasantly the aesthetic consciousness of the reader. "Whatever feelings," Victor Cousin writes, "art proposes to excite in us, they ought always to be restrained and governed by the feeling of beauty. If it produces only pity or terror beyond a certain limit, above all physical pity or terror, it revolts, it ceases to charm; it misses its proper effect, for an effect which is foreign to it and vulgar." It is only by reference to this principle that we can attach a definite significance to the terms "realism" and "realistic" as applied to works of creative literature (and of art in general). No work of creative literature can be "realistic" in the sense that the author has reproduced reality and not the mental aspect of reality: for if the author had attempted to do this his composition would not be a work of creative literature at all. If it is used as a term of reproach, the word can only be properly applied to the work of an author who has so far neglected to select his material—to idealize in fact—that his work has lost the quality of giving pleasure. As, however, this quality of giving pleasure obviously depends upon the nature and character of the individual reader, as much as on the nature and character of the book, the term cannot be used with any precision unless we credit the individual whom the given work fails to please with an average degree of artistic and moral perception. And, since the latter—moral perception—is the more commonly developed, the term has come to bear a significance which is almost equivalent to "immoral," or repugnant to the general sense of mankind. But in thus using the term it is necessary not to forget that its original and wider significance is different. In its wider significance it characterizes any work of literature (or art) in which the author (or artist) has reproduced any subject, or any aspect of a subject, which lessens or removes that "beauty" by virtue of which a work of art gives pleasure.

The most prominent application of the principle of idealization is the doctrine of "poetic justice." According to this doctrine the plot of a work of creative literature should, with the sole exception of the tragedy, "end happily," and so give expression to the deeply rooted sentiment of optimism, which results from the belief that the universe is governed and controlled by an all-powerful and all-wise Being. In a clear and splendid statement of the principle of idealization as applied to creative literature, Bacon gives us the philosophic basis upon which this doctrine—the propounding of successes and issues of actions more just in retribution and more in accordance with divine Providence—rests.

"Poetry . . . is nothing else but Feigned History, which may be styled as well in prose as in verse. The use of this feigned history hath been to give some shadow of satisfaction to the mind of men in those points wherein the nature of things doth deny it; the world being in proportion inferior to the soul; by reason whereof there is, agreeable to the spirit of man, a more ample greatness, a more exact goodness, and a more absolute variety, than can be found in the nature of things. Therefore, because the acts and events of true history have not that magnitude which satisfyeth the mind of man, poetry feigneth acts and events greater and more heroical. Because history propoundeth the successes and issues of action not so agreeable to the merits of virtue and vice, therefore poesy feigns them more just in retribution and more according to revealed providence. Because true history representeth actions and events more ordinary and less interchanged, therefore poesy endureth them with more rareness, and more unexpected and alternative variations. So as it appeareth that poesy serveth and conferreth to magnanimity, morality, and to delectation. And therefore it was ever thought to have some participation of divineness, because it doth raise and erect the mind by submitting the shows of things to the desires of the mind, whereas reason doth buckle and bow the mind into the nature of things. And we see that by these insinuations and congruities with man's nature and pleasure, joined also with the agreement and consort it hath with music, it hath had access and estimation in rude times and barbarous regions, where other learning stood excluded."[1]

---

1 *Advancement of Learning*, Book II, iv.1-2.

It will be noticed that the tragedy is excepted from that application of the doctrine of poetic justice, which justifies, and, in general, requires that the plot of a work of creative literature should be so constructed as to finally convey a sense of satisfaction to the mind. The reason is this. The tragedy is a special form of creative literature which depends for its effect mainly, though not entirely, upon *pathos*, or the presentation of human suffering in an acute form. Here the poetic representation is intended to work upon the passions of "fear and pity," to use the terms of Aristotle's definition, and the most powerful means by which this effect can be achieved is to so construct the plot that it ends in a "disaster." For it is by the presentation of a final picture of universal gloom, into which no ray of hope is allowed to penetrate, that the dramatic artist produces that artificial excitation of the emotions of the spectator, to which the special and humanizing effect of tragedy is due. In other words, whereas the termination of the plot in a disaster is essential to tragedy, it is merely incidental to any other form of creative literature: and it is only in such poems or novels as are designedly tragic in motive that the final disaster is necessary. In all others—that is in the general mass of fictions in prose or verse—the natural optimism of healthy humanity can be legitimately satisfied. Indeed, the effect of artistic beauty which belongs to creative literature is in part directly due to this characteristic application of the principle of idealization.[1]

---

1 Since writing the above it has been pointed out to me that there was a further and non-artistic reason for the prominence of the "disaster" in the plot of tragedy. The religious motive of sacrifice is present in the Greek tragedy; and where sacrifice or atonement must be made for sin, even the innocent must be involved in disaster.

There is, however, a limit to idealization. The principle is itself controlled by the operation of the test of truth, which is the supreme and final test of merit in literature whether creative or non-creative. But it is necessary in estimating the effect of this limit upon creative literature, to remember that the truth of creative literature is the truth of idea, not the truth of logic. Realistic treatment, —that is, realism in the acquired sense of the presentation of subjects, or aspects of subjects, repugnant to the moral sense—is sometimes defended on the ground of its superior truth. Art, it is said, has outgrown the stage of the fairy-tale: adult art should present things as they really are. But this argument admits of a very definite answer. The kind of truth which is here required is not the kind of truth that a work of art can yield. For this kind of truth—the truth of science—we must go not to a novel, or a poem, but to a treatise on politics or economics—to the blue-book or the criminal reports. Nevertheless, there is a real and genuine sense in which the principle of truth limits the application of the principle of idealization. When the poet or novelist represents his character as surrounded by the conditions of real life, and, at the same time, as able to act ideally, his presentation is deficient in truth. For the idea so presented is essentially false. Similarly, if he represents his men and women as acting as they would in real life, while the conditions by which they are surrounded are plainly ideal, the idea which he presents is one which has no correspondence with reality. Such works have neither the truth of science nor the truth of art. What is ideal is false because it is made to look as though it were real, what is real is false because it is offered to the reader in the form of the ideal. In short, the whole picture of life is distorted. A work of creative literature cannot be made to present the facts of life in the sense in which these facts are presented in history, biography, or in a scientific or philosophic treatise: if the attempt is made, such a work ceases *ipso facto* to be "creative," and it loses forthwith the characteristic beauty of a work of art. On the other hand the principle of truth controls the application of the idealizing process in two ways. It requires that the idealization shall be consistently applied throughout—otherwise the work will convey a distorted and therefore untruthful idea of the realities upon which it is based; and it requires that the idealization shall be itself guided by that wide and yet exact knowledge of men and things which is expressed by the term "philosophy." If there is no such basis of wide and exact knowledge to guide the artist in the formation of his mental originals, the characters and scenes which he presents will bear no resemblance to the realities which these mental originals are intended to interpret and explain. The effect of such idealization, uncontrolled by the principle of truth, is to be observed especially in prose-fiction. In the words of Mr Meredith, the art of Fiction under this influence has become "a pasture of idiots, a method for idiotizing the entire population." The ideal of character which it presents is a "flattering familiar," which has become "the most dangerous of delusions." It is only when the novelist has learnt to control his idealizations by the principle of truth, to mould his mental originals into the forms in which philosophy teaches him to express the essential facts of life, that the art "now neither blushless infant nor executive man," can attain its full stature. And he exhibits with perfect felicity the limit to idealization which is set by the principle of truth in respect of that dominant form of creative literature of which he is the greatest living master.

"We can then," he says, "be veraciously historical, honestly transcriptive. Rose-pink and dirty drab will alike have passed away. Philosophy is the foe of both, and their silly cancelling contest, perpetually renewed in a shuffle of extremes, as it always is where a phantom falseness reigns, will no longer baffle the contemplation of natural flesh, smother no longer the soul issuing out of our incessant strife. Philosophy bids us see that we are not so pretty as rose-pink, not so repulsive as dirty drab; and that, instead of everlastingly shifting those barren aspects, the sight of ourselves is wholesome, bearable, fructifying, finally a delight."[1] But the knowledge of the qualities which contribute to excellence in literature, and of the principles which alike require their presence and control the method of their production, is not in itself sufficient to enable us to exercise a correct judgment, to recognize merit and detect deficiency in works of literature. In order to do this we require something further: we must know how to apply these principles to the works we read. Truth is the test which reveals excellence of matter, symmetry is the test which reveals excellence of manner, beauty is the test which reveals the due exercise of the power of idealization. But how can we apply these several tests to any given work? There is only one answer that can be given, and it has been given more than once. The method by which these tests, and the principles which support them, can be applied is *comparison*. Assume that we know not merely that we should look for truth in any given work, but also the sort of truth for which we should look—that is to say, the truth of logic, if the work be non-creative, the

---

[1] *Diana of the Crossways.*

truth of art, if it be creative, —if, then, we would ascertain the extent to which the work in question possesses this quality, we must compare it with a work of recognized merit—a masterpiece, or a "classic" as we say—in the same department of literature. Gradually by the study of the best work which has been produced in the several departments of literature, our minds will become so familiarized with the several and characteristic excellences of each, that we shall almost instinctively welcome their presence, and resent their absence. Literary taste, Addison says, is the faculty "which discerns the beauties of an author with pleasure and the imperfections with dislike. If a man would know whether he is possessed of this faculty, I would have him read over the celebrated works of Antiquity which have stood the test of so many different ages and countries." [1] And Arnold gives the same advice. If we are to learn to detect the distinctive accent of poetry of the highest class, the high seriousness of absolute sincerity, we must fill our minds with the beauty and the music of the masters—Homer, Dante, Shakespeare, Milton. We must keep in our minds "lines and expressions of the great masters, and apply them as a touchstone to other poetry." A few such lines, he adds, "if we have tact and can use them, are enough even of themselves to keep clear and sound our judgments about poetry, to save us from fallacious estimates of it, to conduct us to a real estimate."[2]

It is by the study of the masters that "taste" is formed in literature as in

---

[1] *Spectator* No. 409.

[2] *Essays in Criticism* II. (The Study of Poetry).

art. And by using our knowledge of the work of the masters as a "touchstone"—or more correctly, as Mr Dowden has pointed out, as a "tuning-fork"—we can decide on the general character of any new and unrecognized work. But if we wish to add precision to this general estimate, we must proceed to apply our tests by a more searching and exact comparison, or rather series of comparisons. There are certain passages or scenes which are admitted by common consent to be of transcendent excellence in each branch of literature, and there are other passages in recognized authors which each one discovers and cherishes, because they appeal in a special degree to his own mind. If we desire to estimate the merit of a new work more exactly, we must select a given passage or scene (or several passages or scenes) and compare it with one of these standard passages; taking care, of course, that it is one in which the subject admits of identical treatment, and that, therefore, it affords a fair basis of comparison. In plain words, if we wish to know how X has succeeded, we compare his work with the work of the same kind which A, B, and C have done, and admittedly done well. To give definition to this statement let me take one or two examples from prose fiction.

At first sight, a farmer's walk to church with his family would seem to be a very unpromising subject for artistic treatment. But if we want to know how this or any similar scene can be done, and well done, we have only to read the first half of Chapter xviii in *Adam Bede*. "George Eliot" knew the difficulty of investing so commonplace a subject with artistic, grace and philosophic sense, for she tells us as much in the previous chapter: but she succeeded. And we are not surprised to learn—as we do from her diary—that when she read the MS. to George Henry Lewis he was "much pleased." Here, then, is a "standard" passage. If we come across a description of a like subject in a new work, and wish to measure the success which the author has attained, we have only to place the two passages side by side, and read first one and then the other. Or, again, to take an example of a different subject. Most novelists, when they have brought their hero and heroine to the point of a declaration of love, evade the inherent difficulty of describing actions and speeches which are meaningless or ridiculous when separated from the background of intense emotion by which they are accompanied in real life. They generally leave us, therefore, to ourselves, to imagine the scene, or tell us that what took place concerns nobody but the lovers themselves, and would have no interest for the reader. Nevertheless, Mr Meredith in his "Ferdinand and Miranda" chapter of *The Ordeal of Richard Feverel* not only tells us every word that Richard and Lucy spoke when they met "amid the breath and beauty of wild flowers," but he creates in the mind of the reader such a sense of external beauty, and such an atmosphere of vibrating emotion, that each simple speech and act is welcome, significant, and beautiful. To realize the full meaning of this supreme exhibition of Mr Meredith's art, we should compare this chapter with the corresponding scene in *Romeo and Juliet*. This comparison will serve to bring out the essential agreement in the general method of these great artists in words, and, at the same time, those differences of treatment and thought which naturally result from a difference of literary medium and of mental and social environment.

In both play and novel there is the same love at first sight, the same opposition from parents and kinsfolk making the concentration of the lovers in themselves—*the égoism à deux*—absolute and supreme. In both a brief realization of happiness is followed by separation, and in both alike the final catastrophe is complete and overwhelming, although it arises in each case out of the merest malignity of fate. In the play, Juliet's bearing is the bearing of a woman of the Elizabethan age; her words are direct and outspoken. In the novel, Lucy Desborough's feelings are wrapped in the reserve of a nineteenth century heroine, and her broken speeches convey her meaning by allusion and half thought.

> "O, gentle Romeo,
>
> If thou dost love, pronounce it faithfully;
>
> Or if thou thinkest I am too quickly won,
>
> I'll frown and be perverse, and say thee nay,
>
> So thou wilt woo; but else, not for the world.
>
> In truth, fair Montague, I am too fond;
>
> And therefore thou may'st think my 'haviour light:
>
> But, trust me, gentleman, I'll prove more true
>
> Than those who have more cunning to be strange."

Contrast this frank speech with the dialogue in which Lucy admits her love for Richard, as he holds her hand in his.

" 'You will not go ? '

" 'Pray let me,' she pleaded, her sweet brows suing in wrinkles.

" 'You will not go ? ' Mechanically he drew the white hand nearer his thumping heart.

" 'I must,' she faltered, piteously.

" 'You will not go?'

" 'Oh yes ! yes !'

" 'Tell me. Do you wish to go?'

"The question was subtle. A moment or two she did not answer, and then foreswore herself, and said, 'Yes.'

" 'Do you—do you wish to go?' He looked with quivering eyelids under hers.

"A fainter yes responded to his passionate repetition.

" 'You wish—wish to leave me?' His breath went with the words.

" 'Indeed I must.' . . ."

Then finally she returns.

" 'I think it was rude of me to go without thanking you again.' she said, and again proffered her hand. And so she left him, and . . . The sweet heaven-bird shivered out his song above him. The gracious glory of heaven fell upon his soul. He touched her hand, not moving his eyes from her nor speaking; and she, with a soft word of farewell, passed across the stile and up the pathway, through the dewy shades of the copse, and out of the arch of light, away from his eyes."

These examples have been taken from prose-fiction, a branch of literature which is probably most familiar. But they will, I hope, serve to show how general tests and principles can be applied by similar comparisons in all fields of literature.

Chapter VIII

Forms of Literature—Classical and Romantic Methods—Style

First in order both of artistic merit and literary evolution is Poetry, or creative literature in metre.

The arrangement of words in combinations which possess a more or less vivid musical expression can be traced to a primitive impulse in man. The nature of this impulse in its connection with poetry is well set out by Emerson.

"We are lovers of rhyme and return, period and musical reflection. The babe is lulled to sleep by the nurse's song. Sailors can work better for their *yo-heave-o*. Soldiers can march better and fight better for the drum and trumpet. Metre begins with pulse-beat, and the length of lines in songs and poems is determined by the inhalation and exhalation of the lungs. If you hum or whistle the rhythm of the common English metres,—of the decasyllabic quatrain, or the octosyllabic with alternate sexsyllabic, or other rhythms, you can easily believe these metres to be organic, derived from the human pulse, and to be therefore not proper to one nation, but to mankind. I think you will also find a charm, heroic, plaintive, pathetic, in these cadences, and be at once set on searching for the words that can rightly fill these vacant beats. Young people like rhyme, drum-beat, tune, things in pairs and alternatives; and, in higher degrees, we know the instant power of music upon our temperament to change our mood and give us its own: and human passion, seizing these constitutional tunes, aims to fill them with appropriate words, or marry music to thought, believing, as we believe of all marriage, that matches are made in heaven, and that for every thought its proper melody or rhyme exists, though the odds are immense against our finding it, and only genius can rightly say the banns."[1]

The best division of the several forms of poetry (*i.e.* poetry in verse) is that adopted by the Greeks. Under this system of classification the following chief forms are distinguished—Epic or Narrative, Lyric, Elegiac and Dramatic.

The first of these, Epic, or Story-telling in verse (ἔπος, word; ἐπή, word-poetry), is the longest form of composition in metre. In addition to the narrative in which the poet speaks in his own person, telling the story to the reader—or to the audience to whom such works were originally recited, or chanted with a musical accompaniment—it has a large element of dialogue, in which the poet speaks through the persons of his characters. As compared with a drama an epic possesses two advantages. In the first place, the period of the action is practically unlimited, and, besides the fact that the main action can cover more time, it admits of a greater number of episodes, or subsidiary stories, and of the treatment of these episodes at greater length; and in the

---

[1] *Poetry and Imagination.*

second, a greater element of marvel can be introduced, since the actors or events represented are not subjected to the scrutiny of the sense of sight, as is the case when the scenes and actors are before us on the stage. In other words, the poet can use his imagination with greater freedom in an epic than in a drama; and, in point of fact, many of the subjects of great epics are obviously supernormal, and many of the characters and incidents are supernatural. On the other hand, the composition of this form of poetry is characterized by an essential difficulty which makes its successful execution exceedingly rare. Its form is so great that it requires a vast volume of thought, and thought of the highest kind, to endow it with dignity, and a genuine and powerful source of inspiration to endow it with life. Properly it should sum up the thought of an epoch or give expression to the aspirations of a people; and that is why in the nature of things the great epics can almost be counted upon the fingers of two hands: —the Hindu epics, the *Ramāyāna* and the *Mahābhārata*, the Iliad and Odyssey, the *De Natura* of Lucretius, the Aeneid, the *Niebelungen Lied*, the *Inferno*, and Paradise Lost. And of these, some are the work of more than one mind and perhaps of more than one generation.

Lyric poetry, as the name implies (λύρα, lyre; μέλη, song-poetry) is poetry originally intended to be accompanied by the lyre or by some other instrument of music. The term has come to signify any outburst in song which is composed under a strong impulse of emotion or inspiration. The last stanza of Shelley's lyric *To a Skylark* illustrates the complete fusion of personality and subject which characterizes such poetry.

Higher still and higher

From the earth thou springest:

Like a cloud of fire,

The blue deep thou wingest.

And singing still dost soar, and soaring ever singest.

*   *   *   *   *   *   *

Teach me half the gladness

That thy brain must know;

Such harmonious madness

From my lips would flow

The world should listen then as I am listening now.

Elegiac poetry (ἔλεγος, a mourning song) is composed under deep feeling, but in a different mood. It is reflective rather than impulsive, and as such it is marked by a note of seriousness, often of melancholy. Gray's *Elegy written in a Country Churchyard* is a familiar and exquisite example.

The boast of heraldry, the pomp of power,

And all that beauty, all that wealth e'er gave,

Await alike th' inevitable hour,

The paths of Glory lead but to the grave.

*   *   *   *   *   *   *

Perhaps in this neglected spot is laid

Some heart once pregnant with celestial fire;

> Hands, that the rod of Empire might have sway'd,
> Or wak'd to ecstasy the living lyre:
> But knowledge to their eyes her ample page,
> Rich with the spoils of Time, did ne'er unroll;
> While penury repress'd their noble rage,
> And froze the genial current of the soul.

Dramatic poetry (δρᾶμα, act, stage-play) is poetry composed for the purpose of stage-representation, or written in the form of poetry so composed. As every line is intended to be spoken by one or other of the actors who take the parts respectively assigned to the several characters, there is no direct narrative and no direct reflection. I say no "direct" narrative or reflection, because both these elements are to some extent retained by various devices. In the Greek drama, for example, the epic element of story telling was retained in part by means of the ἄγγελος, or messenger— a character into whose mouth long accounts of events outside the immediate action of the play were put. And at the same time the element of "reflection" was provided by the chorus, whose function it was to express in their songs and chants such feelings and reflections upon the events represented on the stage, as the poet would have uttered directly in a lyric or elegiac outburst of song. The Greek drama as a literary composition, was, therefore, a union of the epic and lyric forms of poetry. In the modern drama, both the narrative and reflective element have been curtailed, but the essential elements of plot and dialogue (or the plot expressed in dialogue) have been correspondingly enlarged and developed.

Dramatic literature is divided by a broad line of demarkation into Tragedy and Comedy. The characteristic motive of tragedy is the exhibition of man in unsuccessful conflict with circumstances. In the Attic Tragedy the apparently undeserved disaster which thus overwhelms the man of average morality is explained by the doctrine of *Nemesis*, or inherited curse: that is to say the man himself has not deserved the punishment, but he is punished for the sins of his fathers. In this doctrine the existence of evil is sought to be explained in a manner identical with the declaration of the second Commandment, and in harmony with the general purport of the Jewish and Christian theology. In the Elizabethan drama this undeserved suffering is rather connected with contemporary circumstances; and in the novels of "George Eliot," which were written in respect of their philosophic basis under the influence of the leaders of the positivist school of thought, the same problem is presented in close connection with the scientific principle of heredity, or the transmission of physical and mental defects from parent to child.

In comedy the motive is furnished by the same conflict viewed from an opposite point of view. In unexpected and even in undeserved suffering, provided that it is not so acute as to actively enlist our sympathy, there is an element of satisfaction which arises from the contrast thus presented between our own good fortune and the bad fortune of our neighbours. If a man's hat is blown off by a high wind, and we see him chasing it, or if a passenger arrives on the platform breathless and excited, only to see the train steam out of the station, we laugh: for these are such slight disasters that our perception of the comic element is unrestrained. But if the same person, instead of losing his hat, were to be run over by an omnibus, the sight of his suffering would at once command our sympathy, and instead of mirth an instant sensation of pain and alarm would arise in our minds: for this would be not comic but tragic. Further, if the person to whom the unexpected disaster happens is an evil character, or a character possessed of anti-social qualities, a sense of satisfaction, or even of downright pleasure, will arise in our minds, even if the disaster be one that is really serious. But this disaster, if it is to be comic, must not involve the sight of actual physical pain, for a spectacle of human suffering in this extreme form will always provoke a sense of horror, unless, indeed, the nature of the spectator be exceedingly hardened, or the circumstances are altogether abnormal. The central motive of comedy is, therefore, to present an exhibition of the irony of circumstances, and the effect which it seeks to produce upon the mind of the spectator is admittedly one of complete satisfaction. It shows him that a great deal of the suffering which he sees around him is deserved—for one of the legitimate motives of comedy is to satirize, or exhibit the ugliness of vice, the ludicrousness of pride based upon conventional distinctions, and the unhappiness of excessive self-regard—and by teaching him to view his own misfortunes as part of the general life of the community, and to himself look upon them from the point of view from which he would look upon the same misfortunes in others, reveals to him the fact that there is a "light side" to the darkest events.

But the drama, that is the representation of a tragedy or comedy in the theatre, includes two further elements besides the literary element—the actual composition in words —with which we are here concerned. These two elements are the interpretation of the words by the intonation, acts, and gestures of the actor, and the representation of the scenery by the various resources, artistic and scientific, which are placed at the disposal of the stage manager. The drama is, therefore, a composite art, in which the author, the actor and the stage manager all combine to produce the total effect: and as the line of development of this art has been rather in the direction of the perfecting of scenic accessories, the importance of the literary element has tended to decline in the modern drama. The greater convenience of prose as a literary medium, and the closer resemblance of speeches in prose to the practice of real life, has caused contemporary dramatic writers generally to abandon the more rigid poetic forms in which the dramatic masterpieces of the poet have been mainly, though by no means exclusively, composed. Moreover, poetry (strictly so-called) has tended to become reflective rather than dramatic, and prose fiction has now become the great literary vehicle for the presentation of idealized human action. But while the poets' contribution to the drama has declined, the drama itself, regarded as a composite art, has advanced. It has advanced by virtue of an enlightened realism which is manifested in the assimilation of its literary medium to the language of every-day life, in an increased "naturalness" in the actor—due to closer and more intelligent methods of study—and in a gradual approach to complete "illusion" in the *mise en scène* by virtue of a higher regard for historic accuracy and a more complete command of mechanical contrivances.

Creative Literature in Prose.—The dominant and familiar form is the "novel." It is an imagined picture of a man and woman in the spring-time of life, in which the love interest is supreme; and the traditionary plot leads the hero and heroine to the point of union in spite of the malignity of fortune, or the opposition of kinsfolk, in illustration of the line;—

"The course of true love never did run smooth."

In the "romance" the motive of "adventure" is mingled with that of love, and sometimes altogether takes its place. Often, too, the atmosphere is frankly unreal, and supernormal or supernatural incidents and characters are introduced. Where a serious meaning is conveyed by fictions which are otherwise purely imaginative in character and incident, we get the allegory, and the satire. Of this class of fictions "Don Quixote," "The Pilgrim's Progress," and "Gulliver's Travels" are familiar examples.

In addition to these, there is a third class of novels which possesses characteristics sufficiently well-marked to be distinguished. It is the novel of "local colour." In it the author uses a thin thread of plot to connect what are practically a series of descriptions in which the natural scenery of a given locality, or the salient features of a particular community, are faithfully drawn. Such novels have a value of their own, although they stand to the higher fiction somewhat in the relationship of the photograph to the painting.

The novel has undergone a remarkable development in the nineteenth century. The general result of this development is expressed by saying that fiction has become philosophic. That is to say, writers of the higher fiction have learnt to base both the development of their plot and the evolution of each separate character, upon principles revealed by the scientific study of the processes of the human mind and the ascertained phenomena of racial and individual evolution. In this way the writer of prose fiction unites the results of the generalized experience of the race with those of his own individual observation of the men and women of his own generation. In thus approaching the study of society from an internal, as well as an external, point of view, he is enabled to present studies of life and analyses of character and motive that are intelligible, and therefore interesting, to the men and women of more than one generation and of more than one country.

Fiction, as thus developed, has become a literary vehicle of extreme importance. To some extent it has usurped the function of the stage as the medium for the exhibition of pictures of life by the display of imagined characters in action. This aspect of fiction is well indicated by the picturesque phrase which has been used to describe the novel—a "pocket theatre." At the same time novels are so widely read that it is impossible not to recognize in them one of the greatest— perhaps the greatest—educational force in literature. Under these circumstances it is not surprising that some of the greatest minds of the century should have adopted this form of literature as the vehicle of their thought. Count Tolstoy in Russia, M. Émile Zola in France, and Mr George Meredith in England, are instances which at once occur of great thinkers, who have definitely contributed to the thought of the century by means of this vehicle.

As a form of literature the novel unites the facts of history and philosophy, and the reflections of the essay, with the element of creation essential to all poetic literature, on a basis of plot, or interwoven action; and while it lacks the music and the structural perfection of compositions in verse, it has the increased precision of prose and complete freedom from the rigid limitations incidental to such structural perfection.

History and Biography.—The characteristic merits of these branches of literature have already been indicated in the remarks which have been made on the principle of "truth." The quality of first importance which such works must possess, if they are to be of permanent value, is the impartiality which results from a natural or an acquired capacity to weigh evidence, united with the power of distinguishing what is essential from what is merely accidental in the mass of material upon which the historian or the biographer respectively bases his narrative. It is by virtue of this impartiality and the exercise of a judicious selection that the essential facts can be disentangled. It then remains to present the facts thus disentangled to the reader in the most effective manner. For this purpose it is necessary to compose descriptions of the several states of society, and of the several localities which form the setting of the chief scenes and incidents in the narrative. In the case of the latter— descriptions of localities— it is generally recognized that the writer should make himself acquainted with the localities in question by personal study conducted upon the spot. And when the events narrated belong to the past, a valuable auxiliary is provided by the historical remains, the inscriptions and the antiquities, which throw light upon them. It is to the extended use of such elements that the greater vitality and picturesqueness which marks the best work of contemporary historians is chiefly due.

While the historian tells the story of the life of a people —or of a single period in that life—the biographer treats of a single individual. If, therefore, the necessary allowance is made for the changes of treatment which naturally arise out of this difference of subject, we may say that the same qualities are required in biography as in history; except, perhaps, that a note of personal sympathy is tolerated or even welcomed in the biographer which would be out of place in the historian.

The *Essay* is distinguished by the brevity of its external form, and by the presence of the element of reflection. It treats a subject from a single point of view, and permits the personal characteristics of the writer to assume a greater prominence than is permitted in the regular and complete treatment of the same subject in a treatise or book. It stands to the treatise in the relation of a sketch to a finished painting, and it has the same kind of merit as a sketch from nature. Just as the sketch is a record of direct and immediate impressions received by the mind of the painter from the study of natural objects made on the spot, so the essay should contain impressions received by the mind of the writer when it has been brought fresh to the consideration of any body of facts. And since the process of selection is employed with more than usual freedom in such writing, the essay is the most artistic of all forms of non-creative literature.

Classical and Romantic.—In the composition of all these works of literature, both creative and non-creative, we can trace the effect of one or other of two opposite tendencies. Of these the first is the tendency to follow the models presented by the works of the masters in each branch, and the second is the conscious desire to break away from these models in one or more particulars with the object of getting nearer to the reality of contemporary life. The danger of the classical method,—as the first is styled—is that of losing vitality by an adherence to those forms and methods of the past which are unsuited for the conditions—mental and social—of the present; the danger of the second, the Romantic method, is to sacrifice one or the other of these qualities in literature which have been shown to be of permanent value by the experience of past ages, by an endeavour to secure effects, which, though they possess a distinct and appreciable value for the contemporary readers, from their close connection with the movement and thought of the moment, may cease to possess an interest, or even to be intelligible, to future generations. Outside of these extremes the pursuit of either method leads to obvious and characteristic excellences, although these respective excellences will naturally commend themselves to different classes of minds. In the works of writers who are influenced by the traditions of the classical method we expect to find a more perfect literary execution, and the "grand air" which is acquired by association with the great intellects and the great artists of all time. But it is among the authors who follow the romantic method that we look especially for the "something new," which is at once the cause and the effect of the progress of the race, and by virtue of which literature becomes essentially a part of the life of man.

Style.—Finally, a word must be said upon the quality, at once so apparent and so elusive, which is called "style." Just as we are repelled or attracted by the manner of a man with whom we are brought into contact—especially when we make his acquaintance for the first time—so are we repelled or attracted by the style of the author whose work we read. Moreover, as we form an estimate of the character of an individual from our observation of his manner, which is quite distinct and separate from the more precise and definite opinion which we form after we have obtained a more exact knowledge of his actions and qualities of mind, so this feeling for style is something separate and apart from any opinion based upon a deliberate examination of the merit of his work. What manner is to the individual, style is to the writer. It is right, therefore, to say that "style is the man," in the same sense, and with the same reservations, as we say "manners makyth man." For style does not consist in any quality shown in the construction of sentences, or in the choice of words, or even in the use or neglect of characteristic literary methods; but it is something distinct and apart from these which at the same time affects them each in turn. It is that element of literary composition in which, without any manifestation of treatment sufficiently distinct to constitute either the observance or the breach of any literary rule, the writer unconsciously expresses his own temperament, training, or circumstances. It is the bearing which the writer assumes in the presence of the reader.

A List of the chief Authorities to whom reference has been made in the preceding pages.

[where not otherwise stated there is no difficulty in obtaining translations of the foreign authors.]

GREEK.

Plato. The *Republic*. (Also *Phædrus, Laws, Symposium, Hippias Major*.)
Aristotle. The *Poetics*. (Also passages in the *Ethics, Politics, Metaphysics, Posterior Analytics,* and *Physics*.)

MODERN.

Bacon. *Advancement of Learning.*
Addison. *The Spectator* (especially papers on *Paradise Lost* and on *The Pleasures of the Imagination*).
Lessing. *Laokoon: or Concerning the Limits of Painting and Poetry.*
Cousin, Victor. *The True, the Beautiful, and the Good.* [*Du vrai du beau et du bien.* Not translated into English.]
Wordsworth. *Observations* prefixed to the second edition of *Lyrical Ballads. Essay Supplementary* to the Preface of his edition of 1815.
Browning, Elizabeth Barrett. *Aurora Leigh.* ["This book . . . into which my

highest convictions upon Life and Art have entered."]

Arnold, Matthew. *Essays in Criticism* (first and second series).(See also *Culture and Anarchy, Irish Essays*, and his poems.)

Ruskin. *Modern Painters. Lectures on Art.*

Swinburne. *Essays and Studies.*

Meredith, George. Chapter I. of *Diana of the Crossways.*

Besant, Sir Walter. *Art of Fiction.*

Emerson. *Essay on Poetry and Imagination.* (See also Essays on *The Poet* and *The Comic.*)

Dowden, Edward. *Interpretation of Literature* (*Contemporary Review*, 1886).

Worsfold. *Principles of Criticism: an Introduction to the Study of Literature.*